About the Author

The author is a retired college lecturer who has lived in East Shropshire for over 40 years. In 2014 he was diagnosed with Motor Neurone Disease, robbing him of the use of his arms and legs. Having been an active walker, climber and skier, he has redirected his energies into a life-long passion for writing. Recently he published a collection of short stories, *Tales From the Hill*, and his autobiography, *Hard Day's Journey into Night*. He is a keen historian, and feels privileged to live in an area which is rich in Roman and industrial archaeology.

Dedication

To the Nine Men of Madeley Project committed to commemorating those lost in the mining disaster of 1864 and all those other local historical associations dedicated to revealing the hardships and suffering of the past.

A particular thanks must go to Barry Trinder recognised as the major historian of the Darby family in Coalbrookdale, Shropshire. Their work inspired me to want to recreate, albeit fictionally, something of the lives of the men and women in the transformational years of the 1770s to which many now refer to as the origins of the Industrial Revolution in Madeley and Coalbrookdale.

Noel D Conway

God, Land and Iron

Adventures of an English Radical

London • Cambridge • New York • Sharjah

Copyright © Noel D Conway (2021)

The right of Noel D Conway to be identified as author of this work has been asserted by the author in accordance with section 77 and 78 of the Copyright, Designs and Patents Act 1988.

All rights reserved. No part of this publication may be reproduced, stored in a retrieval system, or transmitted in any form or by any means, electronic, mechanical, photocopying, recording, or otherwise, without the prior permission of the publishers.

Any person who commits any unauthorised act in relation to this publication may be liable to criminal prosecution and civil claims for damages.

This is a work of fiction. Names, characters, businesses, places, events, locales, and incidents are either the products of the author's imagination or used in a fictitious manner. Any resemblance to actual persons, living or dead, or actual events is purely coincidental.

A CIP catalogue record for this title is available from the British Library.

ISBN 9781398401044 (Hardback)

www.austinmacauley.com

First Published (2021)
Austin Macauley Publishers Ltd
25 Canada Square
Canary Wharf
London
E14 5LQ

Acknowledgments

Thanks to Crispin Barker for his unstinting help with the initial proofreading and editing. To Colin Muddiman, my thanks for his invaluable help in tracking down some local historical sources.

For help with reviewing the publishers proofs my thanks go to Kimberly Ann Jones, without whose detailed detective work I would not have been able to proceed.

And finally, my lovely wife, Carol, for all her help with almost everything else without whom it would have been impossible for me to complete this project.

Table of Contents

Part One   11
  Madeley and Coalbrookdale (1770–1771)
Chapter 1   13
  Disaster
Chapter 2   17
  Christian Charity
Chapter 3   24
  Conflict
Chapter 4   30
  Help from an Unexpected Quarter
Chapter 5   33
  The Meeting
Chapter 6   38
  Abolitionism
Chapter 7   45
  Freedom?
Chapter 8   51
  A Close Escape
Part Two   59
  The New World (1771–1774)
Chapter 9   61
  The Crossing
Chapter 10   70
  Boston
Chapter 11   81
  Doing Business
Chapter 12   87
  Savages

Chapter 13   **95**
  Albany
Chapter 14   **102**
  Mohawk
Chapter 15   **108**
  The Holy Experiment
Chapter 16   **121**
  The Ohio
Chapter 17   **135**
  Hyacinthe
Chapter 18   **144**
  A Tea Party
Part Three   **151**
  Age of Iron (1775–1777)
Chapter 19   **153**
  The Homecoming
Chapter 20   **168**
  Fares, Rioters and Radicals
Chapter 21   **179**
  A Very Great Bondage and Cruelty
Chapter 22   **192**
  Marriage and Mad Houses
Chapter 23   **206**
  The Cannoneer
Chapter 24   **214**
  The Age of Iron
Bibliography   **224**
Timeline   **227**

Part One
Madeley and Coalbrookdale (1770–1771)

Chapter 1
Disaster

Nathaniel had got used to the dark, the heat and the ever-present pools of water. This was his world. For the past 10 years he had known little else. Sometimes it was hot enough to imagine himself on a tropical island – a pirate hiding his plunder in an unmarked islet in the Caribbean. But at other times, he shivered all over from the icy air as if he had been caught naked in a wintry wilderness. In truth, he wore little but a dirty, ragged loincloth that barely concealed his decency. But so did everyone else – even the young girls who toiled in the pitch black dragging their heavy loads from one dim light to another. For 12 hours a day, he scrabbled away at a face of coal or iron ore, careful to avoid dislodging one of the iron hard wooden props that was his only defence against being squashed like a beetle between ceiling and floor. He now hardly thought about it – except when part of an unsupported roof suddenly crashed to the ground. Sometimes an unwary miner, having sought a quiet place to relieve himself, disappeared in this manner only to be missed at the end of shift when the tally was taken. Instead, he looked for whatever glimmer of beauty he could in his carboniferous environment. Occasionally, the weak light from his cheap, tallow candle, secured precariously on his cap, would reveal the outline of an ancient fern etched into the sleek, ebony surface of the seam he was working on. How had it come to be here? There were also small insects or animals that looked like giant millipedes and pill lice, frozen in death but perfectly shaped. He was told by his father these were the animals that inhabited the earth before the great flood when only Noah and his family survived from amongst the race of men, who turned too evil to be allowed to live. Why then, he wondered, did he never come across their skeletons? It was a mystery.

Before he felt or saw anything, Nathaniel's sixth sense warned him of inexplicable danger. He'd heard of this from other miners who had survived previous disasters. His candlelight did not even flicker, nor did he sense any change in atmosphere. It was almost like, when as a child walking through the woods by himself, he had a premonition of doom and the hairs on the nape of his neck would suddenly stand erect and shortly after he would see a deer shoot from the undergrowth startled by his presence. He became aware of time standing still and the steady sound of his fellow workers further along the gallery sounded small and distant. As he turned his head instinctively to search the inky depths beyond the reach of the yellow light of his tiny candle, he was overwhelmed by a surge of freezing subterranean water. It swept him like a rag doll in a raging mountain torrent sending him racing along the seam, crashing cruelly into the iron hard props, which stood supporting the roof at every metre. He felt the sensation of being lifted as the icy water deepened beneath him. He knew where he was going, though he could see nothing, up towards the jet-black ceiling – a starless void that would suddenly crash down upon him like a lead black coffin lid being closed for eternity. But this was not to be. Gasping for breath and barely conscious, he was vaguely aware of helping hands trying to get a grip on his slithering body and limbs until the searing heat of an acutely intense pain in his right leg became so powerful that he was lost to all consciousness and his mind drifted free seeking release from his bodily trauma.

In spite of the danger and the demanding nature of the work, he was proud to be working underground in his family's gallery. 18 months ago, his father, Gideon, had uprooted the family from North Staffordshire to obtain better paid work in the expanding mines around Madeley where the flourishing furnaces and foundries of the innovative Reynolds and the Darby families were transforming the area. The senior partner, Richard Reynolds, was impressed by Gideon's piety and the fact that one of the reasons he gave for moving into the area was because of the presence of the Rev John Fletcher, a charismatic figure of rapidly increasing national fame. Although a Quaker himself, Reynolds was not dogmatic nor exclusive about his religion and perceived that Gideon, in addition to his collier's skills, would strengthen the small religious community because of his sobriety and God-fearing nature. Reynolds therefore was confident that Gideon would make a good overseer/manager. The house they lived in was newly built by the Madeley Wood Company for its employees and was considerably more spacious than the squatters' cottage they had lived in before. His mother, Sarah, was overjoyed at the improvement in the family's fortunes and she and Rachel, his 10-year-old sister, soon attached themselves to the growing numbers of followers of the Rev Fletcher at St Michael's church. Thomas, his 15-year-old brother, was three years younger than he, but was also hard at work hauling the coal and iron ore to the bottom of the pit shaft where it would be whisked up to the top on one of the modern Newcomen engines, which had been made in the Dale factory.

'Move aside,' the gruff voice of Gideon, struggling to contain his emotions, broke through into Nathaniel's semi consciousness. He shivered with the blast of cold air at the surface and the pain that gripped his leg. 'Go down again and see who else can be recovered,' his father's rough voice ordered once more.

'There can't be any more left alive now,' answered an unseen voice, 'and when the water recedes, we shall have to recover the other bodies and seal off the gallery.'

Even through the pain, Nathaniel realised the significance of what had been said. His younger brother, Thomas, must not have survived and the two workmen, Henry Holbrook and

Richard Sewell, both of whom were working further down the gallery than he, must have perished also. He remembered 10 minutes before the inundation, Thomas going by him and shouting a greeting as he always did. It was a way of keeping their spirits up in the gloomy environment. Thomas lumbered along almost totally naked, harnessed to the small wheeled sledge on which he would heap the coal and ore. When full he would harness himself to it from the other end to drag it back to the main gallery at the bottom of the shaft with the winding gear and platform. From there, it would be wound up to the surface where it would be carefully sorted and weighed by his father. What would happen now? With the gallery lost, his brother and two workmen gone, and he himself injured in some way, was a tragedy of proportions that he couldn't imagine. He drifted in and out of consciousness until the last thing he remembered for a long time was the dreadful, deep sobbing of his mother.

Chapter 2
Christian Charity

Semi-consciously he caught snatches of conversation.

'Compose yourself, Mrs Shawcross,' the voice he didn't recognise, but it seemed compassionate and knowledgeable, 'your son is a strong and healthy 18-year-old. Tis true he has had a very nasty trauma to the lower leg. I have rarely seen the tibia projecting so far with jagged edges and missing bits of bone, but I have reset it to the best of my skill and in time it will knit together, though I cannot say whether his leg will be restored to full strength – I think that's unlikely and he may have a pronounced limp for the rest of his life. The main concern at this stage, however, is blood poisoning from the filth of the mine. He is likely to become feverish as a result and it will be up to God whether he decides to take him now.'

He heard the grief in his mother's voice sink to a greater depth of despair as she strove to control her emotions.

'Come now, Sarah,' it was his father's deep, sonorous voice from which they were all used to drawing strength, 'if the Lord chooses to take him, we cannot oppose it and should rejoice in the knowledge that he will be in a good place.'

'Amen,' came the response from whom he supposed was the apothecary and another more strident affirmation whose voice he vaguely recognised as the vicar.

'I will arrange,' added the voice, 'for someone to come and sit with him and see to his bodily needs for as long as is necessary. I know Gideon and Sarah you will need to find alternative employment until a new opportunity in the mine becomes available to replace your lost income. There are a number of young fervent women in our congregation who will jump at the opportunity of serving the Lord in this way. I can vouch for them myself – they come from godly families so you should have no worries about inviting them into your home.'

When he next came to, he knew it was his mother and father alone. In an anguished voice, he heard the grief in his father's voice, which until now he had mastered to repress. It was then he realised the extent of the tragedy.

'Richard Sewell has two young children under five and whilst Henry Holbrook is single, his ageing mother relies entirely on him, there being no other survivors in her family from the cholera outbreak two years ago. I'm responsible for these people but what can I do? I cannot even feed myself and my own without work. There will be no alternative but to have recourse to outdoor relief.' There was a fierce rustling of skirts and he knew it was his mother reacting to this statement.

'No! No! It cannot be!' From somewhere deep within she had summoned up enough strength to reject such a possibility. As a girl, her own family had been on outdoor relief for long periods at a time and she remembered the cold, the gnawing hunger and worst of all the shame. She thought that when she married Gideon, a successful collier, this was well behind her but now at a stroke the family seemed to be on the edge of destitution. 'I will work, as many of the other women have to, at the pithead and Rachel can help me.' Gideon looked at her in despair but recognised the truth of what she said. He sensed the authority draining from him and slowly he became aware of an intense feeling growing within him, which he didn't at first recognise. It was that of anger. A deep seething anger without shape, without focus, at the sheer injustice of their predicament. Not only had God taken one of his sons, and possibly both, as well as the two young men who worked for him but He had also deprived him of his livelihood. How was this a merciful God? Of course, the Rev Fletcher had promised to make arrangements for the care of Nathaniel but that wouldn't put food on the table nor pay the rent for the company house they lived in. In fact, the more he thought about it the angrier he became realising that the vicar was full of fine words and unctuous piety but little more. Even the help that was offered was not by his own hands. What would our Lord have done? He knew the answer to that – he had washed and oiled the feet of the fallen woman, Mary Magdalen, himself. The vicar's words were empty, like his soul, he fumed inwardly.

At that moment, there was a knock at the door. It was his employer, Master Richard Reynolds. He had been informed of the accident and had gone to inspect the site for himself. He knew that the gallery would have to be sealed off but he also knew what that meant for the Shawcross family. Dressed soberly as befitted a Quaker, he stood humbly before the door holding the old-fashioned broad rimmed top hat that was a mark of his faith, his face showing the sadness he shared with the family, and waited to be invited in. A sharp contrast to the authoritative Fletcher who had entered as soon as the door had been opened. Gideon became aware of the differences in manner between the two men that he hadn't noticed before, but then he reminded himself that the Rev was the official Church of England minister of the parish and would see it as his duty to be present as soon as possible.

Recovering himself as well as he could, Gideon signalled for him to enter.

'Mr and Mrs Shawcross,' Reynolds spoke gently and without the arrogance that someone with his wealth and position invariably did, 'I have come to offer thee my sincere condolences at thy loss. I feel the loss of Thomas as if he were one of my own sons. I can only imagine what thy pain must be like. I am also aware that thou will be wondering what is to happen to thee now with the means of providing for thyself destroyed.'

Gideon's head lowered imperceptibly at these words and he feared what was to come next.

'Thou art probably not aware,' continued Reynolds quietly, 'that we have a small friendly fund for purposes just such as this. Every employee contributes a halfpenny per week to the fund, though they don't often realise it. It is not a great deal but thee and thy family are eligible for a payment of tuppence a week for six months. I know it is insufficient for thee to live on and that's why I'm also going to inform the company, as the senior partner, to waive thy rent until such time as thou art employed fully once again. Thee and thy family have struck me with thy pious and upstanding nature and I do not wish to lose a good man as an employee of outstanding quality. I'm sure that Mrs Shawcross and possibly thy daughter will be prepared to undertake some light work at the pithead as many women do. As thee knowest, I do not hold with womenfolk working underground. I will also speak to my partners and senior supervisors about identifying the opening up of another gallery for thee as soon as possible.'

'Praise be to the Lord, Master Reynolds,' the worry lines on Gideon's face visibly faded and he took the hand of his employer in his pressing it earnestly in thanks. The other pressed his gently in return adding a slight bow in acknowledgement. He then unceremoniously turned around and departed. Gideon and Sarah were left dumbfounded at this turn of events, which did much to relieve the grief they were experiencing.

Rebecca arrived the following morning. Sarah and Rachel recognised her from the considerable number of women who formed the Rev Fletcher's congregation. There were so many wanting to devote their time about the church duties that a strict schedule had been drawn up so as many as possible could participate. She was about the same age as Nathaniel, comely and demure with a fervent, quiet confidence that she was about the Lord's work. Her father was a wheelwright, a business he supplemented with cobbling, so there was no need for his wife or daughter to work. Instead, they devoted themselves to the business of keeping St Michael's clean and tidy, provisioned daily with festoons of colourful flowers. Their beautiful soprano voices rang out clearly in the flourishing choir which was the envy of all the parishes roundabout. In the eight years that he had been attached to the church, the vicar had turned it around from a rather moribund declining group of worshippers to a place which was busy every day and too small for the current congregation. There were advanced plans to extend the nave by a third as well as the building of a chapel room that could be used for Sunday school, Bible studies classes and other meetings.

She noted that Nathaniel was more handsome than she had first thought seeing him covered in the filth from the pit, like a spawn of the devil. Now she saw the sensitive features with the shapely jet-black eyebrows set above an aquiline nose beneath which the outline of his first moustache was beginning to appear. Other than that, he was clean-shaven. She shook herself out of this reverie noticing that whilst he was still unconscious, he was moaning with his head moving slowly from side to side. He looked as though he was engaged in some desperate life and death struggle, which indeed he was. The fearsome pain from the broken tibia had receded as a result of the opium concoction the doctor had provided, but now his blood fought with itself creating a fresh danger evident from the fever that gripped his body dosing him first in fiery sweats followed by icy shivering. What could she do? She mopped his brow, she kept him warm in blankets and then she decided to nourish him with the word of the Lord. But instead of reading from the Bible, which she thought was pessimistically premature, she read from another of her favourite books that she had with her, the Pilgrim's Progress by John Bunyan.

Nathaniel's subconscious oscillated between the horrors of what he had just experienced and imagery that he didn't recognise. He was thrashing about the subterranean gallery one moment, seeing Thomas lifeless as a puppet trapped by the sledge with demonic hands grasping at his limp form; and next, he stood at a wicket gate looking back on a fiery blackened city from which he knew he had to escape. But which way to go? There was one faceless form beckoning him one way and a disembodied pointing arm showing him another. He had no idea which to follow. A kaleidoscope of images, later he was at the entrance to a shadowy, sinister valley, which he recognised instantly as The Valley of Death. There was no other path but a very narrow one straight through it and so he plodded on, feeling the invisible slimy entrails of temptation trying to seduce him from it. At one point, he was quite certain that he heard a soft whispering voice and glimpses of an angelic face that seemed to lighten the darkness around him and to lighten the load that he suddenly became aware he had been carrying on his shoulders. 'This way, Nathaniel…' Thereafter, his torment lightened and gradually receded. He was in bed, in a light airy room. It was his! But beside him sat a figure reading quietly from a book, which at his stirring, shot the most beautiful, beatific smile at him. He was immediately ensnared and realised he must have given in to Temptation.

'Nathaniel,' spoke the beatific one, 'you are awake!'

'Who are you?' he spoke in words which were barely audible.

'I am Rebecca, sent by the Rev Fletcher to care for you allowing your mother and sister to earn some money at the pithead sorting through the slag.'

So, he thought, they had resorted to that, which meant, he realised, that his father's gallery was no longer workable after the accident. Despite the beauty of the apparition beside him, another less charitable thought raced through his quick mind: why did his mother have to work and he be looked after by a stranger? What sort of Christian charity did this Rev Fletcher provide? He dismissed this thought as soon as it entered his mind – it wasn't Christian to think this way.

Then a pressing physical need urged him to enquire when his family might return. It was unthinkable that he be helped to pass water by this beautiful, God-fearing young woman. She wasn't aware, of course, of any of this not having any experience of caring for others to draw on to realise that this might be a requirement, let alone what to do about it. As the urgency of his bladder increased, he was moved to ask her for a jug and beg her for some privacy. She blushed recognising the situation at last and said she would return shortly.

She returned with a cup of broth and he hungrily sucked in the nourishment. After that, they began to accommodate themselves to each other and he enjoyed her readings, stopping sometimes to discuss with her the implications of some of the story. When his mother returned, she was much relieved to find him sitting up in bed and conversing with Rebecca, who didn't stint in her duties over the next few weeks of his recuperation.

When he was strong enough to go abroad, it was agreed they should try to attend one of the Rev's Bible reading meetings in the early evenings during the week.

Chapter 3
Conflict

There was a heady aroma of fresh paint and the white benches shone brilliantly as the early evening sun pierced the tiny lateral windows near ceiling height in the brand-new chapel room that the vicar had commissioned. Despite the long working days for most folks in the area, there was still plenty who flocked to the Meeting House. Not all of them were familiar faces from Sunday worship. The Rev Fletcher attracted an audience of great diversity and encouraged it. He welcomed all and they knew they were in for a good evening's entertainment from his preaching. It hadn't been too long ago when he preached in Madeley Wood near the river, but he much preferred to hold forth either in church or in the newly built little chapel which was now crowded with expectant faces.

'Welcome, my dear friends,' he began in his heavily accented Swiss French voice which added to the magical atmosphere of his charisma. 'You are most welcome. Miners, foundry and furnace workers, agricultural labourers, canal diggers, itinerant craftsmen, ladies' maids and footmen in service, people of high and low station – whoever you are, welcome.' If he could, he would have embraced each and every one in his arms at the same time. His hypnotic voice and beaming smile were irresistible. 'Please join me in a rousing rendition of "Help us to help each other Lord":

Help us to help each other Lord,
Each other's cross to bear;

Let each his friendly aid afford,
And feel his brother's care.'

As the assembled group sat down, the Rev Fletcher immediately launched into his message,

'And this hymn perfectly captures what we are to do. Search inside yourself deeply. Seek out the light that resides therein. Feel the overwhelming presence of our Lord and let it flow up and out towards your neighbour, whom you should embrace in the holy love of Christ. Recall the Sermon on the Mount: if your brother, or sister, asks for a blanket, give him two. Set no limits to your love or compassion for each other. Look out for others as ye look out for yourselves. Store not up your love for special occasions, but look daily for opportunities to help your brethren – remember the parable of the talents, when the one son buried his in the ground where it was safe but flourished not, whilst the other spent it usefully until it multiplied tenfold and it was he whom his father cherished and applauded. This is how we grow in the Lord, not through careful and calculated acts of piety. In this way, your life will prosper and not wither. Now, embrace thy neighbour on each side.'

During this sermon two people at least began to fidget irritated by something that had been said. Through his mind, Nathaniel resurrected the half thoughts he'd had a week or two before on discovering that his mother and sister were having to work to provide for the family. In her hour of deepest bereavement, his mother was forced to leave the care and well-being of her other remaining son to a stranger, not knowing whether he would survive or not. He became increasingly agitated at the hypocrisy of the vicar's words,

'Do you call it Christian love and charity to force a mother at the height of her grieving to leave her remaining son to be cared for by another so that she can earn sufficient to feed and house her family?' Nathaniel was beginning to shake with rage and fear as he threw back the words of the vicar before the shocked group of devotees whose looks expressed their outrage at this attack upon their leader. The colour had drained from the

Reverend's face in this unexpected challenge to his authority, something he was not used to at all. He attempted to stammer a response,

'But… What… I arranged for Rebecca, whom I note is besides you now…'

'Is that what you mean, to get another to do what needs to be done? To exercise the power to instruct another to be the good Samaritan? That's hardly the same as doing it yourself. A few coppers and a helpful basket of food would have removed the need for my mother's additional suffering.'

'Shame!'

'Be quiet!'

'Disgraceful!' The audience now began to respond to Nathaniel's interjection. But before he was left entirely isolated another voice, from an unexpected quarter, spoke out.

'Do you also imply, sir, that when a man cannot provide for his family through no fault of his own that he is less worthy in the eyes of God?' It was his father, Gideon, who had been equally upset by the import of the vicar's words but for a different reason.

'The accident in the mine was an act of God and yet your words imply that its consequences and the losses suffered by my family and employees were a result of a lack of diligence on my part, since I am the overseer/manager of that gallery.'

'We are each of us responsible for our own acts,' the Rev responded, stung to reply and to defend his theology. 'I sympathise with your family's suffering and have tried to help in what way I could. But you are also responsible for doing what you can to remedy your situation and not merely sit back waiting for handouts or the Lord to miraculously intervene. We must be active in the faith and not give in to fate.' How could he tell them what he had done and had always done in similar circumstances? He was paying the wages for Rebecca to attend the young injured miner out of his own pocket. Nor did he want to draw attention to the fact that he was a member of the Outdoor Relief Committee, which provided funds for many in need, particularly those families who lost their breadwinners in the industrial accidents that were frequent in the coalfield and furnaces. He was privy to the Employees Fund, which Richard Reynolds administered, and urged many of his wealthier parishioners to also contribute liberally towards it, as he did. It would be arrogance of the worst kind and to give into the sin of pride to own up to such charitable works. He kept quiet. But the onslaught against him wasn't finished.

'It is a strange Samaritan,' spoke up another voice in the crowd, strong and calm, 'who pays another to provide a hand and at the same time criticises the victim for not helping himself.' The speaker was a silver haired man dressed in the black and white linen of an old dissenter. Neither Nathaniel nor Gideon recognised him. He was not a miner. He also had the bearing of someone confident in his own beliefs, not afraid to challenge the words of the Minister. The Rev was beginning to feel as though matters were getting beyond his control so he now called upon one of the church deacons to read the text for the day, followed immediately by a reading of one of the psalms. He then closed the meeting. As Nathaniel was helped by Rebecca to negotiate his way out of the Meeting Room amid a group of angry staring people, Gideon came up to lend his support. At the same time, their unknown supporter made his way deliberately towards them,

'Brethren, you seem none too pleased by the Rev Fletcher's words? Nor he by yours, methinks.' His eyes twinkled as he reached out his hands to both of them. 'I fear you have pricked his ego and found a chink in his theological armour. The way of the new Evangelicals is full of rapture and emotional giving that lays it wide open to charismatic characters of his ilk who expect devoted, unquestioning disciples and not critical individuals. Allow me to introduce myself: Elijah Smith, a self-confessed, freethinking old dissenter. I have no time for priests and churches, but from time to time I come along to these meetings in the hope of meeting folks such as yourselves. I admire your courage, young man. It couldn't have been easy speaking up before the Rev and his flock.'

For Nathaniel and Gideon here was someone different from those they had been used to associating with in the town. Unlike the earnest, nervous anxiety of the Reverend and his many followers, Elijah exuded calm and a genuine compassion that at that moment was sorely needed by them both.

'I thank you, Master,' replied Nathaniel civilly and on an impulse added, 'I would meet with you again to discuss your ideas.'

Elijah nodded to both of them and then made off towards the door but not before Gideon also proffered his thanks to the stranger.

'Well, my son, I am proud of you, but I think we have both made an enemy that we could have both done without.' His father was not wrong.

The following morning Rebecca appeared at the door in tears to say that she could no longer continue with the service she was providing as her father had forbidden her to associate any further with the Shawcross family.

'But why?' Nathaniel was now distraught at the thought of losing her.

'I don't know,' she said dolefully. 'All I know is that the Rev Fletcher spoke to my father early this morning and afterwards instructed me not to come here again. I shouldn't be here now but I couldn't do that without at least letting you know.'

Gideon was furious. 'I think we know why after last night.'

'Could a man of God be so patently vindictive?' queried Nathaniel. Gideon and Sarah just shook their heads saying nothing. They had seen it all before in the hatred which existed between ministers of the established church and nonconformists who were systematically singled out and repressed until they either left or gave in. It was one of the reasons they had moved to Madeley believing that the Ministry of the new vicar would be more tolerant, welcoming and less corrupt than what they had known. But Gideon remembered the charity they had received from Master Reynolds, who was a well-known Quaker in the area. They had been looking in the wrong direction it would seem – Christ was not to be found amid a pile of religious stones and relics, but in the works of men in their midst. None of them were to know that the Rev Fletcher had specifically instructed Rebecca's father to say and do nothing in the light of the previous evening, but the latter was a stubborn church deacon who felt he had to defend the honour of the Rev in some way.

'I believe,' Gideon tried to cheer up his family, 'Master Reynolds will soon find something for me.'

'But what of me, Father? My leg has healed badly and I will be more than useless down the mine. Am I to sit on the piles of slag all day trying to fill a bucket of reusable coal or ore to put a miserable crust on the table?' His eyes had filled up with self-pity and the knowledge of what a burden he had become to the family, but before anyone could answer there was an outburst from one who was still there,

'No! Not whilst I am here to help you, no matter what my father says!' It was Rebecca whose feelings for Nathaniel were now outweighing her duties to her father and the influential Minister. Nathaniel abruptly ceased his self-wallowing suddenly aware of the emotional bond which had become established between them. He took her hand silently as the tears coursed from her eyes and Sarah and Gideon tacitly acknowledged they had gained a daughter this day. Their family was whole again and little Rachel embraced her newfound sister. They knew that if Rebecca's family disowned her, they would take her in and she knew it too. It was too early, however, and the emotions too raw to talk of other things yet.

Chapter 4
Help from an Unexpected Quarter

Gideon's faith in Master Reynolds was well placed and before the end of the second week after the accident, he had been offered a new gallery in an adjacent mine. For a while, Nathaniel was able to help his father keeping records and accounts in the office at the pithead, but they both knew this was not the solution as there was insufficient work for the two of them. Rebecca remained true to her word and that same day she had returned home to confront her father. He was a churchwarden and a man of some substance in the town so he was not inclined to let matters rest. Rebecca would do as he said or she would be no daughter of his. Her mother tried to lessen the finality of this punishment, but her father was not going to lose face or favour in front of the Rev Fletcher – he was not to be moved. Rebecca collected a few clothes and precious books that she possessed and with great dignity walked without hurrying out of the home she had known since she was born, never to re-enter it. Her heart was full and heavy, but when she knocked on the door of the Shawcrosses to be welcomed with open arms by Sarah and Rachel, she knew she had done the right thing. This would be her new home from now on.

On Sunday afternoon, when Gideon was leading a Bible reading for the whole family, there was a knock on the door. It was Elijah Smith who hoped that he was not disturbing their Sabbath by calling on them like this.

'Absolutely not,' answered Gideon, 'Please enter brother and meet the rest of the family. Your intervention the other evening in our support was most appreciated.'

Elijah nodded at Nathaniel and Rebecca, whom he had already met, and offered his hand to Sarah and Rachel who responded warmly, having heard of what he'd said. He then took his place quietly on the bench next to Nathaniel and waited for Gideon to continue with his reading, which he noted with pleasure was from the Sermon on the Mount.

'That is a most apt reading,' Gideon offered, 'and at the very core of Christianity. It is how I and most other dissenters try to live their lives. There is no need for priests, bishops, archbishops, churches and holy relics. They promote the ego of overbearing men and overawe the gullible into submission. They do nothing but separate us from God. He is in every one of us and if we are prepared to listen quietly, we can hear Him.'

'Amen!' Replied the others.

'I will tell you something about myself if you allow me,' continued the silver-haired Sage, 'and then I have a proposition for you.'

The family nodded approvingly and then waited with some curiosity to discover what his next words might be.

'I am from a long line of freethinking dissenters that realise the importance of communion with one another and frequently, as I do now, associate with fellow Quakers of whom there are a good number hereabouts. You will know your own Master Reynolds but perhaps not so well his colleague and younger friend, Abraham Darby. It is for him I work in the Dale furnaces by the Gorge, as a mould maker. It is well paid and there is plenty of work for the industrious. Young Mr Darby is also a Quaker and excellent employer. For example, I live in one of the newly designed, terraced houses at Carpenters' Row next to the Ironworks, which are clean, warm and even supplied with their own water tapped from that which supplies the Coalbrookdale Works. The proposition I have, is that there is a job for Nathaniel should he wish it, which is in the moulding shop that I supervise. The work is not too physically demanding but requires intelligence and an ability to draw and interpret plans. It does require some competence in working with wood. I have heard for myself words which prove the intelligence of young Nathaniel here and I am convinced that he will have little difficulty learning the skills of my trade. His disability will not be an obstacle in the moulding shop. Furthermore, I think he wishes to learn as much as he can, not only about industry but also of the wider world of which I am well acquainted. I do not seek to make him a dissenter, for I can see that he's his own man and can think for himself, but I would look forward to having someone with whom I could discuss a wide range of topics. What's more, I would welcome his company in the long dark evening hours as I have room in my house and it would save him the long daily trudge from here to the Works if he were to stay with me during the working week. I will charge no rent for I believe not in profiting from the ownership of property and he will be able to return home at the weekend to see you all.' Elijah then stopped talking and waited for the family to reply.

'What do you say Nathaniel, as this largely concerns you?' His father turned towards his son on whose face a broad grin had already appeared. He had warmed to Elijah the previous evening and he wished to learn more about him and his ideas. His only regret was being apart from Rebecca, who would continue to reside in his parents' house and she said, now that Nathaniel was well enough to do some work, she would seek employment herself in one of the more prosperous houses in the district. For his parents, it was literally a godsend as the loss of his miner's income was a considerable blow to the family's standard of living, even after Gideon had obtained another gallery. It was agreed that Nathaniel would go along with Elijah and work with him as proposed, receiving the princely sum of 10 shillings a week whilst he was apprenticed.

Chapter 5
The Meeting

It was a rectangular, almost square, building of hardened local brick. On all sides, there were high arched windows designed to attract as much light as possible from without where the steep sided, heavily forested hillsides diffused what little light there was, which on dreary, wet, dismal days maintained an almost permanent twilight. Inside there were rows of rectangular benches constructed so that they rose up from the first row at ground level to a fourth row standing three feet above the first. Nathaniel immediately realised this was done to ensure that no matter where someone was seated, they could clearly see over the heads of those in front. There was no superior or inferior seating position; all were equal in this establishment and the architecture reflected it. The pine benches were enclosed but unlike churches there was no kneeling rail. There was no ritual of worship requiring people to stand or kneel. All sat, backs straight in a natural poised position, their hands resting lightly on their thighs or holding a Bible. Despite the external newness of the brickwork, the benches were well polished from frequent use. They were not painted nor varnished and the scent of the old pine from which they were fashioned still lingered therapeutically in the air. The only other furniture in the building was a long narrow table against the entrance wall and an array of coat hooks for hats and capes as determined by the weather. There was no altar, no presiding minister, no churchwarden, no one whose presence bespoke a higher status than another. Freedom and self-discipline were combined in equal measure. People were free to sit wherever they would and as people came at the approximately appointed hour, there was barely an imperceptible nod to one or two acquaintances. There was no crescendo of greetings, nor the exchange of idle gossip as one usually finds in such intimate gatherings. Nathaniel was especially impressed by the children present, of which there were six or seven in ages ranging from six to sixteen years, as calmly, self-composed as their elders. Peace reigned here because of rather than in spite of the forty or so people present. This was a meeting of The Society of Friends, as the commonly known Quakers called themselves.

As he tried to compose himself as comfortably as he could besides Elijah, who had encouraged him to attend saying that all were welcome and none turned away, all his senses were alert to absorb as much information as he could of the people around him. As his pulse slowed to a more normal rate, he noticed one or two faces whom he recognised from his first week at the Ironworks. Some of them worked in the moulding shop alongside him and Elijah. Others he remembered from the foundry floor whose job it was to pound or split or bend or puddle the multifaceted iron as it began its journey from ore to useful product. But now, they looked so different. They wore the typical saturnine clothing of the Quaker with the large white cuffs and collars, without frills or fancy, and their hair combed neatly, long and straight falling about their shoulders. Their hands and faces were no longer rough and dirty from foundry or forges, which for most of the week they inhabited amid the smoke and fiery atmosphere of hell. Everything and all were clean in every respect of their appearance. There was no distinction to be observed between master and iron worker. He saw now young Master Darby sitting amongst them, no different to anyone else. There was no privileged box for him or his family. Elijah had told him the meeting would last approximately for an hour but could be longer as the Spirit took them. It was perfectly normal sometimes for nothing to be said.

It was up to him if he wanted to speak, he should do so but it was perfectly all right to remain quiet. No one would lead the service or say that at one point some action should stop and something else begin. There would be no fervent singing of hymns but if someone wanted to read a passage from the Bible or indeed some other work, it was perfectly acceptable. The only thing that might happen is that one of the older members, such as Elijah, would signal the end of the meeting.

At first, Nathaniel felt uncomfortable. He didn't know where to put his eyes because he didn't want to appear as though he were staring rudely at those around him. He observed, however, that he wasn't being scrutinised either. People were either looking into the middle distance or often out towards one of the windows, which he now did. After a while, he felt remarkably peaceful and then he heard a softly spoken female voice begin to say something,

'Dear Lord, I wish to give thee thanks for thy bounty, which is all about us. There is a harmony in where we live and what we do. I thank thee Lord for thy love and the love I see in my neighbours every day. It is a very joy to be alive.'

Everyone appeared to listen carefully to what she said and quite a few nodded quietly. A little while later, a middle-aged man, whom he didn't recognise, began to read from Revelations. The reading lasted 10 minutes or so and Nathaniel found himself concentrating very carefully on the words from the text and thinking deeply about them. It was then, that he too felt the need to say something to the assembled group. It was quite short but heartfelt. He wanted to contrast the disaster of the accident in the pit with the peace and acceptance he had found in the Dale, for which he thanked God. The others listened carefully and courteously to what he had to say and at the end no one tried to comment or respond to what he said. He found this provided him with further comfort.

There were no other contributions and in the quiet of the meeting, he found himself reviewing the events of the week since he had left home and gone to join Elijah in his small, clean company cottage. Even by the standards of the Madeley Wood Company, the Dale Ironworks' cottages were far superior. The ground floor room was large and spacious with wrought iron windows snugly fitting to keep out the cold and rain. There was an iron fireplace providing ample heating from the company's coal, which was supplied freely to its employees, two cooking ovens, a place for the cauldron and kettle, and a little cistern for hot water. The centre of the room was dominated by a large oak table at which Elijah prepared food, ate dinner, wrote and prepared plans for the moulding shop. There was an ash wood rocking chair and two simple dining chairs without fancy fretwork but well made, which Nathaniel assumed was Elijah's own work. Upstairs, there were two small bedrooms and thus for the first time in his life, until his brother Thomas had been lost, Nathaniel had a sleeping chamber of his own. He would have preferred the company of his brother to this splendid isolation and a wave of emotion engulfed him momentarily, but he did not want to appear ungrateful towards Elijah so he hid it as best he could. He marvelled at the provision of running water from a cast-iron pipe that supplied each house with its own water outside at the rear from a brass tap located over a small sandstone basin. It was unnecessary to haul water laboriously from a nearby well as it was on tap from the remarkable system of ponds and watercourses which the Darbys had created for their foundries and furnaces. A narrow garden running up from the small backyard provided Elijah with potatoes, beans, onions, cabbages, peas and carrots. At one end of the workers' terrace was a water closet and wash house, whose odourless cleanliness was a minor miracle, despite servicing around 20 or more people. At the other end, provision had been made for a number of small pig sties for those who felt the need to supplement their normally meat free diets with additional protein. Opposite the terrace of workers' houses, there were walks around the essential water supply of ponds that dropped all the way down from the heights of Sunnyside. In recent years, others besides Quakers had moved into the area looking for work as day labourers, which was plentiful down as far as the River Severn and beyond to the tar pits at Coalport and the glass and ceramic works nearby. There was plenty of work for porters and bargees on the busy commercial river and quaysides that were evident on both sides of the river at this point. Consequently, there were quite a few squatters' cottages which had appeared along the small streams leading up to Lightmoor and Horsehay. So long as they didn't create a problem, the Darbys didn't mind. There was plentiful work also to be had in the bell pits which stretched all the way up to Dawley and Ketley. Despite the crash and bang from the nearby Ironworks during the workaday week, the area's beauty was startlingly fresh and therapeutic in the evenings and particularly on the Sabbath, when everyone was expected to cease work. It was only a few miles easy walk from Madeley and Rebecca took great pleasure during the long summer evenings in surprising Nathaniel by turning up at the little terraced house from whence they would stroll out into the nearby woodlands, arm in arm. Elijah delighted in seeing them both together and on such evenings, when he wasn't working busily in his little garden, he would take a chair and set it outside before the sunset plunged the Dale into its characteristic early evening shadows.

When autumn stole more of the light, and the damp from the Dale was too keen to stand, Elijah and Nathaniel would read the few precious books which were kept carefully in a chest in the living room. Sometimes they read together, one to the other, and discussed new ideas and knowledge about the world from history or geography. At other times, Elijah would read from a pamphlet he had obtained from somewhere and so it was that gradually Nathaniel became aware of what some would consider was dangerous knowledge.

Chapter 6
Abolitionism

One Saturday evening as Nathaniel entered his parents' house, as he was won't to do as soon as he'd finished work at lunchtime that day, he walked into the midst of a hotbed of discussion.

'I'm not sure I can stomach entering that den of hypocrisy again,' he heard his father speaking with some feeling. As he came through the door, they all jumped up in pleasure to welcome and embrace him with kisses and hugs, but his curiosity had been aroused by what he'd heard.

'What den of hypocrisy?' he asked, intrigued.

'The Fletcher Meeting Room,' replied Rebecca at once. She wasn't for concealing anything from Nathaniel.

'Why on Earth would you want to go there again, after the last experience which was none too pleasant?' It was his mother now who spoke up in quite an animated voice and at the same time pushed a leaflet towards him that was headed: "Observations on Slavery: a talk by the Rev John Wesley at the Meeting Room, Wednesday 7 PM. All are welcome." Nathaniel looked at it carefully and with great interest for it had been one of the topics that he and Elijah had most recently discussed. Furthermore, he had heard of the great John Wesley who travelled the length and breadth of the country preaching and talking on various topics. He hadn't until now been aware of his interest in abolitionism, as it was more usually referred to.

'This is a most important topic and I for one would most certainly like to hear what the great man has to say, even if it does mean enduring the hostile gaze of those whom we may have offended in the past.'

'So do I,' said Sarah, 'and I and Rebecca have already agreed we shall attend anyway.' Gideon looked unhappy but he was beginning to bend under the strength of convictions he felt coming from the two women. It didn't take long when Nathaniel added his weight to the argument,

'Come on, Father, you should have nothing to fear nor hide. I'm sure you will have something to say of import at the meeting as I probably will.' Reluctantly Gideon agreed and though it would be difficult for Nathaniel to arrive on time because of the distance he needed to travel, he was hoping that Elijah may well be sympathetic to letting him off early so he could make the long haul up from the Dale to Madeley Green and down to the Meeting Room in time for the start. Thus, it was settled that they would all attend. When he informed Elijah about it, he discovered that Elijah was just as enthusiastic about attending as he was. As master of the moulding workshop, there would be no problem about arranging time off. Indeed, when he informed Master Darby about it, he too was interested in attending and what's more he arranged for them to borrow horses in order to do just that, which meant they could finish at their normal hour and return home the same evening.

The Meeting Room was full to overflowing. Wesley was a well-known figure and anything he might wish to talk about would have attracted a large crowd. But tonight, people were jammed in standing where they couldn't sit. They even opened the doors and windows to allow people outside to hear the speechifying and discussion. As it was a reasonably dry and balmy evening, it was just possible they might catch some of the words.

The Rev John Fletcher was in charge of proceedings but he wasted no time in introducing his good friend and fellow minister. For his part, Wesley didn't hesitate but plunged straight in to his peroration in his characteristic forthright fashion:

'Who here believes he or she is more equal before the Lord than his neighbour?' He paused until there was a response, directing his gaze around the room hovering momentarily on the better dressed and wealthier amongst his audience. When he was satisfied by the vigorous shaking of heads or the peremptory negatives that were gasped out by the fearsome looks of the intimidating visitor, he continued,

'And doubtless you will tell me you have nothing to do with one of the most abominable and loathsome activities on God's earth? I mean, my fellow sinners, the trade in human flesh, the manufacture of human misery, the lucrative exploitation of black ivory... Inhuman Slavery!' he shouted.

'No...! No...!'

'But how many of you have bought rum, molasses, tobacco or soft, smooth cotton lately? Because if you have, you are all guilty in this trade! Why, you ask me? Because, dear sinners, you are oiling the very trade itself – you are putting money into the very pockets of those that buy and sell your fellow human beings. The Africans who are cruelly split asunder from their families, transported perilously over the raging seas, are subject to the most appalling treatment aboard ship where they are beaten, degraded and often thrown overboard when their valiant spirits finally succumb to the merciless hands of your fellow countrymen. You, I, we – are all culpable in the eyes of the Lord and we will be answerable to Him one day. Of that you can be assured. Did He not send the Israelites themselves into captivity in Babylon when they failed to heed His word and release their slaves? For three generations they paid the price of reneging on their word to the Lord. Is that what you want? The African is more degraded by the Christian than by any of his chieftains who sell him and her and their children to the Mohammedan slaver, or worse exchange their African captives for a few trinkets and baubles from the white Christian traders of the interior. They are bought and sold like cattle and treated as cattle – the property of slave traders and slave owners. Our Christian colonies in the Americas survive and prosper only because of their misery. Parents are torn from children, children from their mothers, wives from husbands at the slave markets in Charleston, Georgetown, Barbados, Jamaica and many other places throughout the New World. The slave is not deemed worthy of the most basic human family relations. He is branded with the sign of his owner and should he dare to escape he will be hunted down with dogs and punished by amputation of a limb or strung up high and hanged from the neck as an example to others…'

He paused, satisfied with the looks of horror that had appeared on the faces of his listeners.

'Is this how we should treat fellow human beings?'

'No!' roared his audience.

'Should we allow Mammon to rule our lives and ruin us?'

'No!' roared his audience.

'I have travelled to the Americas. I have seen the destruction this trade brings and not only to the poor unfortunate slaves but also to the slaveowners themselves. They lift no finger of their own – often not even to bathe or dress themselves. Their lives are spent in sloth, gambling, drinking, whoring. Their idleness is so pervasive they have lost contact with their own humanity. They know not how to live by working, worshipping or caring for others. Is it any wonder therefore they are able to treat their fellow human beings so badly? The colonies are a breeding ground for Sodom and Gomorrah. They have descended into the pit and have created a veritable hell on earth. It is a far cry from the original pioneers who set out to build a new Commonwealth, although there are still those who strive to this end. So what can we do my brothers and sisters?' Before anyone could answer, he continued,

'First, we must abolish this trade in human beings. I have brought with me a petition to go before Parliament. I beseech you all to sign it. Secondly, we must pray for all the blighted souls affected. Thirdly, we must show those of our neighbours who accept it, the error of their views. And fourthly, we should think twice before we purchase anything that has been produced by slaves – we shall defeat slavery by making it unprofitable as well as morally unacceptable.'

He then sat down abruptly leaving it for the Rev Fletcher to bring the meeting to order, which he did by asking whether there were questions or comments from those present. The tension which Wesley had created was now released in a general hubbub until the Rev banged a gavel on the table before him and repeated the question. It was Elijah who asked the first question,

'What shall be done about those who own slaves in this country? There are some fine, large houses not far from here who have in their employ Africans. It is not just the colonies who have blood on their hands Master Wesley.'

'Indeed, sir, it is not,' he rose to answer the question. 'Many a fine house and public building, and I would warrant many a manufacturing business, is being built or has been built on the great fortunes which are produced by this heinous trade. But it seems those in power have forgotten the consciences of their forebears who in the last century passed an Act of Parliament forbidding the enslavement of people in the United Kingdom. However, whilst Common Law prohibits the buying and selling of human beings in this country, it would seem that it turns a blind eye to those who do it abroad and bring what they consider to be "fashionable objects" to parade them without conscience before their peers as a mark of their high status and wealth. But then, the immorality and excesses of the aristocratic elite are well known to us and should not be used as a mark of moral compass. I think, sir, we should remind them of what it means to be a Christian at every opportunity, however unpalatable or unpleasant that may seem. Our petition should emphasise that any enslaved person entering these shores will automatically be freed and treated as such. Furthermore, any attempt to re-enslave them should be prohibited by law.' He remained on his feet as he saw others in the audience who wished to ask questions also. The next person was the young Master Abraham Darby himself who had been listening carefully,

'May I ask, Master Wesley, whether thou thinkst that all trade with the colonists is tarred by this evil and that we should all withdraw from it? I think if thou dost that will be a tall order and very difficult to effect.'

'I see by the cut of your cloth, young sir, that you are a man of substance and possibly of business. Nevertheless, it is a pertinent question that needs answering. You are right to reply that many people in this country rely heavily on goods from the colonies and vice versa. I do not think there should be no trade between us and them in the generality but on those goods which I have mentioned there is a Christian duty on the purchaser to ensure they have not been produced on the back of slavery.'

'Thine answer is a good one, Master Wesley,' replied Abraham. 'It is a principle that my coreligionists and family have sought to live by for many years.' Wesley nodded graciously in his direction.

The next question was put by Nathaniel, 'Don't you think it will be difficult to get men of substance and power to give up their wealth? They control Parliament and the laws of this land so how realistic is it they will listen to a petition of commoners, sir?'

'That too is an excellent question young man and originates from a thoughtful mind, for which I commend you.' Wesley paused to ensure all had heard and repeated it to ensure they had.

'You are right, of course, it will not be easy. But do not think that is a reason for not even trying. Remember the way of the cross was not easy for our Lord. And do not despair, as Bunyon's Christian was tempted to. There are many others like us of both high and low station. For example, William Wilberforce is a driving force in Parliament to that end. I believe in time we must succeed because we have the moral high ground and the Lord is with us.'

There were a few other questions after that and most people wanted to shake the hand of the great man and sign the petition. The three from Coalbrookdale went in search of their horses and commented briefly on the event. They all agreed that Wesley had spoken well and replied to the questions effectively but for the most part they were lost in their own thoughts as they trotted carefully home in the moonlight. This was something that Nathaniel had to pay careful attention to because he was not a well-practised horseman and certainly not at night. However, the horses were well used to this path and even if he'd fallen asleep, he would have arrived safely home. On arrival and having taken care of the animals, Elijah and he sat down in the small all-purpose ground floor room and began to discuss the evening's meeting. They were far too stimulated to retire just yet.

'What do you think,' the first to break the silence was Nathaniel, 'will be the response of Parliament many of whom own property in the West Indies and the colonies owning considerable numbers of slaves?'

Elijah looked meaningfully at him, 'I think the same as you that they will not happily give up what they consider to be theirs and to be rightly earned. They don't think like us. They do not regard the slave as an equal human being with them and they do not, and perhaps never have, accepted Christian charity seriously. On the other hand, I have to believe not all parliamentarians are of the same cloth and will like Wilberforce strive to change matters. But not without a fight which I think we must be ready for, and not only on this issue.'

Chapter 7
Freedom?

He was in a dark place. It was the mine. He saw Thomas waving to him at the end of the gallery and then the filthy, murky water began to take him. Just as he was about to disappear, long, strong, black arms grabbed hold of him and pulled him out. The sun was shining but there was a harshness to the glare which added an ominous atmosphere and he couldn't see anything but long canes growing thickly together, so densely that it was virtually impossible to penetrate. Then he heard the dogs and he knew he wasn't safe, but when he looked down, he saw his feet were shackled and though he tried to move, he couldn't, sinking further, deeper into the treacle-like bog. He was caught. He felt a hand on his shoulder and saw that it was white…

'Wake up, Nathaniel, you're having a nightmare,' it was Elijah who had heard him thrashing around and moaning from the next room. 'It's all right. Don't worry. You're safe now.' As he came to himself, he saw he was drenched in sweat. It had been like this now for some months – a recurrent dream with some slight changes in detail but essentially the same. What did it mean? He guessed it had something to do with the antislavery meeting he had attended when John Wesley gave such a rousing talk. He knew it wasn't only this. He was happy with Elijah and his new employment but there were so many stimulatingly new experiences and ideas, things to learn, new people he'd met. Sometimes he felt as though his brain were bursting, but it was intoxicating at the same time.

He loved being able to wander throughout the ironworks, lingering in the various workshops where he would take the wooden moulds for casting or more pounding in the wrought iron shop. He marvelled at the malleability of the metal, what it was capable of, what it was capable of becoming. He sensed being at the core of a great undertaking as the iron was split in the cutting shed or bored out in the drilling shop. He was beginning to learn about each stage of making iron products, from furnace to foundry and more. He lingered as often as he dared in the old furnace mesmerised by the transformation of iron ore, heated to super temperatures by the coke, the collection of impurities with the addition of limestone, and then the final pouring into the sand mould to create the essential pig iron from which everything was born. The immense scale of the undertaking, the complexity and the ever-present danger drew him in a way he couldn't explain. He was well liked wherever he went because of his optimism, his willingness to learn and the respect he gave to his fellow workers. They knew he'd worked down the mines and they wanted to know what it was like, comparing the dangers there with the dangers they daily faced from the volatility of molten iron to the erratic spraying of hot shards which could blind instantly. Sometimes, Master Darby would beckon him to come into the drawing office where he would show him the latest designs explaining in detail what the drawing signified and what part it would play especially in the construction of the new high-pressure steam engines that Matthew Boulton and James Watt had invented improving on the weaknesses of the old Newcomen engine. Nathaniel hadn't been schooled in the same way as Master Abraham and he found it difficult to make the transition from abstract design to practical product. Nevertheless, he understood how all the parts fitted together and how each worked, having seen the individual parts produced and fitted. His was a practical intelligence and a very good one. He didn't initially have any calculating skills but he quickly learned and applied them effectively in the workshop working within very narrow tolerances. In time, there were few others in the works who knew how the whole fitted together and complemented each other better than he, to such a degree that Master Darby allowed him to show visitors around the plant when he wasn't available. In this way, Nathaniel discovered something about other places in the world which were not too different to Coalbrookdale such as northern Germany, Denmark, Holland and Sweden. However, without exception all visitors marvelled at the extent of the production and especially the integrated nature of the overall process, which embraced foundries and furnaces quite some miles distant in Ketley, Horsehay, Kemberton and Madeley. The mining of coal, iron ore, the making of coking coal, which fuelled the whole process connected by iron railways and canals, they all concluded was impressive. Nathaniel himself became very proud to be associated with the Dale Works. From time to time, he would have reason to call on the new house that had been built by the present Abraham's father and was now occupied by the whole family. There he discovered, there were yet more worlds of which he was completely ignorant. Both the young Master and his partner, Richard Reynolds, were keen students of geology collecting as many items as they could and paying their workers for bringing good specimens to them. From this, Nathaniel became acquainted with ideas which challenged his first view of the world that was based on a literal interpretation of the Christian Bible. Some people he was shocked to discover were even suggesting that the earth was far older than the Bible said and had been populated by creatures quite different from human beings. He might be shocked but he was not dismissive of new ideas. He was thirsty for them.

 He found that Rebecca was equally curious about the world around them and keen to know as much as he. She too had been deeply affected by what she'd heard at John Wesley's talk and she had been so determined to fight against slavery that she offered her services to the Rev John Fletcher as an organiser and correspondent. She was often to be found at the vicarage writing letters for him to other groups throughout the country, as well as keeping in touch with the London headquarters and John Wesley's movements. Admiring her ardent spirit, Fletcher too had softened his attitude towards her and even suggested to her family that she be allowed back home. She would have none of this, preferring her own independence in the home of her sweetheart Nathaniel whom she could therefore see whenever he returned. His mother, Sarah, and sister, Rachel, loved Rebecca and frequently assisted with the work she was doing. Gideon kept his distance from the Rev preferring instead to follow what he saw as the purer form of Christianity that his Master, Richard Reynolds, practised. He would often walk the extra miles down to Coalbrookdale to attend a Society of Friends gathering where he would meet up with Nathaniel.

One evening when Nathaniel had just returned from work, he found a pamphlet on the table but Elijah hadn't yet returned so he couldn't ask him about it. It was entitled "Common Sense" and was concerned with the American colonies. Nathaniel knew a little about them since pig iron was sometimes imported from there when there was a shortage at home. But apart from that, he knew next to nothing and when he saw that the pamphlet was addressing what was referred to as a crisis there, he was anxious to know more. He had been reading for more than an hour when Elijah walked through the door,

'Ah!' he shouted happily as he saw what Nathaniel was up to. 'I'm glad you're looking at that. I thought you might be interested. It came quite unexpectedly from an acquaintance who lives in London. I should be eager to discuss it with you when you feel ready.' Secretly, he couldn't wait to find out how far Nathaniel's ideas had developed.

'Well, I've not quite finished but I think I've got most of it. The writer, Thomas Paine, seems to be no friend of the King nor of Britain. Some of what he says seems to make self-evident sense but the stuff on the American crisis I'm really not quite sure about.' He paused thoughtfully and Elijah couldn't contain himself,

'What about all this business that monarchs are nothing but brutish ruffians whose power derives from the sword?'

'Yes, the French bandits who followed William the Conqueror to which line every succeeding King or Queen of England has sought to align themselves, thereby claiming legitimacy for their power. Of course, that cannot be strictly true because the house of the Plantagenets has been superseded by the Tudors, Stewarts, the House of Orange and now the Hanoverians.'

'Well done, my son, you certainly know your monarchs and you have spotted one of the lies that they have perpetrated down the ages. Does it not bother you?'

'I never really thought about it until now. All those great lords and ladies and their great estates? Now, that's a different matter because I've seen at first-hand how they treat us with disdain. They believe themselves to be vastly superior to us, their servants, the farmers and labourers in the fields without whom they would starve. But we are the ones who make them rich by leasing their land for mines, ponds and streams, and on which the whole of our endeavours here are based.'

'Yes, yes. Absolutely…' proceeded Elijah, 'but what about hereditary succession? What does Paine say about that?' Nathaniel reflected back on what he'd read – after all, he'd only read it once and there were lots of other ideas in the pamphlet.

'I think he says there is no justification whatsoever and to accept it is to say that some are more superior than others. In other words, it justifies inequality, the ill-treatment of the weak and the vulnerable by the strong and powerful. It directly contradicts Christian morality when all are equal before the Lord. The parallels with the objections to slavery seem to me now to be very clear. I hadn't seen it before. So, Paine is saying that monarchy is a form of government that should not be accepted and that the people through the rule of law should govern.'

'Well done. You accept that?'

'I need more time to think about it but I'm certainly not strongly opposed.'

'Now what about "the American Crisis"?'

'I'm rather surprised that this fellow Paine, who previously argued from a basis of reason, seems to be urging his fellow Americans to reject any possibility of resolving the dispute with Great Britain through negotiation and to take up arms against us. He seems to equate this with liberty and whilst I can accept his objections to the arbitrary nature of King George's power, I'm not at all happy about his warmongering. Have I got this right?'

Elijah screwed up his eyes and let out a great gasp of exasperation, 'You may well be. I am as unsure about that as you are. You may also have noticed he takes a swipe at the British for turning the native Indians and Negroes against the colonies. Since I know the latter have been sorely mistreated, cheated or enslaved, I can only think better of the loyalists there than those clamouring to separate from Great Britain. I think we need to know more.'

'I agree wholeheartedly,' replied Nathaniel.

'In that case, you may be interested in coming with me to a meeting being held to discuss the American crisis not too far away.' Nathaniel's eyes lit up. He was more than ready to find out what was happening in America.

Chapter 8
A Close Escape

He didn't like this place. It contradicted all his instincts but the Golden Ball in Madeley Wood was loved by many others in the neighbourhood and from much farther afield. Its collection of tiny, disturbingly intimate rooms, for those who didn't wish to advertise their presence or that of their companions, was complemented by larger ones brim-full with disreputable and ungodly locals, sinister ruffians, thirsty colliers, barge men and migrant labourers. It was a labyrinth of seduction and temptation. A focal point for strangers passing through the district in search of profane diversion and unspiritual guidance. He was amazed when Elijah had suggested this as the venue where he would learn more about the American colonies and their "crisis".

It had been difficult even to enter the premises it was so full and it offended Nathaniel's sensibilities to barge his way unceremoniously through the noisy, unsavoury throng. Had he been on his own, he would never have made it to the bar, but his companion of innumerable surprises seemed to know his way well and effectively cut a path for both of them through the seething mass. Elijah ordered small beer for them both, neither of them tempted by the stronger ales and spirits available. As they were swallowed up unnoticeably in the crowd, they detected all manner of folk from their accents and dialects. It was a veritable tower of Babel including travellers from the south-west of England, from the North and Scotland, but especially numerous were the Irish. Here and there they even picked up languages they didn't recognise and some they did such as French and Dutch, but what Elijah was particularly on the alert for were American accents. He hadn't revealed all his past to his young friend such as the fact he had fought in the Seven Years' War in Canada or spent time at sea serving under the colours of His Royal Majesty. As a late-comer to the Society of Friends, he had much to regret about his earlier life and he had no wish to advertise this.

'There are two men over there,' he said nudging Nathaniel in the ribs and shouting in his ear above the hubbub, 'who have New England accents.' Nathaniel looked at him in astonishment. How would he know that?

'Believe me, I know,' he said in reply to his friend's silent query. 'Let's see if we can engage them in conversation.'

They eased themselves carefully towards the two so as not to be too obvious in their intentions. The Americans were in their late 20s, wearing the short canvas trousers and tarred pigtails of sailors. They were weather-beaten, with large rough hands that were clearly used to physical labour, broad shouldered, and above average height with healthy, well fed faces. Elijah affected to have just heard their voices,

'If I'm not mistaken,' he addressed them directly in his strong North country accent, 'I hear the unmistakable sounds of New England?'

The two men were pleasantly surprised at this friendly interruption,

'You are right there, my friend,' and he held out his hand towards Elijah, 'James Walsh from Portland and this is my seamate, Frank Cook from Boston. So, you've heard American accents before?' James now scrutinised both Nathaniel and Elijah more carefully.

'I'm familiar with Massachusetts and Maine, having spent time defending the colonies against the French.' The two New Englanders looked at Elijah with new respect at this news.

'Well, my friend,' exclaimed Frank and clapping Elijah on the back, 'my countrymen and I have much to thank you for. Let me buy you both a drink!'

'Elijah Smith, master carpenter and my young friend here, Nathaniel Shawcross, is my apprentice at the Dale Ironworks, of which you must have heard if you have been long in this area?'

'Very glad to make new friends,' replied James. 'We are up from Bristol where our ship is being refitted after heavy damage during our last crossing. We thought we'd investigate further North up the River Severn and see the famous complex of iron making whilst we have the chance. At the same time, we thought we might be able to find out what people think about the colonies and their arguments with King George.' Nathaniel now flashed a look of understanding towards Elijah. So this was the meeting. He realised that Elijah had guessed there might be Americans here whom they could query.

'I'd be very much interested to know how you see it,' said Nathaniel joining the conversation for the first time and making them aware he was no dummy.

It was James who began outlining the colonies' position. He told them that they felt constrained by the British government in growing their trade because all goods imported could only be brought in by British or Colonial ships which made it impossible to make a fair profit. They also chafed at not being able to trade directly with other countries such as Holland or France. All goods had to come via Colonial or British ships through British ports.

'But do you not accept,' asked Elijah, 'that Britain has had to pay out huge amounts of money to defeat the French in Canada and redefine the border to protect its American colonies from the hostilities of the enemy and the butchery of their Indian allies?'

Frank's eyes flashed with sudden anger, 'My father and brother died in that conflict. The colonialists played an equal part in defending their territory and British interests. And now that the French have been securely corralled into much smaller areas, they are no longer a threat to us. Why should we pay for protection when we can defend ourselves?'

'What's more,' continued James, 'we have no say in the laws that come from the Parliament in London. We have no MPs there. In fact, we have shown for a long time that we can govern ourselves successfully making our own laws and creating law-abiding communities that are God-fearing and prosperous, if we were only allowed to be by a remote, disinterested and unsympathetic monarch. And the last straw has been the recent increase in British soldiers on colonial soil that are now billeted upon us and for which we must pay. We don't need you, we don't want you!' James too was displaying his anger and as the discussion had now turned to hot argument others in the room were beginning to notice, especially the Irish,

'Aye lads, King George is no friend of ours nor of any working man anywhere.'

'Nought but Hanoverian oppressors. These Prussians rule Court and country.'

'Aye, bring back the Catholic Kings and God in his mercy will relieve the lot of the suffering masses when the Cardinals and the Pope are restored to authority in the English church.' As these sentiments began to grow and get louder, it attracted the attention of others in adjoining rooms who added their voices but this time in opposition,

'Papists! There are Jacobites in our midst. We must root them out. No return to divine kingship – we want none of their heresy. Parliament rules.'

'Long live King George!' This was followed by a general melee as partisans on each side launched into each other with drunken fists and feet: the Americans and the Irish on one side assailed by increasing numbers of miners, bargemen and others. Bottles were broken, clubs appeared and blood was flowing profusely. As the fighting reached a crescendo, Elijah grabbed Nathaniel by the arm pulling and shoving him to the exit. It was time to go. Nathaniel was no stranger to brawling as he had done many a time down the mines in defence of his father's gallery. He was still strong and broad enough in the shoulders and arms to give a good account of himself, though his right leg meant he was more easily dislodged from his feet. Around him lay quite a few with cracked heads and jaws, but he and Elijah were on the wrong side of the room in the midst of the Irish whose blood was now well up. As the cry went up, 'Sons of Ireland!' it was followed almost immediately by the Americans shouting 'Sons of Liberty' and they knew it was time to exit from there. The fighting became even fiercer. Ducking low and heaving bodies aside, they finally emerged from the rapidly disintegrating Inn.

Abia Darby was as formidable as she looked. Since her husband died a few years ago, she was the recognised head of the Darby side of the Ironworks partnership as well as the leader of the Quaker community in the general locality. She had sent for the two of them the following day after news reached her of the riot in the Golden Ball Inn. They now stood before her in the large well-lit living room, where she preferred to conduct her business, like two delinquent schoolboys, hanging their heads in shame.

'Well, brothers,' she almost harrumphed as her stocky, tiny body faced them squarely, 'what in the name of the Lord were you doing in the midst of that godless Gomorrah at the centre of a riotous assembly? The magistrate is furious about reports of a Jacobite meeting and has informed the Lord-Lieutenant of the County so that the militia will be instructed to investigate who, where and why such events have occurred. As my employees, and until now good members of the Society of Friends here in the Dale, I think I can expect an honest explanation.' She looked at them both expectantly. It was Elijah that spoke first,

'It was very foolish of me, Abia, to lead my brother Nathaniel astray by taking him into that den of sinners, but we had good cause.'

'What possible cause could you have for being there? Were you perhaps spreading the word of the Lord? Now that would indeed have been saintly. But somehow, I think not, as the reports suggest that you were both giving as good as you got.'

'We were after news of what is happening in the American colonies,' Nathaniel spoke up strongly, raising his head and looking directly into her eyes showing that he had nothing to fear nor hide. 'We'd heard that there could be American sailors present and we were anxious to find out for ourselves what the colonists think of the "Crisis" that is being spoken of.'

'And did you?' She eyed them fiercely.

'Yes, in a manner of speaking we did,' he replied, 'although whether that represents all the colonists, I don't know.'

'And, do you think they want to break off from the mother country to become independent?'

'The two we spoke to certainly were of that opinion,' added Elijah, 'making common cause with the many Irish who were present in the Inn. However, I know that not all colonialists share that view, many being loyal to the King.'

'Yes indeed,' added Abia, 'but I would like to know for certain which way the wind is blowing because it could affect our business interests considerably especially as we import raw materials and pig iron from the Americas from time to time.' She then paused and thought for a few moments before continuing,

'Nathaniel, how would you like to go to the colonies to investigate the state of our suppliers and whether we would be able to continue to rely on them if hostilities broke out, which some of my sources suggest could well happen?' Nathaniel couldn't believe what he was hearing, the opportunity that he was being offered, and his eyes lit up with delight,

'I should like nothing better, Abia…' but then a frown came over his face. 'How long do you think this would be for?' He was thinking of leaving Rebecca for what could be a very long time.

'Oh, I should think between three and six months. Will that be a problem do you think?'

'No,' he had thought it through quickly, 'I think that would be acceptable.'

'Good. I shall make the necessary arrangements with letters of introduction to our suppliers et cetera. It will also be wise for you to be out of the country if there is to be a witch-hunt for Jacobites following last night's riot,' she added with a note of admonition in her tone, reminding them both once again that she was in authority here.

Nathaniel could not believe his good luck. He had never thought in his wildest dreams that he would be going to the New World and in a manner that would mean he could travel in style and comfort. He was excited but nervous. How was Rebecca going to take the news? He could not take her with him and he knew that six months absence was a long time during which anything could happen – illness, misfortune, accident. The greater anxiety would be for her since he would be embarked in a potentially dangerous journey from which he might never return. It was a cruelty he would not wish on anyone. That evening he walked painfully up to Madeley Town, knowing that it would also be a hard blow for his family too. As soon as he walked through the door, they could see there was something troubling him but they waited for him to raise the matter,

'I have something to tell you all,' he said slowly, 'which may cause you some pain. I've been asked by the Mistress Abia Darby to go to Boston to investigate how our interests, that is those of the Ironworks, may be affected by the deteriorating relations between the colonists and the British Government. It will mean putting my fate in the hands of the Lord in the dangerous crossings of the Atlantic, but I know the modern seafaring ships of today are far safer than they were when the first pilgrims ventured forth towards an unknown New World from which there would be no return. There is a thriving sea trade now between these shores and the new ships have the benefit of many experienced captains making the trip regularly.'

As he spoke, he noticed his listeners' faces at first turning white, but then gradually the colour returned accompanied even by smiles and exclamations of joy,

'That's marvellous,' cried his father, standing up and embracing him. 'This means you have earned the trust of the Darbys and you are beginning to make your mark in the world. I am very pleased for this opportunity for you to prove what you are made of.'

His mother also came over hugging and kissing him, but Rebecca still hadn't responded. She was trying to work out the implications of it all for their relationship,

'How long will you be away?' she asked quietly. This was the response he'd been dreading.

'It could be six months, my love.'

'You must go, Nathaniel. As your father says, it is a wonderful opportunity that you cannot afford to miss and, of course, I will be here when you return.' Stoically she masked her deeper feelings and concerns trying to put as good a face upon it as she could. He embraced her fervently recognising the courage she displayed.

'I will write every day and the time will soon fly by,' he said. 'On my return, I think it is high time also that we should be married as soon as possible.' There was general rejoicing at this proposal which was long overdue as they all recognised. 'Perhaps you could post the bans at St Michael's and make the necessary arrangements? I will ask Mistress Darby if there might be a cottage for us in the Dale.'

So, what he had been dreading turned out to be not so bad after all, indeed the very opposite. Dread had been turned into joy.

Part Two
The New World
(1771–1774)

Chapter 9
The Crossing

For once Nathaniel could regard the spume that was draining constantly away through the deck rails without his stomach churning over. They were now three weeks out from Bristol on a packet ship loaded with migrants for Boston. Like him, most of them spent the first two weeks finding their sea legs or bent double over the side of the ship emptying the contents of their stomach, but now most had acclimatised, especially as the weather was mild and the rolling of the sea subdued. Hopefully it would remain that way. When he boarded the ship at Bristol, it was already three quarters full with Dutch, German, Flemish and others fleeing the consequences of a turbulent Europe, having embarked from Rotterdam. Many were nonconformists and Calvinists fleeing the wrath of Catholic France and Austria. Theirs was a one-way voyage and those who he managed to converse with him in English marvelled at the fact that he would be returning in half a year's time. It was enough to risk this perilous crossing once let alone twice. Many hoped to go west and either settle in Pennsylvania, where there were already well-established Amish and Mennonite communities, or to push on further beyond the Ohio Valley where they had heard there was land to be obtained at good prices. Neither he nor they at this point were aware of the sacrifices that would have to be made both in blood and religion if they were to succeed. They were optimistic and excited by the prospect of the adventure before them and so was he. He was aware that Boston was a well-established seaport with thousands of residents both permanent and transitory but he had letters of introduction to iron masters further inland which would enable him to reconnoitre a little of the New World. As in England, iron making and steel production required the proximity of many trees or coal, iron ore and water. He'd heard the terrain was not hugely different from what he was used to except for the remoteness. However, there was more to his explorations than the observation of ironworks. Somehow, he also had to assess the people themselves. Besides finding out the amount of pig iron that might be available for export, he had to discover the likelihood of the continuation of this trade if hostilities broke out between the mother country and the 13 colonies. What was the mood of the people? How advanced was their knowledge of iron making? Was there any market for exports to them such as the steam engines they were producing at Coalbrookdale? These were the questions that Abia Derby had emphasised he should seek answers to. He himself, however, had his own questions. Were they as God fearing as those at home? He knew some of them engaged in slavery but did they all, and more importantly, did their current or potential suppliers? What exactly was their relationship to the native Indians? He would have to converse with as many people as he could. He began to consider how he could do this.

    He hadn't noticed that the wind had picked up and the waves were becoming more robust, but when one of the sailors called for everyone to get below as quickly as possible, he immediately saw the reason for the alarm. Abia Derby had insisted he should travel as a gentleman in the best available accommodation and be provided with good quality, although sober clothing, if he were representing the Coalbrookdale Company. Consequently, he had a tiny cabin in the bow just off the main covered deck where most of the migrants collected and journeyed as best they could. As he was threading his way through the milling throng, he heard a surprisingly refined English accent calling out, 'Thomas… Elizabeth… Where are you!?' The well-spoken stranger was clearly becoming more agitated with each moment and Nathaniel now saw him desperately searching among the crowd for whom he guessed were his children. Feeling sorry for him and wanting to help, Nathaniel asked him what the matter was.

'My children...' came the distracted reply, 'I cannot find them. They were playing above deck when the call came to get below. I thought they were following me down but they are nowhere to be seen.' The gentleman, for that he clearly was from his voice and clothing, wore warm home spun hose and jacket of good quality. He was in his mid-40s with long, well-groomed hair that lay on his shoulders and a neatly trimmed black beard which was beginning to show signs of silver.

'What do they look like?' he asked in his North Staffordshire accent.

'My daughter, Elizabeth, is 12 years old with long curly tresses. And Thomas, my son, is 10 years old and a little shorter than his sister... Ah!' he suddenly shouted as he saw his daughter slipping down the stairs from the upper deck, exhausted and soaked to the skin. He ran to her immediately, sending other passengers flying,

'There you are! Where is Thomas? He was with you last I saw.'

'He's on deck somewhere. It was so wet and slippery... I don't know.' She was so exhausted, she was ready to faint.

'I'll go and look for him,' reassured Nathaniel. 'Don't worry, I'll find him.'

The ship was now pitching so heavily he struggled to climb up the steps and found it unexpectedly difficult to raise the hatch at the top. The storm was beginning to vent its full fury at them and he was beginning to wonder how anyone, let alone a 10-year-old boy, could resist being swept overboard. He saw that grab ropes had been placed by the sailors for their own protection but when he looked around, he could see no boy. He now began to panic and prayed to the Lord for assistance.

Suddenly, a rough voice shouted, barely audible above the fearsome crashing of the waves,

'Get below! Get below…' It was the bosun, whose job it was to see there was no one left on board deck, but then Nathaniel saw he was clutching a boy in his left hand as he struggled against the rolling deck with the other. He was 10 feet away from the pair when a massive crested wave towered above them. He threw himself with all his strength in the direction of the two, grabbing the boy with both hands and, as the massive peak of water descended, he flipped up the hatch they were fortuitously next to and threw the boy down. He was immediately swept away off his feet. He waited fatefully for the final coup de grace to be delivered into a seething watery grave, but the bosun who was tied onto a grab rope, with sea legs that were 20 years more experienced than Nathaniel's, slipped a rope around the latter's waste and pulling it tight through a bowline dragged him towards safety. Once there, both men unceremoniously crashed through the open hatch that the rugged sailor had managed to prise up and down which the boy had already tumbled. Those below had left a wide berth around the steps in expectation of more deluges of water and people pouring through. The boy's father shouted with joy as he saw his son and sweeping him up into his arms, addressed both men now sprawled on the floor before him.

'God be praised,' he shouted, 'you have saved my son's life and I am in your debt.' The bosun sprang to his feet with remarkable agility, knuckled his fist to his forehead in salute, saying,

'All in a day's work Guv, but it's this rash young'un here who risked 'is own neck for the lad – I'm not sure for how long I could've hung on to him till he showed up.'

Nathaniel was still shaken from his near-death experience. For a second time in his short life, water had almost claimed him again. The grateful parent helped him to his feet and bracing his own feet held him steady against the bucking deck. Elizabeth had already wrapped her younger brother in a blanket and was leading him towards their cabin, when her father addressed Nathaniel directly,

'Jeremiah Goodman at your service, sir. Please, come into my cabin so I can thank you properly.'

The Goodman cabin was a captain's-sized berth with a leather couch and fixed chairs, which surrounded a small dining table. There were two other rooms off it, which Nathaniel presumed were their sleeping quarters. When Jeremiah explained that he was a corn merchant, Nathaniel was hardly surprised at the size or opulence of the cabin. He explained that he had spent the last six months travelling the length and breadth of England, visiting customers. He had brought his children along with him because they no longer had a mother, who had died in giving birth to his son, Thomas. They were very close to him and he didn't want to leave them behind for such a long period. It was also a good opportunity to extend their education. When Nathaniel explained to him something of his own background, the corn merchant was full of praise for the advancement he was clearly making in his employer's enterprises. Furthermore, he added there were great opportunities for progress in the colonies for intelligent, diligent and ambitious young men like him. Skills and talent were regarded as more important there than titles and pedigree.

Offering Nathaniel some brandy to recover from his recent ordeal, he noticed the young man's reluctance to take the spirit,

'Do I presume, sir, you have some objection to strong liquor?'

'Well, sir, I'm not really used to taking it and I prefer non-alcoholic beverages where possible.'

'Well, Nathaniel – may I call you that?'

'I'm honoured, sir, if you do.' He had taken a liking to Mr Goodman immediately.

'And please, you must call me Jeremiah. A little brandy for medicinal purposes will not make you a wine-bibber, but I can get you some tea if you prefer?'

'No, Sir… Jeremiah, I'm sure you're right. This will be fine.'

'Should I infer,' asked the older man, 'from this evident preference for non-alcoholic beverage and your sober clothing, that you are a man of some religious conviction – perhaps a member of the Society of Friends?'

'You would be right, Jeremiah, that I do follow the practices of my employers, i.e. the Darbys, and am glad to do so.'

'There is no need to be defensive here Nathaniel as you are amongst fellow Friends. Now tell me, what is your business in Boston?'

'I'm a representative of the Coalbrookdale Ironworks in Shropshire and I'm on my way to visit suppliers of pig iron which we are always in need of, especially good quality material. I expect to spend a week or so in Boston making arrangements to go further inland and explore the country, which I'm very much looking forward to.'

'If you are staying in Boston, I insist you stay with us. I have a large, spacious house in Summer Street and would be delighted to show you around the city, as well as helping you with arrangements for travelling further inland.'

'You're too kind, sir, and I look forward to getting to know you and your family even more over the next few weeks.'

As Nathaniel rose from his chair and limped across the room, Jeremiah observed it and said with some concern,

'I see you've been injured… I'll call for the ship's surgeon…'

'No sir, I'm not. This is the result of an old injury and you need not worry yourself. I thank you nonetheless for your concern.' Jeremiah did not press the issue but thought to himself there was more to this young man than first met the eye.

The children, Thomas and Elizabeth, were very pleased to get to know Nathaniel to relieve the boredom of the journey and they were frequently in and out of his cabin over the next 3 to 4 weeks of what remained of their journey. Tom was keen to learn all about the iron industry, whilst Elizabeth adored the proximity of the handsome young Englishman, being on the cusp of becoming a young woman herself. She took it upon herself to tell Nathaniel all about Boston and the New World as if she were the only font of knowledge on these subjects, prattling on in detail about the millinery, shoe and dress shops which were the centre of her world. He hadn't the heart to interrupt her and in fact it did serve to paint a partial impression of the city for him. He had never travelled to London and Bristol was the first large city he had ever seen in his life. He had imagined Boston to be a rough and ready place – a frontier settlement with basic facilities, but from her flowery descriptions he began to realise that Boston was going to be much larger and more settled than he'd thought.

After a few days, the storm had exhausted itself. The skies brightened and cheery clouds raced across them creating a balmy and joyful atmosphere amongst all the passengers in expectation of a successful completion of the voyage. As Nathaniel strolled along the deck with Jeremiah, the children running hither and thither in a blissful family scene, a woman's voice pierced their tranquillity. Everyone on deck suddenly stopped what they were doing and froze as if time itself had stood still. Then it came again – frantic with fear – followed by a second equally chilling making the hairs on the back of the passengers' heads stand on end. But that had been sufficient to have broken the spell and time once again resumed its normal course as everyone began to search for the source of the voice which could give them some clue as to the nature of the danger. There was a plainly dressed woman with a poor bonnet and equally shabby shawl pointing to something in the sea.

'Look…' She could barely shout now and was close to fainting, 'A… A… Body!'

All eyes followed the arc of her arm, not knowing how far or close to focus on the indiscriminate patchwork of the sea. Then, one after the other began to shout,

'Yes, yes… I see it. There it is… It is a body!'

It was face down in the water, rolling with the gentle waves.

'And there's another...! And yet another!'

More people began to scream and shout whilst sailors grabbed ropes and grappling hooks. Some of them began to climb up the rigging to get a better view all around until, reaching the first yardarm, the full horror of the scene began to emerge before them. They counted twenty human corpses in a wide trail around the ship as if they had been roped together. They were all black – men, women and even a few children. The sailors were perplexed. What should they do? All were visibly dead and it would be difficult and dangerous to try to haul them in. Where could so many be stored?

'Cut loose any that have been grappled!' It was the captain who had assessed the situation quickly and firmly took control. 'There is nothing to be done for them now – except to pray for them, poor souls!'

All the passengers looked on totally bewildered, turning questioning faces towards the captain.

'They must have been thrown overboard from a slaving ship,' he said emotionless. He could see the scene in his head, after all he had experienced it often enough before – before he woke up to the horrors and the evil of working on a slave ship. It had been good money, if you could stand the stench and survive the not infrequent attempts to escape by the slaves who were turned into frantic madmen by the inhuman conditions in which they were kept and treated. After surviving two knives in his ribs, he had decided it was far better to avoid the trade altogether. 'It's what happens if a mutiny occurs. They might have slaughtered the crew, but not knowing how to pilot the ship would have thrown themselves into the sea in their desperation. Or, more likely, these were the mutineers who were made an example of by the crew, by being thrown overboard.' The captain turned away as if that were the end of the matter, but it wasn't for the passengers.

'You can't just leave them like that,' Nathaniel was incensed at the callous disregard being shown by the captain and the crew. His voice had taken on an angry, hard edge, which was not lost on the captain who quietly took hold of a merlin spike that lay to hand. But when other voices in sympathy with Nathaniel spoke up, he released it.

'What would you have me do then?' he asked diplomatically.

'The sea has taken them, but we can still send them on their way with our prayers.' It was Jeremiah who spoke. There were many shouts in agreement with this.

'Very well,' replied the captain, 'I'll be happy to do that and perhaps some of you will too?'

'Indeed, I will, Captain.'

Most of the passengers stood up and arranged themselves respectfully around Jeremiah and Nathaniel as first one, then the other, recited the Lord's prayer and Psalm 23, after which they all dispersed in subdued contemplation of the events they had just experienced.

Jeremiah quietly clapped Nathaniel on the back.

'That was well done and very brave, my young friend.'

'Not as brave as what those people in the sea must have endured. Slavery is the abomination of our age and I didn't think to see it with my own eyes in this way. I will fight it wherever I see it and have no truck with any who profit by it.'

'Amen,' replied Jeremiah, though he knew in his own mind that Nathaniel was going to make enemies in the New World. He, however, would not be one of them.

Chapter 10
Boston

Boston harbour was a forest of tall masts, whose rigging tinkled in a cacophony of magical sound in the early morning sunlight reflecting myriads of sparkling rays. They had come in on the dawn tide, though it wasn't strictly necessary as the harbour was famously deep into which projected the great Long Wharf sufficient for the largest of ships to embark or disembark without regard to the lunar draw. The quietude of night was being replaced by the busyness of the day to come. Dockers were preparing their carts by the keys and awaiting the harbourmaster's signal before they hauled them along the sturdy wharf to unload the passengers, their luggage and cargo from the packet ship that now entered and came expertly alongside. Coaches and smaller carts were now beginning to muster on the harbour side towards which all the disembarking passengers began to walk struggling to readjust to the level plane of dry land after weeks at sea. Enterprising porters ran ahead of the dockers offering to help those passengers loaded with heavy bags and chests, an easy money earner for such a short distance.

    Nathaniel, who had only ever seen the one seaport of Bristol, was overawed by the sight. It was magnificent in the crystal-clear atmosphere of a Massachusetts Bay morning. He hadn't expected it to be so large nor so well established. Opposite the quays of the large harbour were four storey high warehouses from which were pouring workers like ants from a nest. Above them and a little in the distance, he saw many spires and church steeples. It was in this direction that the main thoroughfare between the tall harbour-side buildings led. Now he could see coaches and carts of various sizes and condition, reflecting their owners' status, fighting for space along the quayside. He, Jeremiah and the children made their way jostling amid the crowd. Jeremiah led them to a large covered coach drawn by two fine horses, complete with driver and footman who loaded up their luggage and helped them inside the capacious cabin. On the side of the coach doors was inscribed in beautiful Gothic script "Goodman & Co. Grain merchants". He was beginning to realise that he was now in the company of someone with considerable wealth, and probably power, that had not been conveyed by the relatively spartan quarters of the Goodman's berth. As they passed through the centre of what he perceived to be the centre of town, he observed how it opened out into a large square on the west side of which was a tall, imposing brick and stone building with Doric columns over the entrance, up which ran a wide series of marble steps. He was further impressed by the proliferation of other three and four storey buildings surrounding this central square. The ground levels of these tall and elegant structures were glass fronted shops selling all manner of goods, although he couldn't help noticing the greater number of these appeared to be bookshops. The square was full of people coming and going or simply standing around chatting to each other. A surprisingly large number of them were women of quality, judging by their clothes and expensive coiffures.

It wasn't long after that the coach pulled up a broad street stopping before another imposing four-storey building with a porticoed entrance. As they came to a halt, two men in livery came out to collect their luggage and escort them inside where they were met by a number of assorted maidservants, menservants and a butler. They were all dressed in the same uniform and he noticed a few of them were African Negroes but they seemed to be treated exactly the same as the other servants. Jeremiah and the children greeted them affably and there appeared to be a genuine atmosphere of cordiality and respect between them all. He was courteously introduced as a visitor from England who would be staying with them for a little while. Nathaniel was then shown to a large bedchamber with a window looking out onto the Main Street. There were other pieces of expensive furniture of mahogany, cedar and walnut: two chairs, a chaise longue, a small writing bureau and a glass fronted bookcase. It was opulent beyond anything he had ever experienced. He was almost unnerved by it all until he recalled he was respectfully dressed and here on business representing one of the most important businesses in England. There was a quiet knocking at the door and when he opened it a servant informed him that lunch would be served in an hour in the dining room which was on the first floor – the doors would be open so he would be able to easily find it. In the meantime, he might like to freshen up in the washing room, which led off his chamber and which he would never have noticed had it not been pointed out to him by the friendly servant.

After a light lunch, Jeremiah and the children were keen to show Nathaniel parts of their beautiful city to which he readily agreed. It was a pleasure to walk out in the cobbled and paved streets where people greeted one in a courteous manner. He wondered where all the working people were, but then he'd already seen some of them thronging the harbour and there would be many more servicing the great houses, shops and businesses, many of which were located down narrower side streets from the main square. Jeremiah first led him to the building which had struck him initially as they rode through the centre of town. He proudly pointed out that these were the Assembly Rooms, where the representatives of the people met to make laws and enforce them. This was no less than the equivalent to the British Parliament in London and was the very centre of Bostonian democracy. Next to it was the Exchange where much business was conducted. Jeremiah explained that one of the principal items of trade and consequently sources of wealth in Boston was sugar and it was from there that refined sugar, rum and molasses were bought and sold, much of it being sent to England. Nathaniel immediately wondered how much of this was produced on slave plantations, something he would want to discover. Nathaniel told Jeremiah that he had seen many church spires on the skyline as he looked over this city from the harbour and asked about their denomination.

'They are mostly Presbyterian as Boston was first founded by them and is proud of its nonconformist origins. There are a growing number of Baptists, but I regret to say that Bostonians have had little time for dissenters and there is only one Meeting House for the Society of Friends. As I told you before, I am also a Quaker and I will be glad to introduce you to our fellow brethren. However, it is only quite recently that we have been tolerated in the city and last century one of our number, a martyr, was hanged for her faith. The small but growing number of followers continue to honour her memory.'

Nathaniel listened to this with growing disquiet, finally expressing his horror,

'So, Boston is not quite the open and tolerant city that it appears to be on the surface?'

'Far from it, my young friend, but in that it is not much different from most other places.' Jeremiah knew this to be an understatement but he was not ready to sow disillusion or alarm in the mind of his visitor so soon after his arrival. There would unfortunately be time aplenty for that later.

It wasn't long, however, before Nathaniel became aware of this for himself. One bright mid-morning he decided to explore the town on his own. One of the shops he passed carried the sign "Boston Gazette" and looking through the small, square glass windows he saw that it was clearly the front office for the city newspaper. There were a number of editions highlighted over the past few months, of which presumably the paper was especially proud. His eyes were almost immediately drawn to a title with large bold script reading "Boston Massacre". He was unable to read the small print beneath through the distorted panes so he decided to enter and purchase a copy. He found that whilst the article had been printed a few months previously in March, there were still a few copies for sale. Choosing a shady bench in the square on which to sit, he was shocked by what he read. Apparently five loyal Bostonians had been mercilessly cut down by musket fire by British troops and had died instantly. The subsequent uproar had almost turned into a riot until the governor agreed to arrest the five soldiers, confine the rest to barracks and hold an enquiry. It was said the soldiers were drunk and out-of-control, ill-disposed to patriotic colonials. The paper continued by referring to other equally terrible incidents, the most infamous of which was in 1768 when a Bostonian woman had been raped and murdered by garrisoned British troops. He couldn't help feeling that the emotive language of the article was completely one-sided and defamatory painting the British authorities in the guise of tyrannical overlords. It seemed designed to inflame its readers against the British in a way that political pamphlets were written. It made him feel distinctly uncomfortable as if he were an enemy in their midst. As he continued his perambulation of the town centre, he noticed a number of posters, rather old and weather-beaten, which were headed "Sons of Liberty" advertising meetings long past now for all loyal Patriots. He'd heard that name before somewhere and then he remembered the meeting, if it could be called that, in Madeley Wood that turned into a brawl. The Americans and some of the Irish present were shouting out that name. He would ask Jeremiah about the significance of this organisation. He observed that many of the shops were well-stocked and if the number of books available for sale were an indication of the cultural depth of a community, then Boston certainly qualified as a centre of education and learning. However, it was appearing far from that at the moment to him. He also noticed a number of other shops which appeared to be selling land with titles like "Land Agent" and notices which were urging people to go west and realise their dreams. No prices were indicated but there were many references to "West of the Appalachians" and the "Great Wilderness of the Ohio" complete with colourful maps and routes of how to get there.

On Friday evening Jeremiah arranged for a dinner party at which Nathaniel could meet a number of associates and friends of his, all of whom represented different sections of Bostonian society. The children would not be present at this soirée because they were too young for the conversations that would take place. Nathaniel was introduced as a young iron master from middle England who was here on business to scout out new prospects and re-establish links with old customers. He had purchased a new frock coat, linen hose and stockings, cotton shirt and fashionable buckled shoes as instructed he should do by Abia on his arrival. However, he was not comfortable wearing a wig and so tied his shoulder length, thickish hair behind him in a ponytail. He looked very presentable and his general physical appearance made a suitably good impression on the assembled company. His accent and way of speaking were new to the ears of the Bostonian gentleman and sufficiently different from the common labourers and farmers as to make it difficult to place him easily. His confident and forthright manner, something he had been encouraged to cultivate by Elijah, meant he was listened to seriously. Jeremiah steered the conversation to areas that he knew would be of interest to his young friend. He was now aware that Nathaniel was keen to establish a deeper understanding of events in Boston and New England than a superficial traveller passing through.

'Gentlemen,' he exclaimed as the social pleasantries were concluded, 'our young English visitor wants to understand what issues are of main concern to us here. He has heard and observed for himself that we are not entirely content with our status as colonists.'

'Well, I think you will find there is almost total agreement on one topic that is unifying all the colonies,' opined Thomas Lyndon, the most expensively dressed of the dinner guests, looking the full part a member of the colonial elite which as a successful sugar merchant he was, 'which is the widespread imposition of taxes on many goods by the Imperial Government.'

Nathaniel was, of course, prepared for this, 'Do you accept,' he asked, in as polite and courteous a fashion as he could, 'that some taxes may be necessary? For example, to maintain the upkeep of harbours, a fleet to deter piracy and forts to protect the frontier?'

'Some perhaps,' replied Henry Beach, introduced to him as a tea merchant, 'but mostly not. You see, young man, we do not see the point of all these taxes collected here to be sent to London where they will be swallowed up by the corruption of London politicians or tax collectors who enjoy sinecures allowing them to cream off the large proportion of them.'

'We are capable of defending ourselves now that the French Wars are over,' added Andrew McIntosh, warehouse owner and speculator. 'Furthermore, we resent having to pay for British redcoats who far from defending us, do actual harm. You may have seen posters or heard reference to the Boston Massacres which occurred at the end of last year and is still prominent in people's memories and feelings.'

'Yes, I have but doesn't that prove a point that you do need protection from rowdy mobs and rioters?' This immediately gave rise to an explosive, angry response from the three men who had spoken, but Nathaniel pressed home his point courageously, 'As I heard it, a mob of 50 attacked seven British soldiers on duty in the harbour. In order to defend themselves, they had no choice but to open fire which resulted regrettably in the death of five of the rioters.'

'Rubbish,' said Andrew his cheeks inflamed with passion.

'No, you are quite mistaken, young man,' asserted Henry forcefully, 'and that is proven by the fact the governor arrested all seven soldiers, confining them to quarters and subsequently prosecuting one for having started the firing. What is more, two years ago a young woman hereabouts was raped and murdered by garrison troops.'

'There's actually no proof that happened,' responded Isaiah Box quietly, 'and her body was never found. But you can see, Nathaniel, that these stories have created very strong feelings against the British authorities, whether they are true or not. They are believed by many, although I suspect them to be nothing more than the product of a vicious rumour mill anxious to discredit the British presence in the colonies.'

'But why?' asked Nathaniel. 'I don't understand. Don't you want the British here? Are you yourselves not British?'

'You ask a very pertinent question,' said Jeremiah, speaking for the first time in this discussion. 'Who will answer him, gentlemen?'

There was no immediate answer forthcoming. Eventually, it was Isaiah that offered a response,

'I think you have your answer, my good friend. We seem to be confused ourselves. Yes, we do see ourselves as British, recognise and honour the King, but we don't want his authority, or rather, his Government's authority by which most people mean Parliament.'

'Come, come, gentlemen, let us not be disingenuous with our visitor,' insisted Jeremiah. 'Let's not forget the antics of the so-called Patriots and some may say the intimidation and terror created by the Sons of Liberty. Those who pay taxes to the government collectors or refuse to be swayed by what they demand are tarred and feathered, their houses destroyed and frequently must flee into exile to avoid being murdered.'

'It is true, there have been some excesses in the past few years,' agreed Thomas, 'but I'm afraid that when people see themselves as being enslaved, they will react violently sometimes to throw off their oppressors. To impose taxes on us, which benefit us not one whit, to impoverish us by cutting off our trade with the world and threatening to take away our property is nothing less than slavery.'

'Again, sirs, I'm confused,' said Nathaniel. 'I'm not aware of your property being seized by the authorities?'

'Ah, good Nathaniel, as a Quaker, like myself, as I am told by Jeremiah you are,' interjected Isaiah, 'it would not even enter your mind. By "property", read people i.e. African slaves. Not so much in Boston, although there are still hundreds here too, but more in the great plantations of the southern colonies, Virginia, the Carolinas, the West Indies and so on. A recent case in Britain prevented a colonial gentleman from re-enslaving his released property, who had been given his freedom as soon as he landed on mainland Britain, by trying to dispatch him to the West Indies. The British authorities in its American colonies have also expressed support for the idea that slaves can purchase their own freedom. Southern planters fear this will be the end of their world.' The others present didn't try to refute this explanation but merely looked at their feet or took another drink of brandy. This was quite a revelation for Nathaniel and he felt even less sympathy for the colonists than he had before. Other than for his host and Isaiah, his fellow Friend, he would have left the table and the company in disgust. Jeremiah could recognise his discomfort and sought to bring the evening to an early close.

Mistress Abia

I have now spent over a week in Boston, staying with a good friend I made on the outward journey, Jeremiah Goodman and his family. He has been instrumental in introducing me to various important people in the town and helping me to more fully understand the situation in the American colonies. I will report on these issues later on in this letter. For now, I wanted you to be aware that I had safely reached these shores and, in a few days, I will be setting out for the Sterling Ironworks with a letter of introduction from yourself to the current iron master there, Master Peter Townsend. It will take me at least six days to make the journey as this is a remarkably large country and even though it is a well-trod path, it is not yet suitable for coach travel. I will of course write to you in more detail about my observations regarding the ironworks and the options, if any, for business with them.

I now turn to the more general issues regarding the "American Crisis". First of all, since I've arrived, I've became increasingly aware of how negative the colonies are towards the mother country. There seems to be a general attitude abroad here that the Royal Governors, Agents and senior military officers are corrupt tyrants intent on undermining their local democratic assemblies. They are adamantly set against any laws made by Parliament in London which affect them. In particular, they are seething at the imposition of direct taxes on any imported goods and furious at the requirement for their goods to be exported only to England even though they may be intended for other places in continental Europe. These same laws, of course, would interfere with any exports we may wish to send to New England. The colonists are especially fond of their tea and have resorted to widespread smuggling to avoid Customs and Excise duties, which appear to be ignored with impunity everywhere. It is not unusual to hear of Customs officers being beaten up and their warehouses destroyed by arsonists. So called patriotic associations have emerged over the past few years fomenting disaffection and channelling violence against the authorities. Not all colonists support such behaviour but those that don't risk intimidation and attacks on their property. I don't think it is too much of an exaggeration to say that Boston and, so far as I can tell, many other seaports and settlements in the adjoining colonies have become tinder boxes of rebellion. I don't believe it will take much to start an uprising, unless the Government in London sends more troops to restore and maintain order. Those that are here are too few and skulk in their barracks for fear of being attacked by the mobs.

I'm sorry to paint such a disappointing picture of circumstances here. Other things being equal, the New England colonies and Boston in particular appear to be civilised, God-fearing and economically wealthy communities where it should be possible, maybe in future better times, to pursue a thriving trade in many of the goods that we produce.

I shall write again in a few weeks' time regarding the potential of successful trade with the Stirling Ironworks and others that I intend to visit also such as the Taunton Works in Pennsylvania.

Blessings of the Lord be with you your true and sincere servant Nathaniel Shawcross.

Chapter 11
Doing Business

As he rode along the Old Post Road from Boston, Nathaniel was dazzled by the sheer beauty of the coastline which was hugged almost up to the seashore by a wide variety of deciduous trees. Being born in Staffordshire and now living in Shropshire, he was a stranger to coastline. Of course, travelling to Bristol to take ship for the colonies he had seen something of the English and Welsh coastline, but it was nothing compared to what he had seen since arriving in Boston. The city itself was established along a narrow isthmus which broadened out into habitable country, but all routes in and out had to travel along this thin strip of land. Jeremiah had accompanied him to the end of the isthmus, which culminated in what was known as The Crossing Point where the trail divided going north west, due West or south-west. When he first began to plan his journey, he had intended to take the High Connecticut Road which went first north and then due west making directly for the Sterling Ironworks in New York colony who were expecting him. This was a journey of approximately 200 miles through backwoods territory with only a few scattered settlements along the way. He would have to travel by horse because the trail was not suitable for coaches.

He wasn't particularly looking forward to this lengthy journey on horseback because in truth he was only a novice horseman. He therefore looked for ways to break his journey and began to ask around about other ironworks that he might fruitfully visit.

He was quite dismayed to discover there were only three in the whole of the colony of Massachusetts and the Sterling works was the oldest and largest of them. However, he did learn there was a small business not far from Boston itself in a place called Raynham, the Taunton foundry approximately 32 miles away, but it would mean following the south-west route. On further investigation, he found he could continue on this southerly route eventually joining the Bay route. It had the added advantage of being well provided with coastal settlements where he should be able to replenish his supplies and get further information about the state of the country. Although, he had no personal letter of introduction for this enterprise, he believed that it would still be worth turning up unannounced. It may be a fruitless errand, but at least it was en route and he should be able to obtain overnight accommodation there. Furthermore, he thought, it might be a safer route than the first he'd considered because of its closer proximity to the coast. Most of the Native American Indians had settled further inland over the past hundred years or so with the arrival of the Europeans and consequently he was less likely to meet any of them in the woods. To date, Nathaniel knew nothing about nor had met any of the indigenous people of the American continent. Jeremiah had urged him to take a pistol, musket and hunting knife, which he had at first refused but when his friend explained to him there were potentially dangerous beasts which he could encounter, such as bears and wolves, he relented. However, he had to confess he had no idea how to use the weapons so Jeremiah arranged to provide him with some instruction and practice over the days before he left. His good friend also explained that he may well need to hunt for food on the way because some of the settlements could well have been abandoned or may not have much more than what they needed for themselves.

He was in a pensive and wary mood after he parted from Jeremiah, becoming more sombre as he entered the interior woods. Leaving the city had been a relief, especially as he became increasingly aware of the turbulence which simmered just below the surface, but as he travelled further through the endlessly inscrutable forest, whose denizens he couldn't read, he became more and more uncomfortable. There was not a soul to exchange greetings with and he felt as though he could be swallowed up in this immense world of trees, lost for ever. As the light began to dim it added to his gloom and feelings of isolation, but then he heard the distant, unmistakable sounds of industry which transformed him completely. Coming closer to the source he heard the welcome sound of metal on metal growing louder, transporting him back to his beloved Coalbrookdale with all its intimate associations. The gloaming path suddenly emerged into a noisy and frenzied centre of activity. There was an unmistakable foundry and a hundred yards away a building which must be the furnace judging from the smoke and flames issuing from it. Half-naked men were coming and going too busy to notice the arrival of a stranger. Then, above the happy cacophony, he was hailed by a gruff colonial voice.

'Hey, mister, what are you after here?' a large man with bulging muscles, perspiration drenching his hair and brow, asked him in a none too pleasant manner. He was clearly coming to the end of the shift and exhausted by his daily endeavours was in little mood to be more civil. Nathaniel understood this well and took no offence.

'Good day, sir, I'm looking for the proprietor of this enterprise and should be glad if you could point out where I might find him.' The work man now stopped and looked more closely at Nathaniel in order to take his measure. He noticed he was well shod and provisioned, judging therefore that he should accede to the request. He pointed to a small timber-built cabin that was not easily discernible in the surrounding woods from which there was now the glow of an oil lamp shining,

'Aye, that'll be Mr Dean. You'll find him yonder in the cabin.' Nathaniel dismounted, tied his horse to a tree and walked stiffly towards the cabin door. As he arrived, it opened and he was met by a friendly man in his early 40s in shirtsleeves but otherwise well-dressed.

'Welcome, sir, we don't get many visitors here in the woods so it is a pleasure to relieve the tedium by exchanging words so long as they don't come to do us harm.' He held out a clean and well-manicured hand, which Nathaniel took happily,

'You have absolutely no reason to fear me, sir. Indeed, I hope it will be to the contrary – advantageous to both of us. I am Nathaniel Shawcross, from England, at your service, sir.'

'Well, I'm blessed,' he said with a light southern Irish accent, 'Josiah Dean, at yours. Please, come and take a seat. Tell me how I may be of assistance to you.' Nathaniel was delighted at this reception and seating himself comfortably, albeit gently on his horse weary behind, explained the purpose of his visit.

'I am an iron master from Coalbrookdale in Shropshire – you may perhaps have heard of us – the Coalbrookdale Ironworks? We are one of the largest and fastest growing ironworks in the country.'

'I've heard something of a Dale works run by a Quaker family by the name of Darby and that they have perfected a method for smelting iron using coke from coal,' replied Josiah.

'Yes, that's the very one and I have been working there myself for two years, learning the business from top to bottom with the help of Abraham Darby the third, the young son of the current proprietress, Abia Darby. We produce a wide range of goods for home consumption and we specialise in building steam engines for which we need a great deal of high-quality pig iron. We have already imported some from the colonies but more is needed and when I heard of your enterprise here, I thought I would enquire as to the possibility of you being able to supply some to us. I know for the most part you are all still using charcoal, of which there is a ready supply, unlike England, and the quality of the pig iron is good.'

'Well, my young master, you couldn't have arrived at a better time. I have just acquired the works with a view to establishing a slitting mill and nail factory as there is great demand for such items. However, we continue to run a bloomery and produce a modest amount of pig iron for the adjacent colonies, but recently we have been hit by a surprising downturn in demand that is a great disappointment having just acquired the business. Consequently, your request couldn't be more welcome and may well save this small community from going under.'

'Yes, I'm not surprised you are struggling because people seem to be more concerned with politics at the moment rather than production,' replied Nathaniel sardonically. 'Nevertheless, I'd be willing to take all the pig iron that you can produce as soon as possible shipping it in suitable quantities from Boston to Bristol. I have an open bill of purchase with me which is signed by my Mistress allowing me simply to insert the suitable details of date, cost and quantity. Our credit is good and you could apply to Jeremiah Goodman in Boston as a referee for confirmation, if you doubt it.'

'You may well be right, Mr Shawcross, but I can assure you that without trade this little community will not have much of a future. The people around here are honest, hard-working folk and have little time for the political shenanigans in Boston. If you are true to your word, I'm sure we could settle the details tomorrow morning. I note the hour is late so might I enquire whether you are looking for lodgings for the night? If so, I'd be more than happy to invite you to stay with me and my family in the nearby village.'

'That's most gracious of you, sir. People appear to be so hospitable in this New World, though I haven't seen much of it yet.'

Thus it was, that the first stage of Nathaniel's journey was pleasantly successful and he now felt buoyed up to continue to the next enterprise which was a further one hundred and fifty miles along the route, on the other side of the great Hudson River. His confidence in the locals, his business mission and New England was riding high, but this wasn't to last.

As he thought, there were more settlements in the southern coastal zone than had he followed the more northerly route. He therefore didn't have to worry about finding shelter or sustenance along the way, which was well provided by both along this well-travelled Boston to New York postal path. Wayside Inns were well established so the dangers and rigours of the deep forest were now no longer what they had seemed at the outset. He was also able to take stock of the extent of the disaffection with the mother country that he had become aware of in Boston. People seemed to be remarkably well informed and keen to learn more from travellers, leaflets and the royal post riders who were a most important conduit of news and, as he later learned, disaffection and in some cases outright rebellion.

It was unmistakable when he arrived in New York. There were hundreds of ships in the harbour and a multitude of boats of all shapes and sizes plying up and down what he correctly guessed was the Hudson River. The whole area was busy with land and sea traffic with small industrious enterprises everywhere dwarfing even those of Boston. He stayed overnight in one of the coastal Inns and enquired about the best way to travel to his next destination, which he knew was further north up the river at Monroe, not far away from Albany, a flourishing and important fortified town. He was told he could either take a boat up the river to Albany, although that would be costly, or he could take a well-trodden Indian trail east of the river which would bring him there within three days. He was informed this was safe because a great many settlers had moved into the area forcing the Indians out and further west. As he was aware of having to conserve his money until he reached Albany, he decided to take the old Indian trail.

Chapter 12
Savages

Etow-a-Kaum stood wistfully taking one final look at Shemkaneko. There was not much to show for the settlement where he had lived most of his life – a few rearranged stones and grassed over mounds. He could still see where the long houses had stood radiating outwards from the central nucleus providing shelter, a home for over 400 people. After they had been forced out of their ancestral homes by the invading Mohawk, they had fled across the great River That Flows Both Ways, moving south until they found this haven of peace in a hidden and secluded valley of the Shemkaneko Creek. His mind travelled back across the decades like an ever-shifting kaleidoscope bringing into focus so many friends from his youth and early manhood – so many then, so few now. It had been an indulgence to return to this spot where he knew it was too dangerous to stay for long, but he had wanted to show his family their ancestral home before he joined his forefathers in the Great Beyond. Over the campfire at night he brought back the days of his youth for them when they fished for trout and salmon in the creek; meeting the Moravians with whom they conversed in Dutch that many of the elders could speak; and going from ridiculing them and their beliefs, coming to accept the revelations they brought. They were peaceable, honourable people who treated the Indians as equals, teaching them new farming techniques and telling them of a world from over the Great Waters where the whites lived fighting endlessly and ferociously amongst themselves. There had been peace for many moons for his clan in these quiet eddies, especially when the early Dutch settlers were more interested in trading furs than land. Then it had seemed as if there were space for all, but the whites never ceased coming until, pushing deeper and deeper into the woods away from the coast, began to demand all the land they saw, saying it was God's will it should be theirs. It was true, there were some whites who were different treating them like brothers and seeking to protect their settlements. The Moravians built a school and chapel teaching them about Christianity, until they too were threatened by the new arrivals and expelled just as the Mohican. Their white brothers migrated North and West to a place the whites called Pennsylvania where there were others like them, but they were forced to go south and east to the reservation in Stockport where they had lived now for over two hundred moons. There was little left of the earlier physical settlement, but the spirit of the Moravians remained as nearly a quarter of the Mohicans of Shemkaneko became Christian, as did he. They were now known as the "praying Christians", but it had not protected them from expulsion.

At the moment that Etow-a-Kaum slowly turned away from the visions of his youth, there was a single musket shot. He was immediately alert. It was coming from the direction that his family had taken beginning the return to Stockport. He gripped his long, ancient musket even more tightly and taking hold of his war tomahawk, the tall silver-haired warrior ran with long measured steps towards the sound. Despite his 63 years, his muscles were firm and his resolve even firmer to be prepared for any eventuality. A few hundred yards along the trail he came across what he most feared. There was his son, Sauk, with blood still pouring from a hole in his chest – he saw that he was already dead. As he knelt down, tenderly caressing his still warm face, he heard a rustling behind him. Turning with remarkable speed, his tomahawk poised, he was just in time to recognise his young teenage grandson before he plunged the ancient deadly weapon into his skull. The boy was tearful and bloodied from trying to rouse his lifeless father, but now he stood mastering his emotions.

'Great father,' he said struggling to remain composed, 'we were all travelling together when a shot was fired and my father fell as you see him now. I hid myself in the nearby bushes and my mother, grandmother and two sisters ran along the trail until I heard screaming which suddenly stopped...' At that very moment two more shots rang out reverberating eerily through the forest.

'Follow me,' said his grandfather, 'and bring your father's musket and tomahawk. Quickly!'

For the past three hours he had been quietly moving through a colourful woodland of silver birches interspersed with alder, juniper and brown oak. The trail meandered avoiding rocky erratics and hidden brooks but his horse trotted presciently along the well-defined way and as the sun glittered dazzlingly off the smooth variegated leaves, he felt himself dozing in the warmth of a late morning sun. As he came around the next bend, he was plunged into a scene from Dante's Inferno. He drifted as if in a dream into a picture from hell itself, the air thick with gore and mayhem. A small child stood to one side, frozen and mute at the horror unfolding before it. Another, somewhat older child, lay face down her head cloven in two in a deep pool of blood and brains. In the centre of the tableau were two white men busy at work, oblivious to his arrival. Both were on their knees, one to the left, with his left hand over a young Indian woman and his right clutching a bloody tomahawk, was forcefully raping her, the other to the right was engaged in scalping an older woman, bloodied and beaten, with the largest hunting knife he had ever seen. Nathaniel who had never seen anything like this in his life nor in his wildest imaginations, felt time stand still so that every movement slowed almost to a complete full stop. His mind became detached from his body and he was completely unaware that his hands had reached mechanically towards the loaded musket in the holster besides his horse's raised head, hardly registering the smoothness of the walnut stock or the warmth of the gun barrel and trigger mechanism as he aimed, cocked and fired point-blank at one of the murderous assailants before him. As the other turned around to see who had dared to interrupt his business, Nathaniel had taken the pistol from the small holster at the side of the saddle and fired into the broad chest of the startled man. Then he reeled from his horse and was violently sick before he could do anything else. When his horse neighed and reared, he came to himself at last and secured it to a nearby sapling. He tried to make sense of what had just happened but couldn't. He had taken the lives of two human beings which was unthinkable. How he had reacted in such a manner he would never know, but the reason why was gruesomely evident all around him. He had learned something about himself today, something he didn't like, something that was deeply hidden within him and even in that moment he became afraid of himself. It was a moment that would haunt him for the rest of his life even though he would do something like it in the future. He knew he had to take control of himself and the situation. There were two other human beings now who needed his help and he must think through the consequences of what had just happened.

Looking up he saw the barrel of a long musket pointing directly at him. It was a tall, elderly but fierce-looking Indian staring straight at him. By his side, was a youth, not much more than a stripling, but holding another musket also trained at his head. He realised at once that they held him responsible for the carnage so horribly damning, but before anything else could happen the Indian girl who had been so sadistically violated said something in her own language that he didn't understand. The expressions on the faces of the old man and the youth immediately changed from one of murderous intent to deep relief. She had evidently told them that it wasn't he who had killed her family but in fact was her saviour. Nathaniel stood up shakily addressing the two Indian males in an exhausted voice,

'I am Nathaniel Shawcross from England and when I came upon these two men, they were carrying out an act of savagery that I have never before beheld. I am responsible for killing both of them, which I regret sincerely but could think of no other way of stopping them from what they were about.'

'I am a sachem, a chieftain of the Mohican and these are my family,' he spoke in English. He then went over to his eldest granddaughter and spoke more with her in their own language. There was a moan from the woman that until now, Nathaniel and everyone else had thought was dead. She had only been half scalped and must have been knocked unconscious not to have resisted her attacker further. It was Etow-a-Kaum's daughter-in-law and he rushed to her at once to inspect her wound immediately taking some leaves and moss from a deerskin bag that hung at his side. He applied these gently to her gaping scalp and with leather thongs from the same bag he secured them tightly in place around her head. Meanwhile, the youth had gathered the small child to himself and comforted him as best he could. Nathaniel felt helpless until he remembered the water bottle by his side and offered it to the children and the older girl, who took it with alacrity.

'I and my family are in your debt, English man, and I am grateful that you did not hesitate to strike these evil men. You seem shocked at what you have done, but I'm afraid to tell you that these are the ways of the woods and in particular of the white men against my people.'

'It is against my religion to kill,' replied Nathaniel, 'but I don't know what else I could have done.'

'Do not be ashamed, Nathaniel Shawcross, you may have taken life but you have also saved it. Those you killed were neither women nor children, and yet they did not scruple to do what they did. My religion also forbids me to take another's life but had I arrived before you, I would have done exactly the same. It is now rare to find white men around here who think as you do. Even though I and my family are Christians, they will not hesitate to take our lives.' At this, Nathaniel was shocked and horrified.

'You are Christian? I didn't know any native Indians were.'

'Oh yes, my brother, many of my tribe are. We are Moravian Christians. Perhaps you may have heard of us?'

'I have indeed,' replied Nathaniel, 'there are still a number of such remaining in England and they are sincere and pious people, not unlike my own brothers in faith. I am a Quaker, sir, and hold all men to be equal and should be treated so.'

'Then, give me your hand brother as our beliefs are not unalike. There are others of your ilk in a place called Pennsylvania, but around here you will not be welcome and perhaps in as much danger as we are. Better help me with these bodies – hide them in the deep woods because if anyone comes across them now, we will be in grave danger.' When they had disposed of the bodies by dragging them further off the trail, knowing that wild animals would soon obliterate their corpses, Etow-a-Kaum then wrapped the dead grandchild in a deer hide and strapped it to one of the dead men's horses which they had found. He explained that he would take it back to Shemkaneko for suitable burial along with his son whose body was back on the trail near the old settlement. He also advised that they should leave the trail as quickly as possible now and learning that Nathaniel wanted to go north towards Albany, he said they could travel together part of the way until he and his family would need to turn east towards home. They would have to spend another night at the old village, but the following morning he would show Nathaniel a smaller and quieter trail, unknown to whites, that he should take, which would be much safer for him.

Etow-a-Kaum selected a quiet glade hidden between two small hills, not far from the remnants of the destroyed village. They should not be seen by anyone coming along the main trail. Further along, he chose a peaceful spot to dig as deep a hole as he could with Nathaniel's help. The others collected as many stones as they could find to place on the bodies, after which they covered them with earth and then more, even larger stones to keep them from being dug up by the woodland animals. The Mohican said prayers in his own language and quoted from the Algonquin Bible that had been translated from the English by a devoted Moravian missionary many years ago. Nathaniel read Psalm 23 and recited the Lord's Prayer as his contribution to honouring the dead. That evening they sat around a small campfire where they swapped stories about the worlds that each of them had known. The others sat entranced periodically asking their grandfather to translate some of the words from the English, which although they spoke it on the reservation, contained terms they had never heard before such as engine and coalmine.

Before dawn Nathaniel was shaken awake by Little Blue Dolphin, the chief's granddaughter, who placed a small hand over his mouth as a sign for him to keep quiet. He couldn't help marvelling at the resilience of this young Indian girl who had been attacked so savagely by a white man but who now had come to warn him. She whispered to him to pack quickly and silently as there were riders coming up the trail. The old Mohican ensured their presence that night was obliterated before leading them up a small trail going in a northerly direction but increasingly departing from the main trail. After two hours, and having ensured they were not being followed, Etow-a-Kaum came up to Nathaniel and told him that he thought the dawn riders were probably settlers out looking for the two missing men. However, he was disturbed to note they had two Delaware native trackers with them and it could only be a matter of time before they discovered the bodies, having already read the signs of a violent struggle further back on the main trail. They carried on for a further three hours until they reached a bifurcation, one path going north and the other East.

'This is where we must part, my brother,' holding up his hand in native Indian fashion. 'Be wary when you reach Albany because I fear these pursuers are sufficiently determined to go that far and make enquiries. Don't advertise to anyone that you may have come by the main trail from the south but instead have journeyed in from the East, along the upper post road from Boston. I'm sure we will be quite safe returning to Stockport.' He then paused and took something from the leather satchel at his side. 'It has been a pleasure to meet such an honourable man and I and my family will continue to be in your debt with your name passing from one generation to the next in remembrance of what you have done. I would like you to take this as a token of our eternal gratitude,' and he passed over to Nathaniel a wampum belt that he knew to be of great value to the Woodland Indians of the Hudson River. Nathaniel had half expected something like this might happen and he had considered what he might give in return. Gift giving was a powerful sign of friendship amongst indigenous peoples.

'The honour is all mine, great sachem, and our meeting will forever remain in my memory as sharp as it is at present. In return, I have a gift for you and your family,' and he handed over a beautiful leather-bound King James I Bible wrapped in soft silk. It was a gift equal to the value of the other and the Mohican was visibly impressed. 'Go in peace, my brother, and may God be with you.' The two parties then took their different ways.

Chapter 13
Albany

As he rode through the dank pines it was raining hard and had there not been the slim outline of a trail, he would have been hard-pressed to know which way to go. Since leaving his friends earlier, the path had steepened and the weather had turned dark and ominous. His horse had to pick its way carefully between glistening, gnarled, slippery tree roots and equally treacherous large circular stones. His mood reflected the weather as he ruminated on the events of the past two days. He was beginning to wonder what induced people to travel to this so-called New World – to him it was increasingly resembling a savage prehistoric one. He then stepped out of the menacing forest into a clearing that signalled his arrival at Albany.
There was an ageing stockade, brightened here and there by a section of new pine wood replacing rotted sections. The entrance lay through a guardhouse where there were two redcoats. As he made to go through, he was challenged by one of the guards to state his name, business and where he had come from. They wrote his name in a ledger book and in answer to his query about a good place to seek lodgings, they referred him to the Algonquin Hotel, which he would find if he carried straight on and that would bring him out into the central square of the town. He was anxious to get out of the atrociously heavy rain and cold winds that seemed to be funnelled from all the side streets into the centre. He found the recommended hotel

and having arranged for the care of his horse, he replaced his sodden clothing with a dry shirt and leggings that he had kept secure from the wet. He then threw himself on the bed and slept for a good few hours. He was awoken by a peremptory knocking at his door. It was insistent and aggressive so he roused himself as best he could and opened it in his stocking feet.

'You are to come with us,' said an armed officious redcoat, 'to the governor's residence immediately.' Nathaniel was taken completely by surprise and queried the command,

'What's all this about? I have only just arrived in the city taking some much-needed rest.'

'That's not for us to say. The governor will explain when you are before him. Now, come quickly.'

It was clear these soldiers were impatient to return, complete their duty and seek out a warm room somewhere. They appeared to blame him for the cause of their discomfort having to venture forth in the foul weather. He quickly donned his riding boots and threw a cloak around him.

He was hurriedly led through the central streets to a large imposing mansion where he was cursorily searched for weapons and then shown into a large office from which the governor exercised his authority. When Nathaniel was escorted in, the two redcoats remained at his side until the governor, who was looking distractedly out of a large paned window, turned around and nodded for them to depart.

'Mr Shawcross, pray tell me exactly who you are, why you are here and from whence, via which route, you have travelled.' The governor was in no mood to engage in the conventional social niceties for people of his station. Perhaps he didn't think Nathaniel warranted it or the urgency of the situation demanded it be ignored. Nathaniel thought perhaps it was the latter, since his clothes suggested he was no rough frontiers man. He nonetheless decided to adopt a modicum of civility to the powerful man before him, and bowing suitably said,

'You seem to know my name already, sir, but I have letters here both to confirm that and state my business.' He handed over a letter from Abia Derby, which was the introduction to the proprietor of the Monroe Ironworks in the nearby Orange County. The governor perused it carefully,

'So, you are an iron master recently arrived from England I presume?'

'Yes, sir, I've been staying for a few weeks in Boston, with Jeremiah Goodman and his family, whom I befriended on the crossing from Bristol. I'm hoping to establish some trade with Master Townsend whom I believe has recently taken over the Monroe works not far from here, which is the largest undertaking of its kind in the colonies. They are also said to produce extremely good quality wrought iron.'

'I see. Well you certainly seem to be who you say you are but I must ask you exactly which route did you travel here by from Boston.'

'I was advised to go by the Upper Post Road after a short deviation I made to the Taunton Ironworks, not far from Boston itself.'

'You are quite sure about that, Mr Shawcross?' It was difficult for Nathaniel to lie at all never mind convincingly but he knew if he didn't his native Indian friends would be in mortal danger. It was a moral dilemma but he knew which choice he had to make.

'Yes, I'm quite certain of it.'

'And, you didn't meet anyone on the way?'

'No, sir, I did not. It was a very lonely journey. It seems to be a little used route.'

The governor scrutinised his face closely.

'You see, Mr Shawcross, I have been informed that two settlers' bodies were found in the woods to the south having been shot brutally at close range. They were left for the wild animals to consume in a quite unchristian fashion, which points to the work of Indians, savages that they are, but for the fact that they were shot in the way they were. Savages would probably have tomahawked them as well as scalping them, which they weren't. Furthermore, I'm told that this probably occurred yesterday or the day before and the only person coming from the south easterly direction is you. Ordinarily, I wouldn't be concerned about the death of two settlers, who are often hardly more civilised than the aboriginals, but in this case they happened to be members of a local militia group which has considerable influence in the area and I'm being pressured by unsavoury groups like the Patriots to investigate their murders.' He continued to look at Nathaniel carefully before continuing,

'Tell me, Mr Shawcross, are you a godly Christian man?'

'Yes, sir, I'm a Quaker, as is my employer.'

'Hm… That makes it more unlikely that you are involved in this business. However, I'm concerned about those who won't bother themselves with such detail. I suggest you don't stay long in Albany and maintain a discrete presence only whilst you are here.'

The interview had shaken Nathaniel, not because of the potential danger to himself, but because he felt like Peter denying Christ in the Garden of Gethsemane, when he denied him three times. It was as if he had denied his faith twice now. He decided to take the governor's advice and remained in his room for the rest of the evening, taking his meal there instead of in the public bar. He had work to do. He had to write home to Mistress Abia briefing her about the recent successes he had had at the Taunton enterprise as well as letting her know about the next stage of his journey. More importantly, he had to write to Rebecca in the hope that the letter would somehow get to her within the next few weeks. A lot had happened since he'd arrived in Boston and he wanted to convey as much as he could about this as a way of reflecting and sharing the experience with her. He was missing her presence very much as he was Elijah's so he wrote an additional note for him with more detail and commentary on the volatile political situation which he'd observed. None of the conflict between the Royal authorities and the colonial settlers, bordering on insurrection, was known or understood by those at home. In Albany he had discovered the Royal Governor was limited in his powers of authority primarily because he had so few troops to maintain the King's law with a huge and swelling number of rebels seemingly acting with impunity. He emphasised to Elijah that their pretext was to point out the corruption of royal officials, especially tax collectors and land agents, but in reality they were greedy to obtain more land to the west despite invoking Indian resistance and retaliation. They were also claiming they were become slaves to parliamentary law when they had their own assemblies and could rule themselves. Their laws, however, were blatantly to support the overriding of royal protection for the native Indians and to steal their lands. In one colony the National Assembly tried to pass a law that Indians could be killed with impunity. All colonies supported the right for people to own slaves and to restrict the opportunity for any of them to be freed. Nathaniel wrote that it was hard to reconcile political ideas associated with "The Rights of Man" with what was reality in the colonies of New England.

It was almost midnight when there was another imperious knock at the door. When he opened it, he was addressed by a redcoat officer whom he recognised from his previous visit to the governor.

'Master Shawcross,' the officer saluted him and addressed him civilly, 'I have a message from His Excellency, the Royal Governor…' He looked around anxiously, 'May I enter, sir?' Nathaniel gestured for him to enter and firmly closed the door.

'I'm sorry but one cannot be too careful as none of the colonists can be trusted to be loyal to the Crown. The governor is very concerned about your safety as the militia are going from house to house in search of anyone newly arrived in the city. He has arranged for you to have an escort at dawn out of the city which will take you safely to your next destination at the Monroe Ironworks. I shall be in charge of the detail and will meet you in the side street by the hotel at 5 AM. There are

Mohawk Indians en route but they are loyal to us and we will have no trouble from that quarter.'

They were careful not to be seen as they left Albany, crossing the narrow passage of the upper Hudson into Orange County. By mid-morning, he had been safely delivered to the Monroe Works and introduced to the proprietor, Peter Townsend. When he explained his errand and showed him his letters of introduction, the iron master was delighted to be able to show him proudly around. He'd heard of the Derby Ironworks and was very much interested in the process of using coke from coal for fuel. Equally, Nathaniel was extremely interested to examine the high-quality pig and wrought iron that was produced there. He also showed him drawings of the new steam engines they were producing for pumping water out of the mines. He succeeded in obtaining an order for two such engines from Peter Townsend as well as securing a commitment from him to supply 30 tons of top-quality pig iron to the Darby works each month. In his own mind, Nathaniel wasn't sure how long such a contract might last given the increasing political instability but he thought that whatever they could get would be better than nothing. He asked how the extensive enterprise managed to flourish in the midst of so many potentially hostile natives and was told they had a very good trading relationship with them. The Mohawks traded beaver skins and other furs for iron goods, including muskets, axes and musket balls. They would also take skillets, pots and knives to trade with other Indians further north and west towards the Great Lakes. This mutual relationship had served to keep the peace for many years. When Nathaniel disclosed to Peter Townsend that he was interested in travelling further west, particularly into Pennsylvania to observe how his coreligionists had built the good society, the latter offered to arrange a number of Mohawk guides to go with him. He knew that the Munroe business sent goods down the Hudson for transport to Bristol so he asked Peter to convey his correspondence with the next shipment which he readily agreed to. Nathaniel now looked forward to the next and perhaps most adventurous stage of his journey, although he sincerely hoped it would not extend to include the violence he had recently experienced.

Chapter 14
Mohawk

As they ventured deeper into the great woods, Nathaniel was thankful that he had four mohawk guides with him. There was no recognisable trail so far as he could see and increasingly, they had to urge their horses up steeper and steeper ground. Apparently, there was a mountain range called the Alleghenies between them and their destination. During the journey he had plenty of time to study his companions who seemed to be quite different from the Mohicans whom he had befriended on the other side of the river. Their hair decoration, which comprised of a small circular cluster of tufts on the crown of the head, contrasted with the long narrow band of hair stretching from the forehead to the nape of the necks of the Mohicans. But like all Indians he had seen so far, they used feathers and coloured pigment to adorn themselves whilst instead of shaving all unwanted hair on head and face each one had been carefully plucked out as it appeared. Their clothes were similar too with deerskin loincloths and leggings, which some wore against the cold. In summer, their chests were naked unless adorned by some item of European clothing, a favourite being an old discarded redcoat they had traded somewhere. All had a leather necklace and bracelet decorated with bone or shells. Each guide was well equipped for war with a modern musket, iron tomahawk and a long steel scalping knife. Unlike the Mohicans, however, he had met only a few days before the Mohawk seemed to possess no regard for personal cleanliness.

Their yellow skins were made even yellower by the grime from their physical environment or the bodily fluids and blood of the animals they killed. They were clearly amazed at his daily ablutions whenever he could find running water. Their ability to converse in English was remarkably good, perhaps a result of working so closely with the soldiers and trading frequently with the settlers. He knew, of course that a number of them would also be able to speak French and Dutch, and possibly other native Indian languages. He'd been told that they spoke Iroquois whereas the Mohicans spoke Algonquin, separate languages that defined their ethnicity and kept them apart. Around the evening campfire, they were keen to learn about the England he came from and he astonished them with accounts of the industry which was blossoming there and the importance of the canal system for getting around. In return, the oldest amongst them Metacom, recounted the history of their people.

'In the days of our forefathers' forefathers, the Mohawk were one of the great nations of the Iroquois Confederacy stretching all the way from the north eastern shores of the river Mohawk to the great Lakes in the West and the great St Lawrence Seaway in the north-east to the lands of the whale hunting Innu. In those days of long ago, we were the Keepers of the North East doorway and none from there to the Great Sea dared cross the river to the north or the east for fear of our warriors. We were the most feared in the land and our women the most fair. Our confederacy kept the peace and stifled the predations of the Algonquin Nations until the coming of the white man from North and South upset the balance. At first, we traded furs and allowed him to settle, not thinking there would be many more to come. The French from the North then pressed down giving guns to their Huron allies, our ancient enemies. We were sorely pressed but fought back valiantly and with the help of our Dutch friends managed to repel them. We established our supremacy both south of the Mohawk up to the Delaware coastal line and the Mohican we pushed back eastwards over the River that Flows Both Ways. Thus we stayed for many moons until the Great Sickness nearly wiped us out and we were weak and so few in numbers that our borders were pushed back by the enemy. Then the English came supplanting the Dutch but we became allies with them as they were enemies of the French and the Huron. And so, we have remained since that time, although we are increasingly alarmed at the numbers of settlers arriving in the place they call New York from where they have overtaken our lands progressively moving west and north. However, we have taken comfort from the recent great Proclamation of King George (1763) to draw a line over which the settlers are prohibited from going because they are recognised as our lands. We fought well and loyally alongside the British to crush both our enemies and for this the king rewarded us. Some settlers have crossed over the Ohio River and begun to explore west of the Appalachians – these we have and will push back if the King's redcoats do not.'

Nathaniel listened enthralled to the monologue of the older Mohawk, delivered in near flawless English that he could understand.

'Do you think,' he asked, 'there are enough soldiers to keep the settlers from crossing the line?'

'If they were to use their cannon to do this, it may be possible with our help.'

'Do you think the King's soldiers will shoot on his own people? Already there are many signs that the settlers will not heed the Royal Governors and have set up independent militias, whom they call Regulators to clear the land of the Indians settled therein and kill any Royal messengers or agents who attempt to apply the King's law.'

'What you say may well be true, my friend, but we live in their midst and unless they attack us, we will not raise arms against them, except when they cross the line.'

Thwack! A long thin arrow grazed Nathaniel's ear and sank deeply into the tall, narrow pine he was just passing. Immediately the four Mohawk guides dropped agilely to one side of their horses as if it had been choreographed. Only Nathaniel was left visibly an easy target for the next missile or would have been if Metacom hadn't shouted for him to dive to the ground. He had already signalled to the others to circle around from both flanks in a wide arc in order to detect the unseen assailant. A second arrow had come almost instantaneously with the first sinking painfully into the thigh of one of the guides who, beyond a peremptory gasp, carried on with his manoeuvres. Nathaniel wondered whether he ought to try and retrieve one of his arms but decided to stay unmoving on the ground. He reasoned that whoever it was that had tried to kill him might think he'd succeeded if he kept perfectly still. Again, in the suspension of time that always seemed to accompany such occasions for him, what seemed like an eternity was only a few minutes when two shots rang out and a bloodcurdling whoop signalled to Metacom that his companions had been successful in finding and disabling their attackers. When the others returned, they were carrying the scalps of two Delaware scouts who they said were the advanced party of a much larger group of well-armed Regulators. They must have been tracked from the ironworks and were probably the same as had been searching for Nathaniel in Albany. Metacom decided they must seek reinforcements or be overcome. He knew of a hunting settlement only a few miles from where they were, considering that a good place to make a defensive stand or to obtain help from their brothers. It was, however, likely he thought they would be out hunting until late in the day unless they'd had great success in the previous days, when they would be resting. They hurried through the increasingly dense undergrowth as fast as they could, having to dismount and pull their horses up steep banks or through intimidating thickets. Although they couldn't see them, they knew the settlers would not be far behind and they had to have time to secure effective defensive positions when they arrived at the hunting camp. Fortunately, there were half a dozen hunters just recently returned from a three-day expedition but despite being exhausted they prepared to help defend the new arrivals against whatever came through the woods unbidden. There was a plentiful supply of arrows, powder and shot and in places there were partial palisades to provide some protection. As the first wave of Regulators arrived, they were taken completely by surprise and fell when they emerged into the open. The number of shots served to stall their attackers who then regrouped and decided to encircle the small encampment and destroy its inhabitants with overpowering firepower. One of the Mohawk, however, had been sent to find as many of the other hunters as he could to break the potentially fatal encirclement. Nathaniel and the others settled down for a merciless siege requiring total alertness at all times if they were to survive. He was impressed by the fact that not one of the Mohawks even mentioned the possibility of delivering him up to his enemies. Again, he was plunged into the middle of uninvited violence and had no choice but to kill or be killed. They were well camouflaged but the attackers were numerous and disinclined to break off their assault. They were still incensed by the death of their two companions on the other side of the river. When nightfall came, there was still no relief and periodically the Regulators would sally forth hoping to overwhelm the defenders, who for their part fought with a fearless determination so characteristic of their tribe which had inspired terror throughout the north-east. At one point, Nathaniel had no alternative but to use his tomahawk in hand to hand fighting when the rush was so fierce there was no time to reload his musket or pistol. At least half of the defenders were now severely wounded or dead. From the last encounter, Nathaniel had received a musket ball in the right arm and he was virtually beyond defending himself. There were many bodies of the attackers piling up around them, but he knew it was just a short matter of time before they were defeated as well as knowing that no quarter would be given. Then he heard several volleys of fire in the distance realising that help had arrived at last. The Mohawks overwhelmed what remained of the attackers and in turn gave no quarter, whooping with delight at the number of scalps they took that night. They urged Nathaniel to do the same as they observed he had fought valiantly, but he would not do so, which bemused them greatly because it was common practice amongst the colonial whites.

Metacom inspected Nathaniel's wound and found the ball was still in the arm although fortunately it didn't seem to have broken the bone. Nevertheless, he said it would have to be taken out quickly or he would die, so heating his scalping knife to a red-hot point he dug it out, after which he bound the wound with antiseptic moss. Nathaniel had fainted during this procedure and when he came to, he found he was lying on a bed of dry bracken where he was told he should remain for at least a day before he tried to travel. They were not too far from the border with Pennsylvania and the Mohawks decided it would be better to get him over the line and into an Amish community nearby so he could recover more safely.

Chapter 15
The Holy Experiment

Here he was, again before the shining pearly gates that were adamantly closed fast against him, whilst others glided past him and into the impossible brightness beyond. He strained every sinew and muscle in his body to move but he was stuck fast. He gripped the blood red Bible in his right hand, but when he tried to raise it, he couldn't. When he tried to shout, his throat burned and he felt the heat from the fires of eternity at his back grow hotter as they came closer. Then the great voice boomed out,

'Is that the book you held in your left hand, John Leder, at Castenago?'

He trembled at the righteous anger in the voice, feeling the sound waves crash over him as if they were from a mighty sea.

'And in the other, did you not hold a tomahawk?' the voice boomed again relentlessly.

The heat was so intense he felt his head would explode.

'And with that tomahawk did you not split open the heads of my children, spitting and cursing their very existence?'

It was always the same. The same recurrent nightmare when he woke up bathed in sweat and shivering even in Midsummer. But John Leder had nothing to be ashamed of nor feel guilty about, and this is what he couldn't understand. He had done his duty by protecting his flock against the savages by destroying them before they destroyed the settlers. The Indians in Paxton may have been Christian, but that was in name only. Anyway, he reasoned, they were of the Moravian Church, which was very dubiously Christian. Everyone knew they passed on information to the bloodthirsty tribes on the frontier who then raided the unprotected squatters, torching their farms, scalping and tearing foetuses from pregnant women. It had been going on for over 20 years and they'd had enough. A stand had to be taken to protect themselves as the Pennsylvania Governing Assembly would do nothing to criticise or condemn the Indians. Worse than that, they had even given protection to them in the capital, Philadelphia, providing accommodation and the protection of soldiers. By God's grace and the knives of his followers, Paxton was now free of the vermin and the land properly settled by God-fearing Christian folk. The Quaker leadership had even the audacity to issue warrants of arrest for the brave lads who had carried out the will of God, but no one had lifted a finger against them nor tried to help arrest them, even though their deeds had been done in full view of their neighbours who knew exactly who they were. There was widespread, collective, tacit approval and everyone issued a sigh of relief when it was over. They could relax and enjoy their new lands. No, John Leder, the fighting Pastor of Paxton Presbyterian Mission Church was guilty of nothing more than carrying out the will of the Lord. He was a local hero and fast becoming known throughout the colonies. Yet, he could not sleep easy in his bed and hadn't done these past eight years.

Nathaniel was made comfortable in one of the Amish barns with his horse and pack late at night where he would be discovered by the German-speaking puritans. The Mohawks hadn't wanted to show themselves because they distrusted these strange insular European settlers fearing they would be shot on sight, but this way they had carried out their orders to the British by helping Nathaniel to his destination. They were just over the border in north-eastern Pennsylvania where the Mohawks were aware that Indians tended to be shot without question.

He was discovered in the early morning by a young Amish girl who screamed and ran for her elders. Someone had to be sent for who could speak English before they were able to make sense of the young Englishman's presence. When they realised he was wounded and needed help, they were more than pleased to provide it. A middle-aged man called Carl Stein, a widower whose family had been lost to smallpox, offered to take care of him as he could speak some English having lived in England as a refugee for a few years. It was in this way that Nathaniel was able to learn a little more about Pennsylvania. During the two weeks that he stayed with Carl he began to realise the complexity of American politics. He was told that the Amish were a peaceful Christian German Protestant sect who had been heavily persecuted during the religious wars in Europe, but some of them had managed to survive and eventually flee firstly to England and thence to Pennsylvania in the late 17th century, by invitation of William Penn.

'I believe,' said Nathaniel, 'that William Penn was highly revered by both the settlers he encouraged to live on his land and the Indians with whom he concluded many peaceful treaties?'

'That is true,' replied Carl, 'but today not everyone reveres his memory and his sons have struggled to keep true to his original vision.'

'And what was that?' asked Nathaniel.

'That all men are equal and deserve to be treated equally everywhere and in every condition.'

'Don't you believe that also?'

'Amongst ourselves, of course we do, but we have come to learn that outside our own communities the world is an evil place which we must shun.'

'What about those who are not Amish?'

'They will do what they believe is right but experience has shown us they are not to be trusted and therefore we keep ourselves to ourselves, pure in the way of the Lord.' It was the first time Nathaniel had spoken with an Amish believer whose views he thought were strangely disturbing. Nevertheless, he was receiving their hospitality so he decided it wasn't his place to be overly critical. Instead, he tried to find out more about Pennsylvania.

'How is the colony governed?' Nathaniel wanted to know more but soon discovered that Carl really wasn't knowledgeable enough to be able to help him,

'I'm afraid I cannot answer all your questions as we Amish tend to keep ourselves very much to ourselves, as I've said, taking little heed of the outside world except when we are attacked, as we have been before.'

'Why would anyone want to attack a group of peaceful Christians like yourself?' he wondered aloud.

'During the late French and Indian Wars, a farmstead of the Hochstetlers was massacred by Indians,' revealed Carl. 'While the farmstead was set on fire, three of the family of six were killed and scalped. Thereafter most Amish travelled here from Northkill, at the time very close to the Indian border territory. We have consequently been very wary of Indians since that time.'

'What happened to the others?'

'The other three were taken prisoner and after a few years, the two boys who remained were happily released by British troops.'

'I find it strange,' speculated Nathaniel, 'that you refer to this incident as a massacre, though of course any loss of life is tragic. There do at least seem to be survivors from the incident, thanks be to God.' Carl looked at him dubiously and then said,

'I suggest you visit Philadelphia, Pennsylvania's capital and the largest city in the colonies. I think you will find what you are seeking there.'

Two weeks later, Nathaniel was fully recovered from his wound and took his leave gratefully, but with relief, from the Amish, whose views and ignorance of the world he found claustrophobic. It was refreshing to arrive in the centre of the bustling city at midday, where it was not difficult to find accommodation. He had no contacts here so he thought the best plan would be to attend one of the numerous Meeting Houses of the Society of Friends where he trusted to meet someone who might guide him in his quest.

He decided to attend a very prominent Meeting House in the centre of the city. The times were on public display and there was a general welcome to all, so he attended the 10 AM session. Despite the fact that it was Wednesday, there was a full house with well-dressed, distinguished middle-aged men alongside many women folk whom he expected to see. He too wore his finest clothes which had not been sullied by the past week's adventures. He had also attended the barber to ensure his shoulder length hair was well-groomed as was his fine full black beard which he had grown since arriving in Boston. As usual, he cut a dashing figure, so far as one could wearing the sombre dark clothes of his faith. Unusually, he thought, there were contributions almost from the very beginning. These were all from well turned out patricians and the substance of their comments seemed designed to solicit the sympathies and support of those present about matters concerning the Pennsylvania Council and Assembly. He couldn't follow the significance of much of what was said because it assumed prior knowledge of events and persons whom he didn't recognise. Nevertheless, when there was a lull in these statements, he felt it was appropriate to introduce himself and explain his purpose.

'Friends,' he spoke confidently but not stridently, 'I am Nathaniel lately arrived from England via Boston to undertake business on behalf of my Mistress, Abia Darby, who is proprietor of the world-famous Darby works in Coalbrookdale, Shropshire. She has chosen me as an emissary to this new world in order to test its temperature for future business enterprises. But there is another reason which leads me to Pennsylvania both for myself and for my employer, who is also a leading member of the Society of Friends at home. We have read of William Penn's divine endeavour here since he was granted the charter from Charles II almost a hundred years ago. It seemed to us and many others in the old country that his purpose was to build a new Jerusalem here where men could live in harmony with one another irrespective of their faith and colour. And none would be set over another, with no Kings or Popes dictating what they should do or believe and who they should worship. I have heard it called the Holy Experiment and I am here to observe how successful it has been. I sincerely desire to see the fruits it has borne.' Not a few in the Meeting House cast curious glances in his direction and one or two expressed great concern.

Following the meeting, Nathaniel was in no rush to leave but no one came up to introduce themselves or talk to him. It was extraordinary for such a meeting and it was the first indication that perhaps everything was not as it ought to be in this Holy City.

As he stood on the main street taking stock of his surroundings, he was tapped on the shoulder from behind. Turning around, he came face-to-face with one of the well-dressed and groomed middle-aged men from the meeting he had just attended.

'Friend, if I may be so bold to call you that? I'm afraid your open and honest comments have come at a time when the Society are feeling extremely vulnerable and ashamed of the transformation which is occurring in our once godly country.'

'I thank you, sir, for your explanation, however cryptic it may be. It was certainly not the reception I expected but I see there are many things here I don't know.' The polite gentleman made a slight gesture acknowledging Nathaniel's civility.

'Allow me to introduce myself, Solomon Morris, member of the State Assembly. Perhaps I could treat you to a coffee in a nearby coffeehouse whilst I explain the background of our current situation?'

'That is most gracious of you, Friend Solomon Morris. I would gladly converse with you. My full name is Nathaniel Shawcross.' Solomon led him across the street bustling with horse riders and cabs of all shapes and sizes towards a row of frontages of four glass panes, one of which invited gentlemen of sober temperament to "Partake of Non-Alcoholic

Beverages", an alternative to the public bars which Nathaniel was surprised to see in the city centre. One of the shops they passed on the way was headed "Land Agent – Andrew Penn".

'Is that any relation to the great William Penn?' enquired Nathaniel of his newfound friend. Solomon grimaced,

'Unfortunately, it is and he will figure in my tale as it unfolds.' Nathaniel was visibly shocked. In the coffee shop there were quite a few other men of Solomon's age and rank, who nodded in his direction and shouted a greeting as he entered. They found a quiet corner where they wouldn't be overheard and ordered some refreshments. Whilst they made themselves comfortable, Solomon dug out a small clay pipe from one of the capacious pockets in his three-quarter length coat.

'Good quality Virginia tobacco, Nathaniel. Would you like to try some, we can easily obtain another pipe from here?'

'No, thank you, sir, I don't have the stomach for it. It seems to be a very widespread practice in the colonies and I have observed many of the indigenous natives partaking in it.'

Solomon laughed.

'Indeed, you will, sir, as it is they from whom we learned the use. And now many of the plantations in the southern colonies would be much poorer without it.'

'And without the Negro slaves to plant and harvest it, they would be poorer still,' added Nathaniel with unquestioning certainty and not without some feeling, which Solomon couldn't help but notice at which he flinched.

'I take your meaning, sir, and I for one would wish that were not so. There are still many Friends who denounce the practice of slavery and we have tried to have it outlawed in the colony but without success so far. However, we have achieved some progress by passing a law which states that on the death of a proprietor of slaves they will be freed. First, let me try to acquaint you with conditions here in Pennsylvania.

'It was always the aim of William Penn that his land would be a haven of peace for all people. When he came, there were many Indian tribes here with whom he concluded treaties recognising his ownership of the land but their right to hunt and fish all over it. In the early days, when there were few settlers, Indians and Europeans coexisted peacefully. William had the powers of a king but refused to call himself that – he was a confirmed Republican. However, even at the very beginning there were tensions between him and the other major landowners, all Quakers, about whether he had the right of veto over laws that might be introduced by the Council – at that time, the Assembly had no rights to initiate laws, only to comment on them. He drew up a Frame of Government and after three attempts got it accepted by the Council and Assembly with a much watered-down right of veto for him, the proprietor. All freeholders of land above a minimum amount, or who paid a certain level of rent for properties in the settlements, had a right to vote and stand for election. It was the most advanced democratic republic anywhere in the world. As the population increased, more and more people who were not Quakers began to arrive and by the time of his death in 1718 there was a growing majority of Anglicans, Presbyterians, Baptists and others who did not subscribe to Penn's belief that all men could live in harmony. The newcomers brought with them their antipathy for the Indian and a willingness to use violence against them. Matters began to come to a head when Andrew Penn converted to Anglicanism and renounced the aims of the Holy Experiment. In fact, he took every opportunity to obtain more lands from the Indians by deception and fraud, which he sold off in lucrative parcels to incoming settlers. They began to encroach considerably on Indian territories which caused hostilities to break out and savage massacres by both sides became common. When the French and Indian Wars started in 1755, the savagery reached a climax so that no settler on the frontier could ever trust the native Indians and believed they had to protect themselves by slaughtering as many as they could root out. The era of peaceful coexistence was over. In Pennsylvania there were many Christian Indians who still believed in Penn's promise but that came to an end in 1763 with the brutal massacre of the unarmed and peaceful Conestoga Indians in Paxton. No one was ever tried for their murders and the power of the newcomers was established when they marched in their hundreds towards Philadelphia and the Council Assembly. They were only appeased when the Assembly agreed to create a 300 strong militia to protect the settlers. Since then, we Quakers have lost control of the democratic Assembly and our New Jerusalem is dissolving before us, as you have so keenly observed already. What have we done that has brought this about? We continually ask this question amongst ourselves, whilst we do what we can to follow the way of the Lord. So you can see, Nathaniel, why we were ashamed to address you.' Nathaniel was quiet for some time mulling it all over in his mind.

'It grieves me deeply,' he finally said, 'to hear that the Holy Experiment is a failure.'

'I know, but don't despair totally. We must continue to have faith in the Lord. Perhaps there was something fundamentally wrong with the Experiment right from the beginning? We must look positively at what has been achieved, such as our system of government. It would not do to have a dictatorship no matter how benign or godly it seemed. Maybe this is the price we have to pay for democracy and it looks like many of our colonial brothers in the 13 colonies recognise that a hard price has to be paid for freedom against tyranny. Soon we shall have to make up our minds where we are going in this New World.'

Nathaniel wasn't quite sure what he meant by this.

'Do you think there will be war?' he asked genuinely.

'It very much depends on the degree to which support for the Rebels or Patriots, as they call themselves, grows. There is considerable animosity and ill feeling between the Royal Governors and the people in those colonies where the will of the Assemblies is ignored or not even allowed to be expressed. People are still seething over the Sugar Tax and I fear that should the Crown attempt to impose further taxes it will precipitate open revolt. People feel they are paying for nothing since security on the frontier is not guaranteed and has been secured only by the settlers' organisations themselves.'

Nathaniel could say nothing in response to this because he knew that while some of it was clearly true there were other ways of looking at the issue. In particular, he had decided he wanted to talk directly to the Pennsylvanian Indians.

Solomon was bemused when Nathaniel asked him where the Indians may be found in Philadelphia. It hadn't crossed his mind apparently that they might be interested parties. Nathaniel was not slow in coming to that conclusion and wondered what it might signify. A collection of less than 20 predominantly Moravian Christian Indians were located in a rundown tenement block in a poor area of the city. Most of them had been there since the Paxton massacres in 1764, some eight years before. When Nathaniel found them most of them were partially dressed in threadbare European clothes attempting desperately to fit in to this alien culture. Most were elderly or infirm and there were noticeably no children present. They clustered around makeshift fires sharing what little food they had, but one amongst them held himself more proudly than the others and it was to him that Nathaniel addressed himself. He told them briefly of his background and his business in the colonies and then came directly to the point. Most of the others could hear their conversation:

'I am a Quaker here from the old country who seeks to learn the truth about William Penn's attempt to create a peaceful, godly society where Indian and whites could live side-by-side. I have spoken to one of the Quaker leaders here and am beginning to draw a picture of what has happened but I cannot do that fully unless I know your story too.'

Russell Feather was the tall, proud Indian to whom he addressed these remarks. He now spoke without hesitation as a leader of these people.

'Tell me, Master Shawcross,' he asked in excellent English, 'what possible interest can our affairs hold for you and what possible benefit can there be to us?' he spoke quietly but confidently with a tired look of scepticism, behind which lay depths of suffering and pain.

'The truth, Mr Feather, is a many-sided mirror which tends to reflect itself more strongly from those with the most power, but that doesn't prove it is the whole or accurate truth. My countrymen may soon be at war with their brothers here in the colonies and they want to know why there is so much unrest here. There is talk of freedom from tyranny, both here and at home but from what I've seen so far it is a very one-sided reflection of the facts. I'm told by colonists they are being taxed to protect the frontier settlers who are being massacred by the Indians, but that the taxes are siphoned off for luxurious living by Royal Governors here and politicians in London. I'm told about massacres suffered by settlers and yet when I look into it, I find it is the massacre of peaceful, innocent Indians instead. I walk about this godly city and see many black slaves being bought and sold like cattle to work until they drop maintaining lavish and privileged lifestyles of the great landlords and plantation owners. In short, I want to know why the Holy Experiment of William Penn has so singularly failed?'

'Very well, Mr Shawcross, you make a strong case and I can see you will not be unsympathetic to whatever tale I may tell. Let me start from the beginning:

'In 1701 William Penn reached an agreement with the Conestoga who lived in Indian Town, east of the Susquehanna River in which both Indian and white would respect each other's territory living in peace – this was referred to as the Peaceable Kingdom. During the French and Indian Wars, this agreement was tested severely when frontier settlers and Indians attacked and slaughtered each other at the behest of their respective allies, the French or the British. During the preceding decades many settlers had travelled west in search of land and settled wherever they wished. They ignored the Pennsylvanian Council who declared that Indian territory should remain intact but they did little more than that. In 17 63 over 50 Scots and Irish frontiers men attacked Indian Town killing the residents and destroying it by fire. The following day they broke into the Lancaster County jail house where the remaining Indians had fled for safety and massacred them all, even mutilating the bodies of the women and children. No one was ever brought to trial for this despite the Council recognising that the Indians had been murdered. Some of us here are direct kin to those people. In 1768, the Treaty of Fort Stanwix stated that all the remaining Indian territories in Pennsylvania had been sold legally for $500 to the state and via a land agent to the settlers squatting thereon. The authorisation signature was provided by three Susquehanna/Delaware Indians who didn't even live on the land. Other Susquehanna, Creek, Delaware and other tribes were not even consulted and didn't even know about the transaction. Now so far as the Pennsylvania Council are concerned Indian Town no longer exists and the land is occupied by legitimate settlers. From our point of view this is a complete breaking of the treaty with William Penn. We also regard him as bearing some of the responsibility because when he was granted over 2 million acres of land here by the British King Charles II, it was not the latter's to bestow. It belonged to the people who lived on it – the six members of the Iroquois Nation.'

Nathaniel's face revealed his feelings of horror as the sombre Indian recounted his story. There were tears in the eyes of many of the others standing around listening.

'We are the only ones remaining from that time not too long ago and soon we too will be gone. The younger and stronger of us have already departed for the West.'

During the Indian's narration, Nathaniel had already decided what he was going to do.

'I would like to go West also to see where your people have gone and how they are faring. Can you put me in touch with someone, one of your people, who could guide me there? I will of course pay all the expenses and make whatever contribution I can to ease a little the life you lead here.'

On his return to his room at the hotel, he looked in at one of the many bookshops, not unlike Boston, to see if there were any pamphlets covering what he had been told. He was overwhelmed by the number available and selected two which he thought would present the arguments on both sides. The first was written by the Presbyterian minister of Paxton entitled "Remonstrance and Demonstration", which explained the aims and justification for the actions of the Paxton Boys, as the frontiersman were called. The second was entitled "Events of the Late Massacre" by Benjamin Franklin, who denounced the action as an inhumane event and one which was politically inspired to destroy the Holy Experiment. It seemed to Nathaniel that Pennsylvania had become the site of a Holy War, rather than a Holy Experiment. He was plunged into a deep slough of depression.

Chapter 16
The Ohio

'What do you think you're doing Mr?' asked the burly, rough-looking farmer who had been observing Nathaniel for some time as he sat on his horse simply watching the comings and goings of people in Paxton town centre. Children were playing amongst the wagons parked along the Main Street and there was a flow of worshippers entering the freshly painted Presbyterian church which was one of the dominant buildings of the small town. Without breaking his gaze, Nathaniel replied,

'Well, sir, my business is no business of yours but as you seem to be a local, I will tell you,' he said with a hard edge to his voice. 'I'm curious to know how those damned to hell go about their daily lives.' He said no more and the farmer was left wondering what to make of this, though he didn't like the overall tone of the stranger and continued aggressively,

'What do you mean?'

'How long have you lived here?' asked Nathaniel calmly, now changing the hidden meaning of his voice to a more neutral one. The former was now quite perplexed.

'Four years next harvest…'

'Ah, so you weren't here at the time of the massacre, although you have certainly benefited from it.'

Now it began to dawn on the man to what Nathaniel was referring,

'You mean the clearing out of the Indians in '64? No, I wasn't here but I would have helped if I had been.' Now Nathaniel looked at him directly.

'You mean to murder women and children by smashing their skulls, scalping them and cutting off their limbs?' he asked venomously. The farmer now seemed to lose his nerve and began spluttering,

'I think you'd better be on your way, Mr. We don't like Indian lovers 'round here,' and as his hand began to move towards the long knife at his belt, Nathaniel whipped out his pistol saying,

'I wouldn't do that if I were you or your brains will be the first to splatter over the building behind you.' Nathaniel had developed a degree of coolness in dealing with people in such circumstances that some would liken his manner to steel. However, he realised that he'd now lingered long enough and should be on his way. He had arranged through Russell Feather to meet with one of the younger Susquehanna who had already travelled further west, at a fork in the trail 20 miles further on. He would not come closer to the town and he would steer well clear of squatter settlements en route to the river.

When he arrived at the agreed rendezvous, he could see no one present but he guessed his contact would be in hiding. The other would take some time to observe him and confirm from little details that it was the man he was supposed to meet. After 20 minutes, he heard a voice from behind,

'If I rustle something, what do I get?' asked the deep, heavily accented voice of his contact.

'A feather,' was the agreed response. 'Nathaniel Shawcross at your service, sir.'

'My name is Choctow of the Susquehanna, formerly of the Conestoga. Follow me in single file and remain quiet. If we meet other whites, point your pistol at me and we will pretend I am your prisoner but I intend to avoid meeting others of your kind if at all possible. It will be easier once we reach the river because there are fewer squatters on the other side.' As they rode, Nathaniel studied his guide. He clearly disdained to wear European clothing wearing buckskin leggings and shirt. His hair was not unlike other tribes of the Iroquois nations he'd met, half of which grew long on one side whilst the other had been plucked out leaving it quite bare and on which were elaborately scrawled tattoos. He wore two feathers on the hair side and red ochre had been used to tint the long strands that reached beyond his shoulders. He had the usual bone and shell necklaces and bracelets but there was no paint on his face, which Nathaniel knew was only used in times of war. Nevertheless, he was well prepared for action if necessary, carrying a long musket, the obligatory war tomahawk and long scalping knife in his belt.

In half a day, they reached the Ohio River where Choctow had decided they would cross. Nathaniel had brought a packhorse with him loaded with gifts for the Indians he was about to meet, but he also carried something far more valuable than trinkets, which would only become useful when they reached their final destination. However, the packhorse was heavy with these goods which would need to be unpacked and placed in a canoe for the crossing. The horses would then be tethered to the canoe and steered carefully to the other side in a diagonal direction as there was a strong flowing current, although it was less dangerous here and the crossing was shorter and shallower than elsewhere. There was only one canoe available so Choctow crossed the river first with a full load and one horse. On the other side, he unloaded the canoe, tethered the horse and returned. This was by far the safest way of proceeding as even at this crossing place, it was twice as wide as that of the River Severn, which Nathaniel knew so well near his home in England. Safely on the other side, he began to take stock of his surroundings noting the intense density of the trees right up to the waterline. In the near distance he could see heavily wooded hillsides and what were evidently ridges along hidden escarpments. He knew this was a major waterway and a very important channel of communication from the north to the south-west which had probably been used for centuries by the native Americans but was equally well-known to the French and British in the savage French and Indian Wars that had ended about eight years ago. He presumed rightly that there were trails in the woods but there would also be much traffic on the river itself so it would be important to hide their canoe well from prying eyes, particularly those of opportunistic and illegal European adventurers looking to carve out a place in the woods for themselves. When they were well clear of the river, his guide said they should secure themselves for the night in a small clearing he knew where they could light a discrete fire for food and warmth.

After having eaten a roasted rabbit that Choctow had caught earlier that day, they sat reclined around the small campfire beneath the myriad of twinkling stars that comprised the Milky Way. It was a perfect atmosphere for philosophical reflection and conversation.

'Tell me, Mr Shawcross…' Nathaniel interrupted him to say he should use his first name, 'why are you making this expedition? You are not a settler or hunter.'

'I'm not entirely sure. On the one hand, I wish to see for myself the extent of settler penetration beyond the Proclamation line of '63, but I could just have easily asked other frontiers men about that. In truth, I think I wanted to judge for myself the quality of the frontiers people, including the squatters, and of your people and other Indian tribes whom I might encounter. I still want to know why the Holy Experiment failed – was it an inevitability because of human nature and the endemic corruption which I seem to have met amongst the Europeans of this continent? Or, does the answer lie, as some have suggested, with the idea itself – even in the mind of its founding father, William Penn? Alternatively, does human nature simply come down to factors beyond the individual's control and in this case the thousands of exploited and dispossessed Europeans simply looking to survive by obtaining land which is virtually being given away here – a glimmer of hope in their squalid lives that would otherwise not exist? And, faced with this invasion of their lands, a struggle to survive by repelling them by the Indians? Simply, a power struggle for land?'

'It is for the Great Spirit to ask these questions,' replied Choctow, who had never considered such matters before because in his world how to behave and what to do was obvious. A warrior was brought up to defend his honour, that of his kin and his right to hunt or farm whenever and wherever it was threatened. You were either successful, taking the goods of your enemy and even his strength by scalping him and eating part of his flesh, or you were defeated becoming his slave or killed in like manner. A trial of wit and strength. Perhaps the medicine men thought about such questions, he didn't know. He wondered whether Nathaniel was a medicine man for the whites. He knew they had preachers or ministers who talked about a God that lived a long time ago and allowed the people to kill him by nailing him to a tree and for some mysterious reason, which he didn't understand, would save them after they were dead. It didn't make any sense at all – if gods were any good, they were there to protect you from death and suffering.

They spent two more days travelling up and down through the endless woods. Sometimes they would come to a little high clearing which gave them a good all-round view and evidence of illegal settlements could be seen from the tiny wisps of vertical smoke which drifted upwards in the clear high pressure. Around them was an endless sea of green, but, Nathaniel thought, it would not remain that way for long. Periodically, they passed a small lake with low hills surrounding where they would either stop for something to eat or make an overnight camp. He was struck by the incredible peace and beauty that permeated the land. Sometimes he would just sit and immerse himself entirely in his surroundings, whilst his companion was off hunting, finding the intense blueness of the sky and the perfect stillness of the water so serene that he lost consciousness of his own body. He knew it was an illusion because wherever Native American and settler came into contact it was likely to result in a bloody conflict. Eventually, they arrived at the Susquehanna encampment which was by a small lake, well-hidden between surrounding hills on one of which was a fortified palisade. He could see a few acres of crops neatly laid out and weed free with irrigation ditches interlacing the fields of maize, corn and other crops he didn't recognise. People were busy with the latter whilst others were coming and going into the palisaded settlement. When they arrived, everyone stopped what they were doing to stare curiously at the white man. They had been expecting him, but now that he was here, he became an object of great interest. Many crowded around when he was brought before the sachem and Choctaw introduced him to Chief Saqhanaa, who was old and grey but stood erect without any suggestion of a stoop.

'Tekwanonwerá: tons…' said the ancient one to Nathaniel followed by a stream of other words which the Englishman could not understand.

Choctaw interpreted for the sachem, 'He gives you a great welcome. He has heard you are of the same belief as the great father William Penn who was a good friend to our people. He hopes you also will be as he knows you come here to learn about us and with peace in your heart. You may stay as long as you like and you will be made comfortable.'

'I thank you sincerely for those kind words and I hope that my stay here will be as beneficial to you as I hope it will be to me. I would like to present these small gifts as a token of my gratitude and a sign of my friendship to you and your people.' Nathaniel then passed over to him an ornately carved German made smoking pipe, a brass ship's bell and a fine naval telescope, which the chief was visibly delighted with. Choctaw was also highly admiring of the gifts and commended Nathaniel on his choice.

The Susquehanna made room for him in one of their long houses, but he already had ideas about building a small room for himself off which he planned to build a small smithy and forge to make himself doubly useful to his native hosts. He told

Choctaw of his plans showing him some of the ironstone he had brought with him.

'Have you seen rock like this before, my friend,' handing him a piece, which the other scrutinised closely and marvelled at its weight.

'No, but there is a place not far away which has glittering speckles in it similar to this.'

'Good,' said Nathaniel, 'that's what I was hoping, as I have here only a small quantity which won't last long.'

'What is it for?'

'This my good friend is what the power of the white man is based. It is the raw material from which knives, muskets, axes and all other iron goods are made. And, I am one of the few skilled in being able to produce them. I am an iron maker.' Choctaw was open mouthed at this knowledge, although of course he had seen small smithies before but he didn't understand the processes associated with them.

'Did you know, Nathaniel, that the Mohawk, a related tribe, are known as the People of the Flint and before the arrival of the whites used to produce the weapons for people all over the north-eastern lands from the coasts of the Great Sea to the great Lakes and the Inuit in the frozen north?'

'No, I did not and I marvel at the coincidence of our meeting.'

'I do not think it can be a coincidence, Nathaniel, but part of the Great Spirit's plan and I think the Chief is certainly likely to see it that way, but how he will interpret it I don't know. We must show him the stone and reveal your ideas so he can decide what to do.'

When Saqhanaa listened to what Nathaniel proposed and the observations by Choctaw, he said it was possible this could be both a positive or negative sign that could bring the Susquehanna great blessings or great distress. He would have to think on it and put it to the Council when he had deliberated for their agreement or rejection. After many days of private counsel followed by consideration of the broader Council, it was agreed that Nathaniel's proposal to build a smithy could go ahead. They had finally interpreted it as a good sign from the Great Spirit.

Nathaniel spent the next few weeks constructing his smithy cum cabin. The Indians showed him where he could obtain the different varieties of wood he required at a place not too far away, but one which would not undermine their defences or despoil the surroundings. He had brought various items with him for the small forge that he wanted to build such as a pair of leather bellows for blowing, a variety of small wooden patterns for arrowheads, tomahawks, small pots, and, most importantly, a white powder which he could mix with clay to produce fire hard bricks. He had many willing hands to help him as the young people were intensely curious about his activities and even some of the older ones marvelled at the unknown skills he possessed in handling wood with the carpentry tools he brought with him. As the building began to take shape, Nathaniel then set about preparing to make the charcoal fuel and locating the right saplings of birch and beech. He demonstrated to his most dedicated helpers how to construct a small charcoal kiln so that they could erect others when required. As woodsmen, they were quick to learn although they did not fully appreciate yet the purpose of this. When his fire bricks were ready, and the forge in place he was ready for his first firing. The Native Americans were amazed at the heat he produced, required to extract the iron from the stone, and when they saw it run like a river as he poured it into the moulds, they were struck dumb. As the metal cooled and he knocked away the burrs, filing the item into shape, so that it became a long hunting knife just requiring a handle, they whooped with joy.

He had slept quite happily in the space made for him in one of the longhouses, but now that his own quarters were ready, he moved in preferring a bed off the ground with his tools neatly arranged in his workshop nearby. There was a constant stream of people coming to him to repair various metal items which they were not able to do for themselves. The women would often bring him such items and provide him in return with cooked food or items of clothing such as moccasins. Indeed, he now often wore Indian clothes of deerskin leggings and shirt, as did many of the frontiers men he had noticed. Choctaw and the other young men encouraged him to come out with them on hunting trips, which he often did. On these occasions, he would leave his firearms behind and practise using a native bow or javelin in which he became quite proficient. One day, Choctaw took him aside and said he ought to learn the use of the tomahawk for his own protection. Nathaniel was conflicted because he knew these were items of war for killing the enemy and was most reluctant to comply but at his friend's insistence he agreed, telling himself it was more a sport than anything else. In this way he learned how to throw and wield these deadly weapons.

When his stock of ironstone began to deplete, he asked Choctaw to take him to the place where he thought there was similar rock to be found. It was a day's travelling to the North East so Nathaniel decided to combine it with reconnoitring the land for squatters. He was anxious to discover their number, condition, ethnicity and manner. In particular, he wished to know what kind of a threat they posed to the Indians he was currently living among. He therefore dressed in European clothes for any possible encounters so as not to be mistaken for an Indian. They were only half a day away from their camp when they came across a squatter cabin in the woods cut out of the surrounding trees producing an open space between it and the woods. A family was in evidence from the washing on a line, a fenced off area for three horses and the chopping down of more trees being undertaken by a man and a youth. Choctaw remained hidden whilst he presented himself unthreateningly before the two men. They were immediately startled by his appearance and ran for the nearby muskets that were present, but relaxed a little when they saw he was dressed soberly as a Quaker.

'Good day, sirs. I wonder if I could trouble you for a little water as mine is getting low.' The two men still regarded him with some suspicion.

'And who are you, Mr?' he detected a distinct Scots'-Irish accent, which suggested they were recent immigrants to the continent having been forced West in search of cheap land, without knowing the dangers.

'Nathaniel Shawcross, at your service, sirs. I am researching the area for trails and minerals as I am a miner,' which was the truth, though not perhaps the whole truth. As a Quaker, he could not lie unless it were to save lives, as he had, he reflected regretfully, done before.

'Get Mr Shawcross some water from the barrel lad,' said the father. 'It is good to see a white face hereabouts and it would certainly be welcome if there were to be mining in the area, which would draw in many more over the river. We have seen Indians in the woods but kept clear of them. We won't bother them if they don't bother us, but we are well armed and protected,' he gestured towards the cabin where Nathaniel could now see slit windows for shooting from.

'How long have you been here, sir?' he asked conversationally.

'Nine months in Connecticut and Massachusetts but we were forced West because of the high price of land there. Here in the woods just under two months, but our provisions are almost gone and we need to hunt and fish for survival. Eventually, when we have a large enough plot carved out, we will be able to plant and that we must do before winter or we will starve. If we have any furs to trade there is nowhere close enough to get a good price for them and all the other squatters in the area are in the same situations we are.'

'You could try trading with the Indians?'

'I fear not, Mr Shawcross, as they don't want us here and will scalp us soon as look at us. We have been forced this side of the river because on the other we have to pay land tax to the State Collectors. We can't afford to do that as we have spent all our savings getting here providing ourselves with the basic necessities to survive. My wife and I were indentured for seven years in Ireland before we could obtain the money and permission to emigrate here. This is our last chance and this winter could be our last.' Nathaniel's heart reached out to them – there were so many similar cases both here and at home in England. Life was hard but he knew the Society of Friends was committed to helping people just like this.

'Sir, I will call in upon you again in a few days if I may after my business is complete?'

'We would be very glad of it, Mr Shawcross. My name is Sean Connor, this is my son Donovan and my wife Kathleen is in the cabin. Perhaps you would share a meagre meal with us when you return?'

'I would be honoured to, Mr Connor,' he replied sincerely.

As he returned to his friend in the woods, he was deep in thought. How could he criticise or condemn these people – they were no different from most folks he knew back in Coalbrookdale and Madeley. And yet, by their very actions they posed an existential threat to his Native American hosts. That evening he asked his companion about the squatters.

'Well, Choctaw, will they last through the winter?'

'Not unless they harvest sufficient crops, salt away sufficient game and fish, and stock up on plenty of dry, seasoned wood. They are just about high enough to avoid the melting floodwaters in early spring, which will swamp much of the lower lying woodland.'

'Will the Chief allow them to stay unmolested?'

'We don't want trouble with the white squatters because we know it would provide an excuse for Regulators on the opposite bank to war on us. We have had enough of that but if the squatters attack us, we will respond.'

'Is it possible, perhaps,' asked Nathaniel, 'that you could trade with the squatters on this side of the river if they prove to be peaceable?'

'They have nothing we need,' said Choctaw dismissively.

'They have tobacco and sugar,' responded Nathaniel quickly having given the matter more thought earlier anticipating this response from his friend, 'and they could likely get more from the nearer settlements to the east of the river if they needed to. You know, my friend, the alternative to war is trade because it is mutually beneficial. You know this from your history as do we Europeans.'

'You may have something there and of course your little smithy might prove just as valuable to them as it is to us. We can put it to the sachem on our return.'

Nathaniel was pleased with this outcome. He even wondered whether it might be possible to restore a little of the Holy Experiment here on the west bank of the Ohio. He knew it would not be for long, if they could, and that in time the two races were likely to return to conflict. He was beginning to see that whilst the Native Americans lived in the woods and were a part of it, the Europeans lived on the land and wanted to own it. These were irreconcilable ways of thinking.

The following day, they arrived at the place where Choctaw thought he had seen the ironstone and sure enough he saw, revealed beneath a low escarpment, a seam of rock that had been exposed by an ancient landslip. It was 6 feet deep and stretched as far as they could see. It would prove to be a very valuable source of ironstone, more than they could ever possibly need. Before they went to see Saqhanaa, Nathaniel asked Choctaw to wait a day until he had prepared a small gift for the sachem. He had previously prepared a wooden mould for a small, replica but usable tomahawk with scrolled indentations in the axe heads. He then spent the whole day forging two tiny tomahawks from some brass which he had brought along for just such an occasion. He polished and sharpened them so they glittered in the sunshine looking very attractive. He was sure that the chief would be very pleased with these gifts, which would he hoped place him in a positive frame of mind for his proposal. He wasn't wrong.

'You are a true son of the Peacemaker William Penn, truer than his real sons. I think the Council will agree to the idea of trading with settlers within a day's ride of our settlement so long as we are not met with hostility. If you are prepared to inform them of this and weigh them up with regard to our safety, then it may be possible to open up the settlement to them.'

The Council were initially very wary of the idea but when Nathaniel emphasised the opportunity to obtain good quality tobacco and sugar, which were in short supply, they slowly came around to the idea. It was then that Nathaniel himself became aware of his responsibilities for a greater number of people than he was used to and, if his judgement was misplaced, it could result in disaster for the Indians and bloodshed for the settlers. There were a hundred and fifty people in the settlement of whom approximately a third were warriors, whilst the squatters, who continued to grow slowly in number, came to about four hundred in the area, half of whom would be capable of carrying and using weapons. He decided, therefore, to proceed cautiously, firstly by inviting single families like the Connors who might then spread the word to their neighbours of the advantages of trading. Choctaw was convinced that none of the squatters knew where the Indian settlement was nor that they lived so closely to them. It was only a matter of time, however, that the two came into contact whilst out hunting in the woods as the latter's numbers grew. It was better, therefore, to establish positive relations on which they could hopefully build. When Nathaniel returned to the Connors, accepting their invitation of a meal, he waited until the end before he revealed his circumstances and proposition. At first, they were shocked and angry at what appeared to be his deception but when he told them more about what they could gain, especially his services as a Smith, they began to recognise the advantages. They would be freed from the daily fear of Indian attack and obtain a source of fresh vegetables before their own were available. The clincher was Nathaniel's workshop and they agreed to accompany him there in a few days' time. When the day came, he met them at their cabin and the whole family accompanied albeit with muskets and knives. The Indians were as tentative as Nathaniel and the Conners, but they had prepared a feast for their arrival and showed them willingly around the settlement, pointing out the crops they grew and what they could trade. The Connors had brought a little of their precious supplies of tobacco and sugar and some coils of spare rope which they happened to have. There was too little for everyone to trade but promises were made for later and orders placed. Nathaniel presented them with some small cast-iron pots and pans which he had produced for the occasion. These went down extremely well with Mrs Connor. They agreed to return in a fortnight's time feeling much more secure about everything, especially from Nathaniel's presence in the settlement. He also took the opportunity to explain how important it was that anyone they might mention it to should not be hostile to the Indians in any way otherwise the whole venture would be destroyed. They agreed that should they detect such an attitude in any of their neighbours they conversed with, they would inform Nathaniel immediately. He suggested the best plan would be for the squatters to travel together to the next market in the settlement. So it was good that year for all concerned, though Nathaniel did not delude himself that they may all be on borrowed time.

    It was during this time that Nathaniel met Hyacinthe.

Chapter 17
Hyacinthe

She remembered the smoke and the noise. Sitting quietly on the riverbank playing with her corn doll, the world suddenly turned upside down. Someone grabbed her hand pulling her roughly away and amid the shots and the bloodcurdling war whoops, she vaguely saw her father, tomahawk in hand, running towards the enemy when there was a mighty noise, like a lightning bolt striking a tree in the forest during the storm, and he was no more. The hand gripped her more tightly and pulled her in the opposite direction. She felt water up to her waist as they waded through the giant lily leaves that clustered near the dark forest's edge. The noise was awful, a combination of savagery and intense painful shrieking as the living turned into the dead. She was about to cry out herself when a hand covered her mouth. It was her mother who dragged her into the forest and ran as swiftly as her young child could go, far from the butchery, the heartache and the demoniacal yelling. When she collapsed and could go no further, strong hands picked her up and they continued escaping through the woods. Next, she was thrust into the centre of a light canoe, her mother behind her and an unknown person in front. They paddled swiftly and quietly away from the tumult along with many other canoes pointed in the same direction. This was the first terrifying memory from her childhood after which she later learned her people had been attacked and scattered by a combination of their mortal enemies, the Huron and the French. They were swept out of the

St Lawrence waterway fleeing for their lives south and west towards the Great Lakes. What was left of her tribe, the Iroquois Senecas eventually made their way down one of the rivers from the Great Bay to their present settlement where they joined up with the Susquehanna who took them in. There were other ugly memories from this earlier time in her life such as when all the Indians were at war with the British soldiers. She had been to the fort once or twice with her mother and uncle where she was struck by the beautiful colour of the redcoats of the soldiers. She even coveted one, but she knew the only way to obtain one was to kill the person wearing it, which some of the young Braves amongst her tribe had, though they made sure only to wear them when there were no British soldiers around. One day, the men of her tribe and of others of the Delaware, even their former enemies, the Huron, attacked and captured the fort. They killed all the soldiers except the commander, taking prisoner many of the white settlers who had fled there recently for safety. She saw how the women and children were divided up amongst the warriors and taken off to their own settlements to become slaves. Worst of all, she remembered what happened to the chief of the redcoats. He was scalped and burnt alive tied to a post with a slow burning fire beneath his feet so that it took him three days to die in agony whilst the Warriors danced around him inflicting minor wounds with their sharp hunting knives to enhance his pain. His pitiful screams and the smell of his burning flesh were inscribed indelibly in her mind.

 Since then there had been peace and their chief had found this secluded place to build their settlement hidden away between the hills, surrounded by the woods where fresh clean water was available from the small lake into which trickled a number of freshwater springs. She knew that the white settlers were not meant to be in this area and she had not seen any since her earlier days until the young white man, Nathaniel Shawcross, was brought into the camp, but not as a prisoner. He seemed to be treated with great honour and like all the other members of the settlement, but especially the young unmarried girls like herself, she was intensely curious about his activities. Before very long, she became aware that it was more than his behaviour that excited her interest but also his appearance. She watched him discreetly and cautiously building his little workshop and going about with the other men of the village, sometimes wearing his own European clothes but increasingly adopting the clothes of her people. His chestnut dark coloured hair was worn long tied behind him in a ponytail. His skin was not adorned or painted with tattoos like the other men and she found this oddly more attractive. His Quaker simplicity of dress and humility in demeanour were in stark contrast to what she was used to. She began looking for opportunities to visit his small workshop, bringing items to be repaired. At the same time, she ensured her clothes were clean, wearing her best beaded moccasins, combing her long thick black hair so that it shone brightly in the sun and scented with oil from the hyacinth, after which she was named. However, she realised there was little possibility of communication between them beyond sign language because neither of them spoke the other's language. Then, as if the Great Spirit had designed it, she learned that the chief was looking for someone to teach him their language. She immediately offered to do this, explaining that as she spoke some French, a little of which their white visitor might also speak, she was well qualified for the role. Thus it was that Nathaniel and Hyacinthe began to spend more time together.

Was it the scented hair that excited him? Or the abnormal stigmata in her feline eyes, that flashed orange streak that penetrated his innermost self? The curvature of her body accentuated by the deer hide skirt and tunic that was perfectly contoured to her form. He didn't know, but one day he suddenly discovered he was entirely intoxicated by her presence and thereafter was agitated by her absence. Where was she? What was she doing? Who was she with? He could detect her at a distance in a crowd of people, seeing only her. As she came towards him, his body trembled with desire and he was incapable of concentrating on anything he was doing. He knew she felt the same way about him. She was always stood or sat very close to him. Slowly their fingers began to find each other as he turned a page or she passed him a broken knife to be repaired. Such occasions brought unalloyed joy. He knew he had fallen rapturously in love with her.

'I love you,' he whispered gently in her ear as their heads subconsciously came close whilst they examined a broken silver bracelet she had brought to see if it could be repaired. There was no one else around at that moment in his workshop and she looked up into his earnest, handsome face overcome by the same feelings as he nuzzling her face in his, in the Native American way of expressing tenderness, until his mouth found hers giving themselves totally to each other in that embrace. She understood the English words, and when their lips parted, she repeated them the way he had said them and then spoke the sentiment in her own language. They were still in the first stages of each other's languages and both felt frustrated at not being able to say more. But, for the moment they were content to bask in the acknowledged love for each other. These were the pinnacle days of his stay in the settlement. It wasn't long before they stole away into the hidden corners of the embracing woods consummating their love in secret glades, hoping that no one would notice, but of course they did.

'What are you going to do, my daughter?' asked her mother, Running Deer, one evening as they both sat quietly sewing in a corner of the longhouse.

'About what?' Hyacinthe asked innocently, knowing full well the meaning of her mother's words. Her mother didn't answer immediately but looked her straight in the face with an expression that signalled she was aware of everything.

'I don't know, Mother, but I know Nathaniel is the only man for me. What can I do? What should I do?' she corrected herself dutifully. Her mother placed her sewing on one side and taking her daughter's hands, said,

'You must either stop this now or approach the sachem for permission to marry this man. If you don't, your reputation will be reduced to the level of a slave and you may well be asked to leave the tribe. It wouldn't be the first time that a Native American and white man have married.'

'Would you approve, Mother?'

'He's a good man, a man of peace and many skills. But I would not be honest with you, if I said I was happy with the possibility because you would be marrying outside the clan and none of his family are here to join with us as is the custom. I would also be fearful of how other whites would treat you. I also wonder whether he would be content to remain with us always. If not, I might never see you again. But I will not stand in your way if that is truly what you want.'

'I know I love this man, Mother, and I cannot see me with another.'

'Then, if it is what he wants too, you must be married.'

When Hyacinthe related this conversation to Nathaniel, he became very thoughtful. He hadn't stopped to think about where their deepening relationship would lead. In particular, he had refused to consider the implications for Rebecca with whom he acknowledged he had an unofficial engagement and agreement to marry on his return. He knew he should have already gone back to England and had stayed well beyond the planned six months of his trip. If he stayed longer, he didn't know whether he would ever return and the thought of not seeing his old friends and family again was extremely painful. Was it possible, or even practicable, to take Hyacinthe back home with him? It was a very different world and she may not be accepted by those close to him, let alone the broader community. It was difficult to convey these feelings and thoughts in a suitable way to his Indian lover but he tried as best he could. She could see he was riven by doubts and she understood very well the potential loss of his family. She could not imagine being without hers, which included far more than Nathaniel's because of the extended clan system to which she belonged. The dilemma was eventually resolved when Hyacinthe became pregnant and for Nathaniel it was now unquestionable that he could ever leave her. He would seek permission from Saqhanaa to marry, not realising that beside him he would have to seek permission from her mother as these were matters decided by the females in Iroquois society.

Permission from the old chief and Hyacinthe's mother was really never in doubt. Choctaw and the other Braves had already started to treat him like a brother and never thought that he would someday leave them. Nathaniel decided to ask the Connors to represent his own family at the ceremony, which they were more than glad to do. Traditionally the groom and bride's families would produce a corn basket containing ritual items of clothing for the married couple, which Kathleen Connor was delighted to help make. Nathaniel decided he would fashion two thick silver rings for each of them in the European style. He also made little gifts of iron or brass for his bride's family, including her stepfather who in the Iroquois manner had little to do with the ceremony, thus winning them over to his side. Two of the other squatter families, who by now were well acquainted with the Indian settlement and Nathaniel's workshop and trusted to keep the secret, were also invited. So, the happy couple were united in the eyes of both of their peoples after which they settled down to get on with their lives very much as before, except Nathaniel took to wearing Indian clothes more and more. Instead of living in the communal clan longhouse, however, they lived in Nathaniel's self-made accommodation. In the spring, Hyacinthe gave birth to a beautiful little girl, whom they named Bright Eyes because of her blue eyes acquired from her father. Life was good. It remained that way for over a year with the tribe flourishing and the settlers roundabout content to accept their native American neighbours and live in peace.

It was late summer. A few of the less hardy deciduous trees were showing signs of early autumn. Bright Eyes with the other small children was frolicking in the safe, shallow waters of the lake, many of the women working and chatting in the vegetable strips nearby. Half of the young men were off hunting whilst Nathaniel busied himself in his workshop. An ear-splitting yell, followed by a fusillade of shots and then momentarily by complete silence, shattered the air until heartrending cries totally destroyed the Palladian scene. Nathaniel was frozen still, the hackles on his neck fully erect until the adrenaline kicked in and he immediately grabbed his musket, always loaded and ready to use, his tomahawk in the other hand. At full speed running down the slope as fast as his lame leg would allow, he took in the scene with a clarity of vision which normally would have been blurred from the swiftness of his movements. He saw the puffs of smoke at the forest's edge, followed by the accompanying explosive reports, and the grotesque postures of the dead and dying. Men were now emerging from the woods having reloaded and firing again at whatever moved. Nathaniel stopped dead, fell to one knee and without thinking targeted a moving figure coming towards him. The man's body jerked backwards as his shot caught him squarely in the chest. He wasn't alone. He was aware of his armed companions doing exactly the same. More men poured from the forest, too quickly for them to reload, but almost as one mind he and his friends surged towards them using their muskets as clubs and their tomahawks. It was hard, close, savage hand-to-hand fighting. Nathaniel ducked and dived as he had been taught, slashing low at the attackers' hamstrings with one hand and parrying with the other. The Susquehanna resisted valiantly but they couldn't hold the onslaught and Nathaniel knew they must retreat to the palisade. He desperately searched the sprawling bodies for signs of his wife and child. Out of the corner of his eye he saw a small child standing stock still at the water's edge and recognised his daughter. He sprang towards her and releasing his tomahawk swept her up clutching her tightly to his body as he turned and ran uphill, all the time sweeping the ground for signs of Hyacinthe. Men on horseback now began to appear more easily slaughtering those on foot, but at least half of the fighting men of the village had retreated into the palisade helping the defenceless women and children who were still alive inside too. The ground around the fortified settlement soon resembled that of a full-scale battle fought with muskets, arrows and spears. The attackers were relentless and ruthless, sometimes stopping briefly to kill a wounded child or woman, and even attempt to take a scalp but there was little time for this as the defenders picked them off when they attempted to do this. They knew it would only be a matter of time before they were overwhelmed by the numbers and their defences breached, but they were prepared to fight to the death as they sensed there would be no quarter given by their unknown enemy. At the bleakest moment, the attackers found themselves under attack. The hunters hearing the shots from afar had returned quickly and from another quarter came further relief as a dozen of the neighbourly squatters, also hearing the din of battle, had come to their assistance. Together they made short work of their assailants keeping half a dozen alive who had surrendered in order to discover who they were. They learned that they were a troop of unofficial Regulators from Virginia who, hearing of the Iroquois settlement, had decided to wipe them out. Not all of the Virginians had been involved in the attack, a few remaining with the pack horses but these were pursued with most of them being killed and scalped; only two or three survived by escaping.

Nathaniel desperately searched amongst the scattered human wreckage, hoping beyond hope that he would find his beloved Hyacinthe. But, down at the water's edge he saw her familiar smock with the embroidered wampum belt that she always wore as his wedding gift to her around her slender waist. She had been shot twice. Once in the left breast and the other in her stomach. Her end would have been swift. Fortunately, she hadn't been scalped. He raised her gently and carried her back up the hill, tears streaming down his face. There was so much death and destruction around them that most were too preoccupied with their own personal tragedies to pay him much heed. But Running Deer had seen him and came running towards him with other members of her clan, taking the lifeless body of her daughter with the help of her sisters into their long house to be prepared for her last journey. Nathaniel found Bright Eyes and clutched her to him for the rest of the day, oblivious to all else. When his mother-in-law later came to rescue the child, she also took Nathaniel quietly by the arm into the longhouse and gently pushed the listless man down beside his daughter to take healing refuge in sleep. The following morning, Nathaniel's mind was made up. He didn't care to endure the barbaric ritual torture and death of the captives, nor did he want Bright Eyes to be witness to it. He was going home and he was taking his daughter with him. He would stay only long enough to see Hyacinthe ritually cremated.

Chapter 18
A Tea Party

'This tea tax is a direct assault on our freedom,' Sam Hutchinson was in full spate with his fiery oratory. 'If we pay it when it lands on our soil, it turns us into slaves. Brothers – there are your chains – waiting in the harbour. Is that what you want?'

'No!' came the full-throated, passionate response.

'No Taxation without Representation,' he yelled.

'No! No Taxation without Representation,' they yelled back.

'Well, what are you going to do about it?'

'Destroy it!' a strong voice from his audience rang out. 'To the harbour!'

The hundred plus strong crowd surged out of the meeting room into the chill, frosty midwinter night. Henry Miller was glad of the blanket he wore Indian style, over his shoulder and tied around the waist. He felt for his pistol, assuring himself it was still stuck in his belt and fingered the keenness of his hatchet blade as he strode out in the direction of Griffin's wharf. He felt his face to ensure the oily soot was still there. He was damned if he was going to be recognised and accused of breaking the law by any of the bemused onlookers whose numbers increased as they reached the harbour. There were the three ships waiting to unload the damnable cargo. They had been warned by their leaders not to damage any other property or they would pay for it. Nor were they to do any injury or take the life of anyone on pain of death. The Sons of Liberty were not to be ignored. They all knew they would be severely punished if any of these instructions were ignored. They divided into three groups boarding the ships meeting no opposition. There were no guards. The captains had been ordered to stay locked in their cabins, whilst the crew were told to remain locked in their quarters below decks. The hatches to the storage bays were wide open and they could clearly see the items they sought. The cargo was reasonably light to handle but shifting 60 or 70 chests of tea was nevertheless tiring because of the number and one or two were dropped spilling the black powdery gold everywhere. More of it scattered around the decks as they smashed open the tops of the chests and manhandled them onto the gunwales where they poured the contents into the deep waters of the harbour. The water began to bubble up with the air trapped in the intense black China tea. Henry couldn't refrain from grabbing a few handfuls where he could and stuffing it into his pockets. It was just too valuable to let go, even at two shillings a pound. When they'd finished, they dispersed into the night whooping trying to convince whoever was looking they were Native Americans.

'Have you heard what happened last night?' asked Jeremiah Goodman of his recently arrived guest, Nathaniel.

'No, I can't say I have as I slept like a log following our exhausting journey.'

'It would appear the Sons of Liberty were busy last night. They have tipped the total contents of a valuable cargo of tea from three ships into the sea. The town **is** buzzing with the news and liberty poles have been erected in all the squares. They claim it is the work of Mohawk Indians but why on earth would they do something like that? It's rumoured that the governor will issue a proclamation forbidding any ships from entering Boston until the tea has been paid for. People are furious at the news and it is becoming dangerous for anyone who is a British sympathiser to be abroad in the town.'

'Are they allowing ships to leave the harbour,' enquired Nathaniel, 'because if not, I may have to prevail upon your hospitality for a little longer?'

'Don't you worry about that, my good friend. You and your daughter are welcome to stay for as long as you like.'

Just at that moment there was a commotion as the toddler came rushing through the door giggling and shrieking in high merriment pursued by Jeremiah's two children. They absolutely doted on her, and were willing to play with her as long as she wanted. Since Nathaniel and she had arrived, they had been enthralled by the brief accounts he had given of his journeys and stay with the Iroquois Seneca-Susquehanna of which Bright eyes was the living embodiment. They had of course heard much about the Indians but had rarely seen one. Nathaniel swept his daughter off her feet and threw her up in the air catching her neatly as she came down. He was besotted with her even though she reminded him painfully of his dead wife.

When he'd appeared at Jeremiah's door a few days before, he was welcomed like a long-lost son who'd been given up for dead. The sight of the little girl excited all their imaginations and they listened with growing dread to the culmination of his tale, weeping silently, sharing his bereavement at its conclusion. It hadn't been an easy journey after the fight at the village. It was painful leaving his friends, his wife's family and even people he'd come to love and trust like the Connors. They all pressed him to stay, but he just couldn't stay in that place of death where every inch reminded him of his beautiful Hyacinthe. It'd also been a dangerous journey as the countryside in Pennsylvania and Massachusetts was seething with Regulators and Sons of Liberty, holding impromptu mass meetings and stopping travellers demanding to know their business in the hope of detecting British Loyalists. They were aggressively inquisitive as to why Nathaniel was travelling with a small Indian child and he had to tell a story that she was the child of his slave who died from the smallpox. Some of them wanted to kill her there and then but his furious protection of her made them back off. This convinced him more than ever that he had to leave the colonies as soon as he could before complete anarchy prevailed. His report to Abia Darby couldn't help but conclude that future trade with the colonies was unlikely to be possible in the short term. He had to write to his family and employer before he left but he had no idea what he was going to say to Rebecca. He knew it would have to be the truth, which would be terribly painful for her. How they would receive Bright Eyes he couldn't guess. However, he resolved that if he could not find a welcome at home, he would settle elsewhere.

'Do you think it will be possible to obtain a ship from here?' asked Nathaniel as he sat down one evening with Jeremiah after the children had been put to bed.

'At the moment, nothing is coming in or out and anyway it would be impossible to brave the midwinter storms of the Atlantic. You would be asking for certain death for both of you. I think you'll have to resign yourself to staying here until spring, Nathaniel.'

'But how can I possibly impose on you for so long?'

'It's absolutely no imposition, my young friend. I enjoy having you here and being able to discuss so much which would not otherwise be possible. One has to be very careful these days for fear of being branded a traitor to independence. You will also have to take great care of what you say when you are out and about. The Patriots are trying to control the situation but the mob in the form of the Sons of Liberty are stopping people everywhere, searching them and reading whatever correspondence they may have.'

'I hear the governor has recalled all troops to the citadel and has forbidden any ships to enter or leave the harbour. Is that right?'

'Yes, you are correct. I heard it from one of the members of the Assembly earlier today. They are furious with him for curtailing their businesses and currently there is a stand-off between them with the redcoats being confined to barracks and the mob dispersed to their homes. However, as you know the countryside is full of armed men arrived recently from further south, from Virginia, Maryland and the Carolinas. Boston has become a cause celebre and focal point for those who want complete independence from the Empire.'

'Where does it go from here?'

'It's hard to say, but don't imagine all the people are of the same mind. Many of the elite and business leaders are very concerned about an uncontrollable mob even though they may have grievances against the Crown. Many of them would rather negotiate a new settlement which granted recognition and a greater degree of independence for the colonial assemblies whilst remaining part of the British Empire, thus benefiting from the security of its army and navy. Others, however, want complete independence from Parliament and the Crown. There is also probably an equal number which is totally loyal to King George and condemn the Patriots as traitors. Then there are those who are simply neutral, wishing the whole controversy would just subside.'

'What about you, Jeremiah, where are your sympathies?'

'I will always opt for a peaceful path so negotiation is my preferred option. There is good and bad on both sides of the argument. For example, I detest the way the colonists demand freedom for themselves but denounce it ruthlessly when their African slaves cry for the same. Indeed, it has reached such a pitch now that even free Africans are being detained by Regulators and sent in chains to the southern plantations. However, I also observe the greed and corruption of His Majesty's servants and tax collectors here in Massachusetts. As things are developing, I think it will be extremely difficult to maintain a neutral position, even for a Quaker. Do you know that now there is a saying amongst the Quakers in Pennsylvania that: "only powder secures freedom"? I find this incomprehensible, especially when a hundred years ago

Quakers were hanged here in Massachusetts for their pacifist beliefs and the remainder expelled from the colony.'

'Yes, I know, I have seen the confusion amongst them close up for myself in Pennsylvania. But they have not all capitulated, nor all will, I think. Why don't you come back with me to England?'

'I cannot. This is my homeland and I need to stay and shape it for the good in whatever way I can.'

They both paused in their conversation for some time, deep in thought from what had been said.

Jeremiah proposed that they take in a female African servant to see to the needs of Nathaniel's child, Bright Eyes, as she really needed the constant, close attention of a mother. They employed Abigail, a young free single mother herself providing all found accommodation for her and her six-year-old son, Jacob. She was delighted to have found the position in the house of Jeremiah who was well known as a good employer, paying above the going rate and treating all his employees as members of his family. Nathaniel wondered whether he might find employment as a Smith or Ferrier at the barracks but Jeremiah advised against this as being too dangerous and drawing unwanted attention to him from the Patriots. Instead, Jeremiah suggested he accompany him on occasion to the Corn Exchange to observe how business was done. In addition, Nathaniel decided to make a close record of events as they unfolded in Boston, going along to observe the debates in the Assembly Meeting House, reading the Boston Gazette daily and obtaining all the pamphlets he could which were produced in that period that supported one or other faction. He also attended the Boston Society of Friends' Meeting House two or three times a week because he was still deeply disturbed by the blood he had on his hands. He spoke to Jeremiah about it too, who listened compassionately and non-judgementally. Jeremiah surprised him when he said that human beings were little removed from the animal kingdom and could behave with great savagery in given circumstances, which were sometimes beyond their control, as he had found. He asked Nathaniel what might've happened had he not taken action when he came across the outrage perpetrated on the Mohican women and children. Equally, in each of the other actions amongst the Mohawk and the Seneca he had defended himself and others. Had he not, he would now be dead. There was a difference between proactively seeking to kill others for money or revenge et cetera and reactively defending oneself and one's loved ones. He admitted that the most devout amongst them would not lift a finger in defence, even if it meant the injury or death of another, but he didn't know what he would do in similar circumstances. There was much evil in the world and it was difficult to know how to negotiate a pure path through it unless one lived completely apart such as the Mennonite and Amish communities, or had sufficient wealth to purchase a protective barrier, as he admitted he had done.

In January the news arrived that the British Parliament had passed The Intolerable Acts, as the colonists called them. A complete trade embargo was placed on Boston whilst the East India Company was effectively allowed to sell its tea tax-free. The colonies and the Empire were now set on a collision course and many more people joined the Sons of Liberty and the Patriots. In that year, the First Continental Congress was held thus signalling the intent of the 13 mainland colonies to become independent. Nathaniel realised he had to leave as soon as possible.

Part Three
Age of Iron
(1775–1777)

Chapter 19
The Homecoming

He had a strange feeling in his stomach as their boat navigated the dangerous shoals into the main harbour. They had been lucky with a relatively calm crossing. It hadn't been easy securing two berths in a small private cabin as so many people were anxious to leave Boston now that the port was virtually under siege. The Green Mountain Boys from Virginia and Kentucky had infested the hinterland, whilst the Royal Navy blocked the seaway. However, with Jeremiah's help and wealth sufficient hands had been prepared to take money to allow he and Bright Eyes a passage. It had been a tearful parting from Jeremiah and his family whom they had become very close to after their four months' long stay in their home. It was unlikely they would ever see each other again and the two men felt a deep foreboding about the future. This was compounded now as he saw eight ships of the Royal Navy being loaded with men and horses in the Royal docks at Bristol. During the long voyage he'd had plenty of time to think about his experiences, speculate about what the future may hold in the colonies and consider what he would say to his family. He was still daunted by the prospect. As they disembarked and found a barge journeying to Shrewsbury, which would take them for a small price, he decided he would go straight to Abia Derby. He would seek her wise counsel before entering Madeley.

He'd been absent for three years and as soon as the coach neared the Darby Works, he became immediately aware of the increased volume of industry. There were many additional buildings, both industrial and domestic, that had been erected since his departure. Nevertheless, he still recognised familiar features and the one he was heading for in particular, the Darby home. It was mid-afternoon but he hoped the Mistress would be at home. She frequently visited neighbours, sick employees or attended business meetings with her sons so he couldn't count on her being there. Fortunately for him, this afternoon she was. When she heard his voice at the door, despite her strict self-discipline, she almost rushed towards the entrance embracing him as one of her own.

'Nathaniel, welcome home my boy,' she said trying to suppress the emotion in her voice. 'And, who is this?' she asked bending down to the toddler that was grasping her father's leg. 'You must be Bright Eyes,' she said with a mother's obvious affection. She ushered them into the large living room and ordered tea, and milk for the child. 'It's been so long, Nathaniel, I wondered whether we would ever see you again.'

'I wondered whether I would ever return,' he said dolefully.

'I can see there is a lot you haven't disclosed in your letters. You have experienced much heartache and loss, I fear.'

'Yes, but there is plenty of time now to tell you more for I have no plans beyond returning home.'

'And your family? Have you told them everything?'

'No,' he replied hesitantly, 'that's one of the reasons I came straight here. I would like your advice.'

She accepted this recognition of confidence with great pleasure and satisfaction.

'Well, first of all perhaps your daughter might stay here with me for the present. In fact, I think it might be a good idea if you were both to stay with me for a while so that Bright Eyes – we must find a Christian forename for her – will not fret at your absence for a few hours whilst you see your family initially.' Nathaniel had looked up with some consternation at the digression regarding his daughter's name, but he agreed with the idea that he should visit his family alone for the moment, so he left this unchallenged.

'That's very generous of you, Mistress Abia. Once my daughter is settled here, I will pay a visit to my family.'

'Excellent, I'm so pleased to be able to help and we can discuss business later. Now, Abigail will show you to your rooms and I will find a few toys for the little one.' At the mention of the familiar name, Bright Eyes looked up with delight but on seeing the white face rather than the African nurse maid in Boston, she was dismayed and began to whimper. Nathaniel explained and Abigail rose to the occasion by coming down to the child's height to comfort her and then made her laugh by tickling her ribs.

Abia put a horse at Nathaniel's disposal but before he left, he asked whether anything had changed at home and after Elijah.

'Everything has gone on as before,' she said noncommittally, 'I'm sure they will have plenty of news to share with you on your arrival. As for Elijah, he is here with us and has fretted somewhat these past two years when we heard nothing from you, until just recently. He was overjoyed when he heard you were returning home. I don't doubt he will want to discuss the latest news and politics from the colonies – as would I later. Now be off with you. Your daughter will be safe here with us for a few hours.'

It was a very difficult ride from Coalbrookdale to his family's home in Madeley. So many sights and smells redolent of a time that seemed to belong to another world. He may have been only a few years younger but he now felt aged beyond his years. Did age bring wisdom? Abia had sent a servant yesterday to inform them that he would be arriving at midday to allow them to make arrangements to be present. He noticed there were more squatters' houses en route than when he left and more smoke was pouring out of the chimneys that had also multiplied since his departure. The environment seemed to have turned much greyer and drearier, but he recognised this could well have been because he had become used to the rich, colourful landscape of New England. Madeley seemed to have grown exponentially with the profusion of shambling redbrick buildings everywhere that he could hardly find his parents' home. Eventually he found it and lingered for a good while outside, taking time to secure his horse as if dreading the next few steps. He knocked on the door and opened it scanning the occupants to see in what condition they were in. They all looked up expectantly and, save for his father, gave a cry of joy on seeing him. His mother and his sister, Rachel, jumped up to embrace him, tears in their eyes. He noticed how tired and shoddy they looked, their clothes threadbare and slightly grubby, no doubt from the work they had to do. Rebecca hadn't moved. It was as if she was stunned by his presence – she wanted him so badly but not in front of the family and she had an unshakeable premonition that this wasn't her Nathaniel, the one who had left her three years ago professing his love and determination they should be married on his return. The last letter she'd had from him was two months ago from Boston and it spoke little about his feelings for her and whether they would marry. It contained details of Boston and other places he had visited as well as his new friends in Boston, the Goodman family. But he'd been careful not to refer to his Indian adventures. She knew he was keeping something from her and dreaded what it might be. Then he looked at his father who had not even registered his son's arrival, sitting there vacantly. Nathaniel knew there was something not right with him. He looked to his mother for clarification.

'He's been like this now for the past year, ever since the explosion in the mine.'

'I didn't know. Why didn't you write me?' grief and anger present in his voice.

'We didn't know where to write or, indeed, whether you were still alive,' she replied with a hint of anger of her own. 'And anyway, what could you have done so very far away?'

'I could have sent money…'

'We have been well provided for. Mistress Abia Darby paid for a physician, Master Reynolds continues to abate the rent and the Rev Fletcher has provided better, more congenial employment in his household for Rachel and myself.'

'But what about Father? Can he no longer work?' he asked with growing concern.

'I'm afraid not. Since the firedamp erupted destroying two galleries and killing 10 men, he is as you see him. He was lucky to survive with only minor cuts and bruises but something seems to have snapped in his mind. He hasn't spoken a word since, just sits and stares.'

'I'm so sorry,' responded Nathaniel, barely able to keep the tears from coursing down his cheeks. He went over to his father and kneeling down hugged him closely. There was a slight glimmer in his father's eyes but then they went dull again. His mother had noticed and she wondered silently whether she dared hope that in time with the return of Nathaniel he might return to them. As he sat down by his father, he felt a hand on his as it lay upon the table. It was Rebecca's. He turned towards her to see that she was too full of emotion to be able to talk. He had to tell them.

'My very dear ones,' he struggled for the right words, 'I have something very important to tell you.' The three women looked at him in alarm.

'You are not leaving us again!' It was Rachel who spoke for them all.

'No, absolutely not. I'm here to stay, but there is something you need to know. You have a little sister who is with Abia Derby at the moment, but I would like to bring her to meet you all if you allow it. I know this will be very hard for you, especially you Rebecca,' and he sought her hand as she began to withdraw it alarmed at the significance of what he'd just said. He then began to tell them something of his travels and adventures from Massachusetts to Pennsylvania and finally to the Ohio. They listened in awed silence and when his own voice faltered as he told them about the death of Hyacinthe, the tears sprang afresh from their eyes. Rebecca was totally numb. She wasn't able to say anything, although soon she began to feel plenty – a complete kaleidoscope of compassion, anger, jealousy, dejection, heartfelt sadness. The only thing she could do was to withdraw her hand roughly from Nathaniel's and rush outside. She didn't know where she was going – she just had to get away from him. It was too crushingly painful to hear any more. He would have run after her but his mother restrained him.

'Let her go. It's too overwhelming for her to take it in at the moment, but she will want to know more as we all do. Of course, your daughter must come to us. She is our family. Now, what is the dear child's name?'

That evening after dinner, when Abigail had taken her charge to her room, Abia Darby sat opposite Nathaniel and asked him to tell her of his dealings in America.

'We have already received consignments of 30 tons each of pig iron from the two suppliers you contacted. I'm told it's excellent quality.'

'Yes. The Taunton mine in Connecticut is quite small and I found it by chance because of its proximity to Boston. However, I doubt whether it will be in production for very many years because the supply of ore is limited. The Monroe mine is much larger with an excellent supply of nearby coal and ore mines, but whilst it can meet our orders for the present I have no confidence it will continue to do so because of its proximity to the Hudson and its strategic position in any future conflict between Britain and the colonies, which I will comment on in a moment. I believe it already supplies many of the Royal naval facilities by way of anchors, chains and the like. It is very close to Albany and the military college of West Point.'

'This is the crux of the matter,' said Abia. 'How likely are hostilities between the Crown and the colonies do you think?'

'When I left, Massachusetts was already a hotbed of opposition to the Royal Governors, although not specifically against the king. The anger was directed at the British Parliament. It rather depends on how the King's agents conduct themselves. In fact, it could almost be too late now given the fallout from the tea fiasco in December, which alienated many more colonies than Massachusetts. That's not to say that all colonials oppose British government. My friend Jeremiah Goodman estimates they constitute at least a third of the current population and he is well informed. My judgement is that we really should look elsewhere for supplies of good pig iron or just simply produce more ourselves if we get the raw material.'

'Yes,' she said in a surprised voice indicating that she was rather taken aback by him daring to suggest company policy. But then she thought that Nathaniel had grown in stature and confidence since his journey abroad and it may well be valuable to reconsider his role in the Darby Works. 'Now, the other issue I wish to discuss with you is your trip to Pennsylvania, which I was surprised by as it was not part of the business purpose of the journey? Furthermore, it was shortly after that you seemed to drop off the end of the world without any communication with anyone here. We dreaded hearing the worst news but happily here you are.' He had been expecting this enquiry and wasn't sure how she would react to his news, although her positive response to meeting his daughter was a good sign.

'You're right,' he said shamefacedly, 'I did keep you all rather in the dark. I'm sorry. I could have contacted you easily enough from Pennsylvania, although after that in Ohio it was more difficult and then... Well, life for me began to run a different course. I'll be truthful. If events had been different, I would not have returned because I was very happy with the life I had amongst the Susquehanna Indians. Not to put too much of a face on it, I was carrying out my own little Holy Experiment.' She looked up and started at this – quite confused.

'Ah, you may not be acquainted with William Penn's aims in Pennsylvania although I'm sure he must have written back to English Society of Friends about it, though that would be nearly a hundred years ago.' He then proceeded to explain what the term meant as well as the treaties Penn agreed with the Native American Indians. He also described how the Experiment had unravelled and been betrayed by his two sons, who had become blatant land grabbers. Abia listened earnestly to these accounts.

'No man can behave like God, whose ways are mysterious and not always clear to us. Despite his piety, I suspect you are right that there were flaws with his intentions right from the beginning. It's no surprise that others later challenged his autocratic rule, no matter how benign it seemed. All men should be equal and free to make their own choices. So, what happened in your case if his failed?'

'It was very short lived but within the area defined the squatters and the Indians found peace and common cause for a while through the medium of trade. I believe the French were much better at this than the British have been and consequently secured a greater degree of loyalty from their Indian allies in the recent wars.'

'Now Nathaniel you haven't explained whose Bright Eyes' mother was?'

'She was the most beautiful, graceful and kind person that I met in the whole of the colonies. Her name was Hyacinthe of the Seneca – Susquehanna, whom I fell in love with when she was teaching me their language. We led an idyllic life until one day without any warning we were attacked by Regulators from Virginia looking for escaped slaves but also keen to slaughter any Indians they came across. They murdered my wife but few of them escaped to tell the tale.'

'Nathaniel,' she looked at him in consternation, 'did you take a life in revenge?'

'I took life to defend myself and my daughter, not out of revenge nor for any other reason. And each time I have taken a life has been for that reason.'

'You mean, you have killed other people…?' she asked in horror.

'It is a savage world over there and had I not, I would not be here now. What would you have had me do?' She thought long and hard before answering,

'I just can't answer that, Nathaniel. It's not for me to judge you, but the good Lord. There are many things here I just don't understand and I sent you into that new, strange world not knowing what I was doing.'

'I am a man and I am responsible for what I do and the choices I make. You must not blame yourself, Mistress, for my actions.' She looked at him with great affection acknowledging the sagacity in his manner. She had decided what she was going to do with Nathaniel.

'Nathaniel, I want you to become a working director of the company. I believe you now have the insight, experience and maturity that is needed to help and assist my sons. As such, I think you ought to have a house of your own and I propose to build one for you and your family just along the road from my house here. I would hope, if you accept, that you and your daughter along with your family in Madeley will become my neighbour when the house is built.' Nathaniel was staggered by the offer and daunted by the prospect of becoming a working manager, but then he thought he could do the job as he had made many important decisions affecting the company over the past three years. The prospect of living close by both the Works and the Darbys was attractive and being able to rehouse his family in a much larger, more congenial house was ideal, especially now his father was incapacitated. But, he thought, what about Rebecca?

Early the following morning: there was a loud, insistent knocking at the front door. They breakfasted early in the Darby household but even they hadn't yet come downstairs. The maid admitted a tall officer from the Shrewsbury militia with six men waiting outside on horses. He knew whose house this was and offered his credentials courteously to the Mistress and then explained that he was here to escort a Mr Nathaniel Shawcross to come before the Lord-Lieutenant at Shrewsbury Castle. He would give no other details but insisted they depart at once. As he rode by the silent officer, Nathaniel tried to think what it might be about but he was simply at a loss. On arrival, he was escorted smartly into the Lord Lieutenant's office. It was the Deputy Lord Lieutenant who turned around to face him with a thunderous expression on his face.

'Well sir, what seditious purpose do you here? And, don't give me that holier than thou, innocent look. I have your accomplice here,' pointing to someone in the corner of the room guarded by a militia man, whom he hadn't noticed until now. He was mortified to see it was Elijah whose hands were chained. He hadn't seen him in three years and he appeared demonstrably older, thinner and greyer than he remembered. Nathaniel tried to go over to him but was prevented by a musket with a cruelly long and vicious-looking bayonet.

'So, you don't deny knowing this man? Your actions betray you, sir. He is a self-confessed purveyor of radical tracts…'

'I have no intention of denying him. He is my honest, good friend Elijah Smith, whom I haven't seen these past three years, though I'm glad to see him now, but not in these circumstances. I don't understand why you have arrested him.' Nathaniel would not be browbeaten by the Deputy Lord-Lieutenant – he had certainly acquired a level of confidence that he hadn't possessed before he left for America. Was this a legacy, he wondered to himself, of having killed? He didn't know and couldn't dwell on it but maintained a strong pose of self-confidence. The Deputy was momentarily taken aback by this unaccustomed show of defiance from a commoner and wasn't sure how to deal with it.

'Well… I… Hmm. Do you know he is a radical with antimonarchist ideas?'

'He is a Quaker, sir, and a freethinker but he's not dangerous to anyone. I thought the days when we persecuted people for their religious ideas were over in this country?'

'But sedition, sir, is criminal and punishable. You are both said to have attended a meeting some years ago at which the antimonarchist Irish Sons of Ireland were present. Do you deny it?'

'Oh my goodness,' said Nathaniel with exasperation, 'not that old hoary issue! Yes, it's true Deputy Lord-Lieutenant and I know there was some consternation about the riot at the Golden Ball Inn just before I left for Massachusetts, but I will tell you truly what happened. Elijah and I had heard there was to be a meeting at the Inn that evening addressed by two seamen from the colonies in the Americas. We were keen to attend because we had come across pamphlets claiming that for the first time all men were free, which we couldn't fully understand as we know that slavery flourishes in the American colonies. When we arrived, the Inn was full of workmen – navies, barge men, miners and foundry men – a complete assortment from many parts, but a large number who were Irish. When the two colonists began to talk about their home countries and how they were being enslaved by the British Crown, the Irish supported them wholeheartedly in denouncing the King and Parliament as corrupt and tyrannical. But I have to tell you, sir, that this was not received well by the rest of the clientele who began to object and defend King George. This is what precipitated the exchange of blows between the two camps which led to the virtual destruction of the Inn. Elijah and I got out as soon as we could.' The magnate listened carefully to what Nathaniel was saying but there was a sceptical look on his face.

'Please, my Lord, my Mistress Abia Derby will vouch for both Elijah and I as loyal, hard-working employees as well as God-fearing subjects of the King. I would also add, if you write to the Royal Governor in Boston he will also vouch for my loyal credentials as I stayed with a foremost member of the loyal community there who he knows well, Mr Jeremiah Goodman. If you need more confirmation of my loyalty, you can also seek it from the Royal Governor in Albany whose protection I was given when I arrived on business in that country.' The Deputy Lord-Lieutenant was now beginning to view the matter in a whole different light, especially impressed by Nathaniel's confident manner, dress and excursions to the colonies.

'I will check with the people you mention and, in the meantime, will give you the benefit of the doubt but be under no illusion my men will be keeping a close eye on both of you.' Nathaniel was glad to take Elijah home on his horse providing them both with an opportunity to catch up.

'You aren't the man who left Coalbrookdale three years ago,' Elijah said admiringly. 'I believe there is much we will be able to talk about when we get home. You act more like a gentleman than a hired iron worker.'

'I'll tell you everything, Elijah, in time and you might judge for yourself. However, you should perhaps know I will be living at Mistress Darby's house until my own is built nearby.'

'My, you are going up in the world.'

'My family will also be coming to join me. Oh, and the other thing you might need to know is that the Mistress has asked me to become a working director, to which I have agreed. Don't worry, we shall still see each other and no doubt I will still be seeking your good advice and opinions on many topics, as I used to.' Elijah smiled to himself, content that his old friend hadn't changed so much after all.

'And Rebecca?'

'I'm not sure… It will be up to her as much as anything. Something you don't know Elijah is that I have a daughter now, although her mother is no longer with us having been murdered.' Elijah was aghast at this news but realised now wasn't the time to find out more.

He got around to finally confronting the issue with Rebecca by sending her a note and asking her to join him for tea one afternoon at the Darby house, when he knew that everyone would be absent apart from the servants and his daughter.

As she was led into the main salon, he stood up to receive her, which made her, along with the opulent surroundings, a little self-conscious of her common status. He ordered tea as though he were quite used to commanding the servants, or so it seemed to her. She knew he had things to tell her, but she was neither sure of her own feelings nor his. There was an emotional gulf between them. Since she dashed out from the family gathering some days before she had cried herself sick with feelings of self-pity at his obvious desertion of her. She couldn't understand what circumstances would have led her Nathaniel to betray her in such a way. When she received his note, she didn't know whether to accept his offer of a meeting or not. In the end, however, she realised that she still felt deeply for him and that by refusing to meet she would only be cutting off her nose to spite her face.

'As I have asked to see you,' he said gently and with affection, 'perhaps I should begin.' She looked at him, on the edge of tears, and merely nodded.

'When I went to New England, as you will know from my early letters, I had no intention of staying longer than six months. However, my travels and unexpected adventures led me to Pennsylvania, where I needed to satisfy my curiosity about events there. In particular, I wanted to know how a state designed and run by Quakers was faring. I was appalled to discover a few years previously there had been the most terrible, savage massacre of peaceful Indians, many of them Christian, in the very midst of that supposedly saintly community. I visited the beleaguered survivors of those native Indians in Philadelphia where, wanting to know more about them, I found a willing guide to take me to their last remaining settlement on the frontier in Indian territory. I found them and they received me well whereupon I began to make friends learning from them about their ways and also teaching them some of the rudiments of iron making. I set up a small smithy which was a great success with them. The idea then struck me that I should try to bring these Indians together peacefully with the settlers in that area, who in fact were there illegally and, with whom I realised, that unless something were done would soon be in conflict with each other. I established a small market and invited them all to participate in the trade. I'm glad to say this worked. it was during this time that I came to know a young Indian woman by the name of Hyacinthe who was assigned to teach me their language. She was my constant companion and helper at the workshop I built and the market I established. Before I knew it, I realised I had fallen in love with her. Perhaps it was inevitable given the length of absence and distance between the two of us. Perhaps I am merely weak willed, although that devalues the love I felt for Hyacinthe. I decided to make my life with the Indians living amongst them and building good relations between them and the settlers. We were married according to Indian custom and before long our wonderful daughter, Bright Eyes was born.'

Rebecca sat silently weeping at his account, wringing her hands. He had turned his face away from her unable to look her in the eyes. He waited for a few moments giving her space in his long explanation to interrupt him.

'But we were engaged. How could you forget me? I was true to you all this time.'

'I was in another world, Rebecca, where you didn't exist. Can you understand that? I had become something else, someone else.'

'What are you now, who are you? Is anything left of the old Nathaniel?'

'I don't know. Yes, I have changed and I am different but I do still feel very tenderly towards you. Maybe, in time you will be able to see who I am now and decide whether you want to know me again.' She realised he was right. They could not just ignore the past three years as though it had never happened. Time was a great healer she knew, but whether it would enable their love to be restored she didn't know.

'Yes, you're right. We need time. It's just possible too I have changed as well. As you will learn, I have not been idle these past few years.'

'Would you like to meet my daughter,' he said disarmingly. She was immediately taken aback, having forgotten there was a child. Her emotions were in turmoil again.

'Of… course,' she could hardly speak but she knew if there was to be any future at all between them, she would have to accept this ordeal. He called for a servant to ask Abigail to bring his daughter down. The little girl hid behind Abigail's skirts at the stranger present but when her father said,

'This is my treasure, Bright Eyes. Come, my darling, this is Miss Rebecca, an old friend of daddy's. Don't be afraid, she's a good and honest person.' Rebecca was again taken aback at the dark-skinned little girl with the beautiful black, long, thick hair and she wondered how much she resembled her mother. Rebecca, however, loved children and held out her arms to her telling her in soothing terms to come to her, that she had nothing to fear. Bright eyes approached her cautiously and smiled curiously at Rebecca, winning her over instantly. As Rebecca's manner relaxed, the child was happy to accept her embrace. At least, thought Rebecca, this was a promising start.

Chapter 20
Fares, Rioters and Radicals

The Rev John Fletcher was a worried man. He always was at this time of year despite it being the highlight of the Christian calendar. For most people, however, in the burgeoning settlement of Madeley, Easter was a time for drunkenness, ribaldry and animal baiting. To him it was more like a bacchanalian revel and he racked his brains to see what steps he might take to protect his flock from the seductions brought by the travelling community of tinkers, gypsies and other assorted ne'er-do-wells. The flotsam and jetsam had already arrived a week before Easter-tide and the otherwise busy, industrial community had descended into a week-long noisy, drunken carousel. He had seen it before in Switzerland and France where the authorities were much more assiduous at moving them on. And he knew the reason why. There are many cutthroats, pickpockets and radicals peddling their anti-government sedition amongst them. He was on his way to meet with the other, godly worthies of the town in his Meeting House he'd built a few years before. As he came around the corner of one recently erected marquee, he came across a large seething crowd, hooting and baying. There were so many people crowded together he couldn't see what was going on. Pushing his way to the front, he was confronted with the most horrific spectacle of three ferocious dogs baiting a massive brown bear. The bear was tethered by an iron spiked necklace and chained to a fixed wooden pole in the ground allowing it to move only a few feet in any direction. It was a powerful beast with great thick arms at the end of which were razor-sharp claws. The fight had been going on for some time and all three dogs showed signs of open, rugged, bloody wounds, which they were unable to feel now as they foamed at the mouth desperate to sink their teeth into the bear's flesh. There were indications that they had been partially successful from patches of matted blood on the bear's haunches, but none of them had been able to get anywhere near its throat, which would enable them to inflict a fatal blow. Money had changed hands on the outcome of this tournament and was still doing so by the dextrous workings of the tout's fingers and hands, the silent but effective way of placing and accepting bets. The Rev tried to exert his authority, but was shoved roughly back by the crowds who were well inebriated and excited to a feverish pitch by the blood-sport that it would have been too dangerous for him to persist. It was not unlawful, although the local magistrate had forbidden dog and cock fighting within the perimeter of Madeley. Local employers like the Darbys and the Reynolds, who also disapproved of such barbaric practices, and with whom he was meeting that very hour, had forbidden the keeping of such animals on their tenants' properties on threat of eviction. However, they knew they had only succeeded in pushing the vile sport out into the countryside where it was even supported by members of the gentry.

When he entered the Meeting House, he looked dishevelled and decidedly dejected. Those present, Richard Reynolds and his son William, Abia Darby and her eldest son, Abraham, along with the Rev's wife, Mary, all looked up with concern at his appearance.

'My goodness, John,' said Mary, speaking for them all, 'whatever has happened to you?' He told them about the bearbaiting going on in their very midst which he was helpless to stop.

'You know,' responded Abraham, 'we really do need to have the militia present at these events, which can so easily turn nasty and even potentially riotous.'

'You may be right,' answered the Rev, 'but it is odious to me at this time of year to have to invoke the might of the authorities to maintain peace. I feel as though I have failed in my mission to bring love and harmony to this community and inviting in the militia I fear would only lead to worse indiscipline and possibly bloodshed.'

'Thou art right, my brother in Christ,' acknowledged Richard Reynolds, landowner, Quaker and local mine owner. 'However, there may be other ways by which we may encourage the people here to turn away from such savage and unchristian acts. Over the past few years, thou hast successfully reduced by half the number of establishments licensed to sell alcohol. At William's suggestion, I have opened up my estates providing beautiful, rural pathways where the local folk may walk and picnic in the beauty of the Lord's great bounty.'

'Yes,' added Abia, 'and I have opened our Meeting Room in Coalbrookdale to as many as will come during the week as well as the sabbath. But I recognise we have to do more. The women and children are not the ones who are the potential troublemakers as they are too busy with work and domestic duties. It is the men who have their hands on the family income and are seduced by the demon drink. What can we provide for them?'

'Well, we do have the school building in addition to the Meeting Houses in Madeley, Coalbrookdale, Horsehay and elsewhere,' offered Abraham. 'What about offering classes in reading and writing to the adults as well as the children? That would be an alternative to the drinking den in the evening.'

Abia Derby reacted very enthusiastically to the suggestion,

'And I think I know some people, in addition to those of us present here, who would be very willing to offer their services in this respect. Elijah Smith, a fellow Friend and widely read employee of mine, and possibly Nathaniel Shawcross, recently returned from a long stay in North America.'

The Rev Fletcher offered both his and his wife's support and also suggested that Rebecca, who acted very much as his secretary with regard to a wide range of matters now, might also be interested. It was agreed that those mentioned would be approached.

'Hey, Nathaniel, have you seen this in today's *Times*?' asked Abraham in the design office pushing a copy of the newspaper towards him. On the front page in large black, bold letters was the headline:

WAR IN THE COLONIES! BOSTON IGNITES THE SPARK.

'So, it has started. I'm not surprised it begins in Boston for the port and the whole of Massachusetts is a hotbed of rebels. I think this is going to have an impact on all our lives in some way beginning with an economic decline. You know as well as I do that the colonies have been a lucrative market in a broad range of iron goods for the last few years and this will dry up.'

'Yes, I suppose you're right, although the army and Royal Navy will increase its expenditure for certain items which may offset some of the loss.'

'Are you suggesting, Abraham, that we supply the Crown with munitions and cannon? I thought we had stopped that practice when Abia took over as being inconsistent with our commitment to pacifism?'

'No, I wasn't referring to that but to all the other non-martial goods that will be needed. No, I absolutely support my mother's policy.'

Nathaniel then took the news through to the carpenter's workshop where Elijah still was. He showed him the news item and they read it through together dwelling on the detail considering the implications.

'Come 'round to see me this evening if you can,' said Elijah, 'I have a few things to show you which you may be interested in. I can't talk here,' he said knowingly. Nathaniel nodded and said he would come around about 8 PM.

Abia had also seen the news when Nathaniel met with her later that day.

'So, Nathaniel, you were right about the outbreak of hostilities. I don't suppose you're able to say for how long this may last?' she said not without a little irony.

'There are so many possible outcomes and as you know from what I told you earlier even the rebels are not agreed on their objectives. It could be a short campaign if the Crown steps hard on the insurgents, but I fear that unless they provide more troops to take this seriously, they won't do it quickly. The action at Bunker Hill, according to *The Times*, showed very clearly that the untrained and inexperienced frontiersmen were more than a match for the redcoats until they brought cannon up.'

When he arrived at Elijah's, he found him excitedly reading from a number of leaflets and pamphlets he had displayed on the table. Nathaniel sighed.

'You really are intent on being arrested for sedition. Why do you keep this material so obviously in your possession?'

'It is our "natural and inalienable right" to read what we want and say what our consciences dictate.'

'Where on earth did you get that from?' recognising that these weren't Elijah's normal words.

'Well, I've been reading a great deal since you went away, as usual. I'd like to draw your attention to these two publications which I've discovered – sent to me by friends who live in London. The first you're probably aware of about John Wilkes, the radical MP who went to prison for sedition a few years ago. He wrote an article in "the North Briton" in which he not only criticised the king but also claimed that every Englishman has a right to free speech. Here…' He passed over a copy of the paper which Nathaniel readily perused.

'Yes, I see where you're going with this. These are very similar opinions to those being expressed by the rebels in the 13 colonies.'

Elijah continued, 'John Wilkes elsewhere has also argued for universal suffrage and annual parliaments, anything short of which he regards as tyrannical. But much more detailed and profound, indeed revolutionary, is this pamphlet by a Birmingham-based man, one Joseph Priestley, whom one or two people have mentioned to me in passing over the last few years. He seems to be a man of many interests, particularly in natural philosophy, as well as political philosophy. In this lengthy tract, "Essay on the First Principles of Government", he sets out the essential characteristics for the good society, which like Wilkes is based on universal manhood suffrage and short parliaments. But he argues for a republic, as of course do some of the colonists. I wouldn't be surprised to hear that he actually supports the rebels in North America.'

'Thank you Elijah, I will be very interested to read this pamphlet, but for the moment you should be very careful about what you say on these matters because now that hostilities have broken out I believe the government will begin to crack down heavily on anyone seen or heard to be criticising the King and promoting radical, Republican ideas.'

Whether by sheer coincidence or the fact that Elijah Smith was still held under suspicion by the Crown's agents in the county, the following day his house was raided, he was arrested and thrown into Shrewsbury jail on grounds of disseminating seditious material. What Elijah failed to tell Nathaniel about was that Joseph Priestley was well-known to the authorities and the magistrates in Birmingham were keen to move against him. Nathaniel didn't know what to do in order to help Elijah because he knew the confidence he had managed to establish last time with the Deputy Lord-Lieutenant was wafer thin at this time. Furthermore, seditious materials had been found in Elijah's possession.

He directed his horse slowly up Lincoln's Hill towards Madeley. He was having Saturday lunch with his family and he wondered whether Rebecca would be present as well. He knew it would take a considerable time before either of them could readjust to their new circumstances. As he came through the Market Square, he heard a strident commotion and sounds of women shouting,

'Give us bread! Our babies are starving.' As they became more insistent, others joined them along with some men who emerged from nearby drinking houses. This crowd converged on the two or three stalls that were selling bread shouting, 'Your prices are too high. No one can afford them. Swindlers!' They then began to turn over the stalls and people ran to grab the rolls and loaves that went sprawling along the cobbles. The stallholders cowered and ran for the shelter of nearby shops, which caused a few in the crowd to hurl stones at the windows. The incident was becoming uglier and uglier and no one could have been sure of the outcome had it not been for the Rev Fletcher storming into the midst of the fray shouting at people to refrain from the madness. When Nathaniel saw him, he decided to lend a hand and rode his horse to the side of the Rev protecting him on one side. John Fletcher was a member of the Madeley Board of Guardians of the Poor Law and he had food vouchers stuffed in his pockets which he began to distribute. This was successful in reducing the emotional atmosphere until he and Nathaniel were able to get people to heed their calls to go home. When they had largely dispersed the Rev turned to him.

'I am most grateful for your assistance here today. It was very brave of you…'

'On the contrary, Rev, it was very brave of you and very clever to have thought to distribute the vouchers. I've seen mob rule before and it can become very nasty.'

'I believe we have more work to do before we can be sure this won't happen again,' replied the Rev.

'I'll inform my Mistress Abia,' said Nathaniel, 'who will no doubt wish to convene a meeting of the local magistrates, landowners and employers.' Nathaniel offered his hand to the Rev who took it warmly and thanked him sincerely.

When Nathaniel arrived at his parents' home, he told them what he had just witnessed.

'The price of bread is doubling every day,' replied his sister Rachel, 'so it's hardly surprising that people have acted this way.'

'The grain merchants say it isn't their fault,' added his mother, 'that that's the price they have to pay if they are to get anything at all because there's such a shortage of imports of grain.'

'Yes, of course,' responded Nathaniel, 'it's the war with the colonies where a great deal of grain is grown and exported to us. This is likely to get worse. However, I have good news for you that the new house in Coalbrookdale will be finished by the end of the month, when we can all move in together.' His family were extremely pleased with this news even though it meant leaving the centre of Madeley, but the town had become so crowded and unsanitary in the last few years because of the influx of so many additional workers in the mines and elsewhere, they were not sorry to be leaving. He looked at Rebecca, who had just returned from the Meeting House.

'There's also room for you too, Rebecca, should you want it. I know you are part of the family now and I wouldn't want to exclude you.' She looked him bravely, almost defiantly, in the eyes and merely said,

'Thank you, you are most gracious.' He wasn't quite sure whether there was a touch of irony in her voice.

When he arrived back at the Darby house, he told Abia about the incident in Madeley market about which she didn't seem much surprised. In fact, she had quite a bit of interesting news for him.

'Just before you arrived,' she explained enthusiastically, 'I received a messenger from the Lord Lieutenant's office informing me that Birmingham was in the midst of serious food rioting that had been going on for nearly two days causing much damage to property and potential injury to life. He wanted to inform me that we could well be on the verge of such happenings here. He knows, however, that we along with the Reynolds have a well-established means of preventing these sorts of disturbances.' Nathaniel looked at her expectantly ignorant of these measures.

'The high price of corn is guaranteed to stoke popular rebellion and for years now we have recognised that the only way to maintain stability and ordered production is to compensate for this directly. That is one of the main reasons we have the farms in the surrounding countryside. They have grain stores available for this purpose, which we will supply to the local traders on condition that prices don't rise and return to the pre-rise level. If there is insufficient, we will purchase corn at market prices for our use. However, I've informed the Lord Lieutenant that this will only be done if he releases Elijah Smith into my parole. I've told him that Elijah is one of us, that he's harmless if somewhat eccentric. I will keep an eye on him through you. Will you do that for me?'

'Of course I will. That's excellent news. You know I don't share Elijah's unalloyed support for the American rebels and am trying gently to lead him away from them. Furthermore, even if I did, I wouldn't want him to languish indefinitely in prison. He is becoming an old man now and I don't think he'd last long in any prison.'

Henry Sharples got up early this morning to drive his three pigs down to the wharfage in Madeley Woods where he was going to ferry them up river to Shrewsbury market. It was the quickest and cheapest way to take his produce to market from Leighton as it was a long way to Shrewsbury town from there and in the last 20 years two toll gates had been erected on that route making it more expensive. When he arrived at Buildwas Bridge, however, his temper erupted explosively when he found a new Tollgate had appeared forcing him to pay a penny a pig and an extra penny for himself. He swore royally with the uncouth, brutish lout who controlled the gate, but it was no use and he feared the great club which lay to hand. It was more or less the same when John Lyttleton turned off the bridge with his cart load of potatoes, carrots and onions with the same intention as Henry. He had to pay a whole sixpence to get through, which was a large hole in his earnings for that day that he hadn't expected at all. Within 20 minutes, he caught up with Henry, whom he knew, and the two of them spent the rest of the journey to the ferry cursing the tollbooth keeper and landowners who allowed this. When they arrived at Shrewsbury market, they met others who had a similar tale to tell and all with the advent of the toll gates in various parts of the County over the last twenty years. At lunchtime in one of the pubs close by the cattle market, there was further talk about the issue which was soon to lead to incendiary intent.

'It's not right and something should be done about it,' added one irate tenant farmer, 'it's getting harder to make a living and prices everywhere are climbing steeply with this damned war in the colonies.'

'Aye, but what can we do?'

'We can show'um what we think.'

'How?'

'Burn't gates down.'

'Aye…' many shouted their agreement.

'We'll start wi' Buildwas and then do Atcham,' said one anonymous potential leader. There were loud shouts of support and when the unknown captain suggested they meet at midnight, almost the whole pub roared their approval and said they'd be there. Whether they were or not, cannot be said, but that night the two toll gates were razed to the ground and any attempts at restoring them were demolished immediately over the next few weeks. The local magistrates and landowners were in a panic. The militia were put on alert, but they had no way of knowing where the arsonists might strike next. A reward of £50 was posted for any information leading to an arrest, but the countryfolk kept their mouths shut and intimidated any who it was feared might go to the authorities.

'We must take action to stop this outbreak of indiscipline,' said Richard Reynolds at a specially called Board of Directors meeting of the Darby Ironworks and Madeley Mining company.

'That's going to be difficult,' replied Abraham Darby, 'since we know these aren't our people and we cannot exercise any direct influence over them.'

'There is a way,' added William Reynolds, who was now beginning to show himself as a formidable business leader in the community. 'We could as landowners purchase the contracts of these Turnpike Trusts and ensure that not only is the income spent on maintaining and improving these roads, but also to keep the tolls as low as possible. People won't object if they see improvements. Furthermore, it is absolutely essential that we control the communications by road to the site of the proposed new bridge we are planning.' All agreed this was an excellent idea and William undertook the business of approaching the current owners to buy them out. It was a good time to make an offer because the owners were terrified of losing the investments they'd made so far. As it was, when the toll booths were rebuilt and the new lower fees advertised, there was no repetition of the attacks. The militia continued to investigate but none were apprehended and the issue subsided.

Chapter 21
A Very Great Bondage and Cruelty

Daniel Rondo had never known freedom. His pregnant mother was sold by a local chieftain to a British merchant in East Africa, who felt cheated when the mother died giving birth to him. When he was not yet 20, his master stopped off in London en route to the West Indies. Mr George Smedley wanted to impress his London and Counties' set friends with his newly acquired wealth. He had spent the last 10 years in India and East Africa and was what was called a Nabob. A few weeks in the capital and he would be off again to further aggrandise himself in Jamaica.

'If I don't take my freedom now,' said Daniel to himself, 'I never will.'

George Smedley was too preoccupied with organising the unloading of his considerable luggage that he didn't notice Daniel slipping quietly down the gang plank to British soil and freedom. At the disembarkation port, a single blackface was not unusual amongst the servants and free sailors from various parts of the world. After that it would be more difficult. He had no idea where to go, but when he saw the skyline of St Paul's great new dome in the distance, for no particular reason other than it was a church, he headed in that direction. It was a lucky move as when he came into central London, he saw a notice plastered on the door of a large rectangular single storied building advertising a meeting that evening for all who wanted to abolish slavery. It was just as well his master had found it useful for him to read and write so he could assist with the record-keeping, or he would never have known. He tried the door but it was locked. He would have to wait somewhere inconspicuously and try again later. He found a small park and secreted himself behind some thick bushes. It was beginning to drizzle with a slight but cold wind blowing. He began to shiver all over as he wasn't used to the cold weather and the clothes he wore of light Indian cotton provided him with little protection against it. He heard the chimes of a clock from somewhere nearby. It was about an hour to go before the meeting started, but he thought there may be someone in the building now preparing for it, so he tried the door once again and was delighted when it opened. Inside, it was quite dark as dusk had fallen and only one light was lit in a rather large rectangular room laid out like the inside of a church with pews, although not quite like the ones he was used to – there was no high altar or red light burning to signify the presence of God. This was a much more simply adorned place of worship, if that's what it was, than the Roman Catholic or lavishly furnished high Church Anglican buildings that peppered the Europeanised coastline of East Africa. He found a dark corner and waited for more people to arrive. In a short while more lights were lit and people began to find places to sit in the front pews. When they began to fill up, he sat at the end of the fifth row and waited. A heavily bearded man in a dark three-quarter length black jacket, wearing a black hat which had a large flat brim, a plain white collar and immaculately white shirt then went forward to the front and turned to face the audience.

'My dear friends, thank you for coming out this evening. I'm very pleased to report that we are gaining ground amongst the parliamentarians and especially since the results of various legal cases which have been heard here and in Scotland. The committee has invited a well-known advocate of abolition and successful lawyer to talk to us about the seminal case in English law of Stuart versus Somerset 1772. You will remember that was a few years ago now, but its significance continues to resonate both here and in the American colonies. We must ensure that more and more people come to be aware of it. To that end, Granville Sharp is here to talk to us.' Now, a rather more elegantly dressed man in his mid-40s came forward and began to speak to them in a refined and academic manner. Daniel was enthralled by the lecture but at the end he also felt some disquiet because he had clearly been under a misapprehension that as soon as a slave entered British soil he would be freed. However, that was not the outcome of the case that Granville Sharp had prosecuted himself. So far as he could understand, English law stated that no man could be the chattel or property of another by being bought or sold in Britain, but slavery was not specifically outlawed in the country. It did permit the possession of slaves bought or sold elsewhere. The Somerset case had shown, however, that servants could not be arrested and taken out of the country for sale or resale elsewhere because the common law right of habeas corpus would be transgressed.

At the end of the meeting, a number of people came up to introduce themselves to Daniel, a few of whom he was surprised to find were African. They were keen to hear his story and when they learned that he had just escaped, they showed great concern for his safety because, they said, there were slave hunters abroad in London. Granville Sharp on hearing this invited him home and said he would take steps to get him to a place of safety.

A few days later, Daniel decided he needed some fresh air, after being cooped up in the Sharp residence, comfortable though it was. He had the address of two of the Africans he'd met at the meeting. It wasn't far away, in Soho, and he decided it should not be too difficult to find by asking the way and following the street signs. However, he hadn't reckoned on the fact that he was an object of complete fascination to most Londoners and his Eastern caftan and fez made him stand out even more. Before long he was the centre of a large crowd, as though he were the main attraction in a circus. As he became more and more bewildered and not a little frightened by the attention, he failed to notice two unsavoury characters elbowing their way through the crowd towards him. They grabbed hold of him roughly.

'There you are, my friend. Now, come along with us quietly and don't give us any trouble or you will be sorry,' said one of them fingering a sharp knife. No one in the crowd attempted to stop them, deterred by the two evil looking ruffians. They held him tightly by his arms at each side and dragged him to a building a few streets away where they let themselves in through a small gate into an enclosed yard. There they tied him securely with rope and discussed what they should do with next, after first gagging him with a dirty, oil filled rag. They'd guessed quite rightly that he was a runaway slave and there would be a bounty on his head. Even if there weren't, they could always drag him down to the docks and sell him to one of the more unsavoury captains bound for the West Indies who would ask no questions, knowing they could obtain a good price for him at one of the many slave markets. When Granville Sharp returned home and discovered that Daniel was nowhere to be found, he contacted a number of his friends who went out into the streets nearby asking whether anyone had seen him. He was conspicuous after all, which was a danger, but could also aid them in finding him. He was right. Before long, they had pieced together the story of what had happened and the rough location of where he was likely to be hidden. Granville alerted some trustworthy Bow Street runners in the vicinity whom he knew and, after obtaining a writ of habeas corpus from a friendly magistrate, went towards the building in which they suspected he was being held. The Runners broke open the gate and found the bound Daniel, who had been left alone whilst his captors made arrangements for his sale. It had been a close thing but now he was safe again.

Granville Sharp thought quite hard about how to help Daniel. He and his companions in the Society of Friends agreed it was not a good idea for him to stay in London, despite the few thousand Africans who lived there. It was too easy for him to be spotted by his Master's employees and no doubt the slave hunters who he would have alerted. It was a lucrative trade clandestinely catching escaped slaves and shipping them off to the West Indies so long as the abolitionist groups didn't get in the way. He looked over his list of correspondents and saw John Wesley's name. As an Anglican minister with a well-established network of contacts throughout the country, he felt he would be the best person to know who to contact. As luck would have it, Wesley was in London at the moment so he went to visit him.

'Welcome, Mr Sharp, I'm very pleased to make your acquaintance,' said the famous Minister. 'The Somerset case was a tremendous step forward for the abolitionist campaign and I wholeheartedly congratulate you. Now I'd be very happy to help you in any way I can.'

'Mr Wesley, a young Negro fugitive from slavery, Daniel, is under my protection at present, but I feel it would be far safer for him to be out of the capital. I know you have many contacts up and down the country and hoped you might be able to recommend someone who could give him sanctuary for a while in a quiet, inconspicuous place.'

'I believe I know the very place,' replied the congenial reverend. 'My good friend, the Rev John Fletcher in Madeley, in the east of Shropshire, has been a strong supporter of the cause for many years. It is a flourishing community, but it is out of the way of London and the major ports. I'll provide you with his address and you can make arrangements with him direct.'

Within a week Daniel Rondo had arrived in Shropshire. The Rev Fletcher asked Rebecca to make the final arrangement, obtaining passage on the mail coach for him which plied between London and Holyhead along Watling Street. Hearing of this, Nathaniel offered his help by agreeing to meet him at the Buck's Head near Wellington with two horses, as the roads were still too rough for a carriage. Nathaniel had also suggested that Daniel could stay with he and his family at Dale End, where there was room enough in the new house. That first evening, Daniel's eyes were agog with what he saw and whom he met. He hadn't seen such a concentration of industry nor so many foundries and furnaces as on his way to Coalbrookdale. He was overwhelmed by the hospitable reception he received being treated as an equal and when he met Bright Eyes astonished and intrigued by who she was. Coming from the East Indies, any news of the West Indies or the Americas was completely fascinating for him. He listened with awe to the tales Nathaniel told of the North American native Indians, of the slave markets in Philadelphia and Charlestown and with horror to the story of the Africans floating lifeless in the Atlantic on Nathaniel's crossing from Bristol to Boston over three years ago. He realised he'd had a very lucky escape. Then it was his turn to relate his story.

'So, Daniel,' prompted Rebecca, 'tell us about your life and how you came to be enslaved.'

'There's really not much to tell. I seem to have had it fairly easy by comparison with many of my fellow Africans. In fact, I have not known anything except servitude to my master since I was born, as my mother, I'm told, died in childbirth soon after she was sold by a local chieftain to Mr George Smedley in East Africa. As soon as I could walk, I was made to fetch and carry until some days I was totally exhausted and fell asleep anywhere, when I was beaten severely. For some reason, as I got older my master decided to teach me to read and write and I began to work in his counting house. There was no respite and I had to work every day experiencing heavy beatings if I fell asleep, or made any errors. That's why I decided to escape when we docked at London because I knew when we reached the West Indies it would be much more difficult. I knew from other slaves I met that the climate there is very unhealthy and the white owners so fear slave revolts that they inflict terrible torture and punishment on any who try to escape. I cannot thank you enough for helping me.'

'It is our godly duty to do so,' replied Nathaniel. 'You are a human being like us and should not be treated like cattle. Thank you for your story. Please, make yourself at home here and should there be anything you desire, please ask. You are quite safe now.'

Daniel stayed with the Shawcross family for two months, after which there arrived a letter from Granville Sharp via the Rev Fletcher, that Daniel should not stay too long with them for fear of attracting the slave hunters who would be anxious to collect on the bounty of £50 that Smedley had posted.

Nathaniel and Rebecca with the Rev Fletcher tried to think where it might be best for Daniel to go. Initially, they had considered Liverpool where there was an established African community, as in Bristol, but it was part of the triangular trade and therefore likely to be frequented by slave hunters and slaveowners. Nathaniel mentioned it to Abia Darby who came up with an ingenious idea that none of them could have thought of. She suggested that the Deputy Lord-Lieutenant of the County, whom she knew, might be approached with a view to offering Daniel employment in his large household. This could provide a high level of security for Daniel, but also provide an opportunity for him to meet with others of his race as it had become quite fashionable to employ one or two Africans in service and a number of the other large landowners in the county had done so. Servants and masters often met at organised soirées and formal balls. Abia said she would approach Sir Anthony Fotheringham herself to put the proposal. He agreed with alacrity for up till now he had no Africans in service at all. When they put this to Daniel, he was overjoyed because it meant he wouldn't be too far away from his new-found friends. It also meant that he would not have to undertake tasks of a heavy physical nature and in time might aspire to become a well-respected senior household servant.

Fotheringham's country house was in the north of the county so it was agreed that Nathaniel would guide Daniel there from Shrewsbury on horseback, travelling up from Coalbrookdale on one of the shallow keeled barges that plied the River Severn from the wharfage at Madeley Woods. Rebecca travelled down with them to wave Daniel off on his short journey. As usual, the Riverside wharfage was busy with traffic of both goods and people, many of whom had travelled up from Bristol. It was whilst Nathaniel was negotiating the price of their excursion with one of the bargees that he became aware of a commotion amidst the crowd behind him.

'Hey boy, come here!' a dangerous voice in the crowd rang out, accompanied by another.

'Stand still, nigger, or I'll club you!' As he turned around, Nathaniel saw two burly men, one with his hand over Daniel's mouth, whilst the other was securing him with a tether to the neck. That morning Nathaniel had been cautious for some reason, probably because of Granville's letter, and he had taken along a pistol and tomahawk, which was hidden by his long coat and tucked in his belt behind him. When he saw what was happening, he rushed up to the group where Rebecca was trying to pull one of the men off Daniel, and shouted authoritatively,

'Take your hands off that man or I will blow your brains out,' as he levelled his pistol at the larger of the two men. The crowd parted in horror. Some of them recognised Nathaniel, but they had never seen him armed before nor behave in such an aggressive manner. The man ignored Nathaniel's threat.

'Ha! You've only one shot their boy oh and there are two of us.' As he said this, he sent Rebecca sprawling with a slap of his huge hand, which was the catalyst for Nathaniel to act. He shot the man in his shoulder at close range, which knocked him off his feet where he would have rolled into the river had not Nathaniel stooped down and pulled him away from the edge of the wharf. The man didn't resist because he was virtually unconscious from the impact and the pain in his shoulder. Then, Nathaniel quickly turned around to see what his companion was up to. He just had time to dodge out of the way as the other lunged at him with a long knife. Daniel was so trussed up, he couldn't move. What happened next became legend. As the man readied himself to attack Nathaniel again and plunge the evil-looking blade into his stomach, Nathaniel agilely stepped backwards and took the hidden tomahawk from his belt which he now swung in the way he had been taught by the Susquehanna, bringing the small but heavy, well sharpened blade down on the wrist of his attacker. The man's hand was severed completely from his arm flying into the deep swirling waters of the Severn. He stood there for a moment in shock looking with disbelieving eyes at the blood pumping from the severed wrist and then fell unconscious to the ground.

'A surgeon, quickly! Someone fetch a surgeon before these men die,' he cried still in command of the situation. Someone ran off to the local barber who came scurrying along to examine the two men. He placed a tourniquet on the one to staunch the bleeding and then examined the other.

'They both need immediate medical attention but who is going to pay the cost?' he asked.

'I'll see to that,' responded Nathaniel without hesitation, pulling some coins from his pocket handing them to the surgeon who looked at them cursorily, grunted and asked for volunteers to carry the two men to his nearby house. 'Don't let them out of your sight and don't let them leave,' said Nathaniel. 'I'll be along this evening to see how they are and ask them some questions.'

Rebecca had got to her feet by now, but Nathaniel's concern was written all over his face.

'Are you all right?' he enquired anxiously. She looked at him as if seeing him for the first time. She had never ever seen this Nathaniel before.

'Yes… I am. Are you?' she looked searchingly into his eyes, but they had become normal again after the fight when she saw they shone with a bright black lustre that made him seem almost demonic.

'If you are sure you are well,' he responded, ignoring her question, 'please go to the magistrate and ask him to detain these two men for what they tried to do. I'll return this evening after getting Daniel to Shrewsbury, when no doubt the magistrate will want to question me too. It's quite clear that Daniel would not have been safe for long with us here either.'

Daniel was very shaken by the experience but he trusted Nathaniel when he told him that he was going to a much safer place with the deputy Lord-Lieutenant. It had been arranged for Nathaniel to drop Daniel off at Shrewsbury Castle where his master was currently in residence. He told Sir Anthony all about the incident who was doubly intrigued by Nathaniel's part in all this.

'Excuse me, sir, but am I not correct in thinking that you are a Quaker? It's just that I don't understand why you had a pistol and a tomahawk.' Nathaniel lowered his head as if in shame but in truth it was to hide his own confusion.

'I try to be, sir, but I don't appear to be very good at it,' he said dubiously.

'Well,' replied Sir Anthony, 'I should be more than glad to employ you as a martial at arms, should the need arise,' he continued with a mischievous glint in his eyes. 'Oh, and please convey this note to the magistrate which will explain that you were protecting my man and they had no right in English law to arrest him, if I understand this note from your Mistress, Abia Darby, which I received earlier today.'

When he questioned the two men later, they confirmed they had been motivated to search for Daniel by the prospect of Smedley's reward. It hadn't been difficult to pinpoint his location from travellers up and down the major waterways. There weren't many Africans to be found in the industrial areas of the Midlands. The magistrate made no trouble for him after receiving the note from the Deputy Lord-Lieutenant and he dismissed the two men from the district warning them not to return at all or they would be thrown into prison for threatening to break the King's law.

A more difficult problem was to know what to tell Rebecca and indeed his Mistress. As a God-fearing Quaker, he shouldn't have gone armed. Was he deluding himself? Would it be more honest to stop calling himself a Quaker since he seemed to have a propensity for violence which was inconsistent with his faith? He'd already received guidance from Abia about his North American experiences, but here he was again repeating the same behaviour. On the other hand, he felt that what he'd done was right. He had tried hard not to kill the men and in that he'd been successful. He also felt that if he'd done nothing Daniel would be on his way back to slavery. Furthermore, there was the prospect of Rebecca being injured or worse by the ruffians and the emotions this aroused in him had surprised him. It evoked the memories and feelings of Hyacinthe, which made him realise that perhaps his love for Rebecca had returned, if it had ever left. When he saw the rest of the family that evening, they expressed their horror about the attack on Daniel, but some of it was clearly directed also towards Nathaniel's actions. They seemed as equally confused as he was in their attitude towards his employment of violence. His mother asked him where the arms had come from.

'They were in my luggage from North America, where almost everyone walks around armed for protection.'

'It sounds like a very lawless society,' she opined critically.

'It is in every respect.'

'But why,' asked Rachel, 'did you carry a pistol and axe with you?' She asked the obvious question the others had refrained from for fear of what the answer might be.

He shrugged his shoulders, 'Out of habit, I guess,' he answered using a frontier idiom. 'Whenever I made a major journey there, I always took with me a pistol, musket and tomahawks. Not doing so would have been suicide.' He realised he had absorbed something of the frontier culture of the North Americans, who strongly believed in providing their own security – they had to for survival. But was that now necessary back in England?

After dinner, he and Rebecca repaired to the small sitting room. He wanted to know what she felt of him now.

'I suppose I have shocked you with my behaviour and I will understand completely if you want to keep your distance from me.'

'Yes, I am rather in awe of you – and maybe even a little afraid. This is a new you for me to accept and I perceive how it is a product of your American adventures. But I believe God must have made you like this so it must always have been present in you. The fact that you showed considerable concern for the injuries to the two men are a great redeeming feature. I can see that what drives you is an intense passion to see justice done – which I find an admirable quality. I think I do still love you, Nathaniel, but I'm still getting used to the complex person you are. You are no longer the boy whom I nursed after the mining accident nor the young man to whom I was engaged over three years ago. If you possess some feelings for me also, then it may well be we have a future together.' He turned to look at her directly.

'I'll be truthful with you, Rebecca, that I didn't fully appreciate the love I still have for you until the incident at the Severn quayside.' They clasped each other's hands and then embraced, finally kissing slowly at first and then more passionately.

'Rebecca, will you marry me?'

'Of course I will, Nathaniel. It's what I have wanted most in the world.'

As for Daniel, it wasn't long before he settled in very comfortably to Sir Anthony Fotheringham's house hold. He had a sharp mind and he was quick to learn, so it wasn't long before he became part of his Master's Secretariat. This provided him with a much greater degree of mobility than might otherwise have been the case and very soon he found a young female African servant, who was a personal handmaid to one of the leading ladies of the county, with whom he became quite enamoured. It wasn't long therefore before he asked his master if he could marry and bring his new bride into the household. Sir Anthony was very pleased with both Daniel's character and work so he was more than happy to comply with this request. It wasn't the only wedding of note that year in the county. Nathaniel and Rebecca had become engaged again and this time they didn't wait long until they too were married, but it wasn't quite as easy as they thought it would be. So far as the family was concerned, however, this was a wonderful outcome and, until Rachel herself became betrothed to one of the iron Masters and was soon married, the house at Dale End was full to bursting.

Chapter 22
Marriage and Mad Houses

The three females of the Shawcross household were closeted together in the small living room arguing quite heatedly.

'I really don't see what you are concerned about, my dear,' said Sarah with emphasis to Rebecca.

'If you love each other, it really doesn't matter where you get married!'

'Oh, but it does,' argued Rachel, taking Rebecca's part. The two of them had worked very closely together in the last few years keeping in touch with groups of evangelical Anglicans and abolitionists on behalf of the Rev Fletcher throughout the country. 'You know that since the 1753 Marriage Act, it has been essential to be licensed by an Anglican priest the ceremony being conducted in the Church of England.'

Sarah wrinkled her nose at this, involuntarily acknowledging the truth of what her daughter said, but continued her remonstration,

'There are, however, examples of dispensation for Jews and Quakers in some areas, so why can't that apply here?'

'Well, I believe it will be necessary to obtain permission anyway from the Bishop and the local clergy. You could avoid all that by simply asking the Rev Fletcher to officiate.'

'It is an important matter of religious freedom,' replied Sarah. 'As a dissenter, it is significant because we must remain independent of the established state church with all its associated hierarchy and authority.' Rebecca now spoke up for herself,

'After all the confusion about whether Nathaniel and I were betrothed or not after these past three years, I don't want anyone to argue that we aren't married. In a dissenters' ceremony, especially of the kind conducted in the Dale, the licensees are any member of the Meeting and whilst we may produce a certificate to say who they are, I'm not at all convinced that at present this is sufficient to be recognised as marriage in the sight of the State.' At that moment, Nathaniel returned home and was intrigued to know what the three of them were discussing so earnestly. When he entered the room, all three tried to make a show of congeniality but he was not to be so easily deceived.

'My, what a coven of witches have we here and, more to the point, what are you brewing?'

'Hello my dear,' smiled Sarah, 'we are just discussing arrangements for your marriage.'

'Well, why should that produce such an air of heated mystery? I can't think the topic of marriage should invoke such disagreement amongst you, which you can't deny as I saw it for myself.'

They all looked meaningfully from 1 to the other.

'I'm sorry, Nathaniel, we don't want to hide anything from you but nor do we wish to weigh you down with our concerns,' responded Rebecca.

'I'm afraid you are going to have to now or I will be thinking the worst,' he said with a wry smile.

'For goodness' sake, let's put the poor man out of his misery. He needs to be aware of the issue anyway,' said Rachel with exasperation.

'We were discussing where the marriage might take place,' revealed Sarah. 'Rebecca would like it to be in the local Church of England, St Michael's, whilst I have been suggesting it would be more appropriate in the Meeting House here in the Dale. Rebecca is worried that the form of the ceremony in a

Friends' Meeting House wouldn't be recognised by everyone as a true marriage.'

'I must confess I hadn't given much thought to that but now that you raise it, I can see the issue,' he said thoughtfully. 'I thank you for raising it.' Turning to Rebecca he addressed her directly, 'Perhaps, my love, we should first discuss this between ourselves?'

'Yes, of course, it's just that it came up in conversation quite naturally and Sarah and Rachel have been helping me to make some arrangements. It was consequent on that which led to this seeming difficulty. No one intended to exclude you from the plans.'

'No, I'm not suggesting that at all. However, given the difficulties you've identified, I wonder whether the solution might be to have two ceremonies? That is, if the Rev Fletcher is agreeable and the Friends have no objections either – I could speak to Abia Darby?'

'What a wonderful idea,' expressed his mother and the faces of the two lit up as well.

'I'll speak to the Rev Fletcher,' Rebecca offered, 'whilst you confer with Abia.'

And, thus it was that no one raised any objections to this proposal. John Fletcher now looked upon Nathaniel very favourably since his support during the bearbaiting incident and the heading off of the potentially very serious food riots in Madeley. Nor could Abia Darby see any reason why a second ceremony could not go ahead in the Meeting House. No one could ever say they weren't now well and truly married!

Who was that shell of a man? Where was he? What had he become? Somewhere deep inside, Nathaniel hoped that his father was still there locked away and protected from the demons that had invaded him. He looked at him affectionately remembering times when as a child he would be thrown high into the air and caught securely in strong arms. On the sabbath, he with his smaller brother and sister would walk to the nonconformist chapel they attended. Afterwards, if it were a clement day they would walk home, the children running between their parents' legs in a game of tag, secure in the protection of their devoted and pious elders. In the evenings, their father would read to them in his strong, rich voice holding them mesmerised by the stories from the Old Testament. They couldn't afford to send their children to the local fee-paying nonconformist school, but instead, despite feeling weary from a hard day's work, they would both settle down to teaching their three children how to read. By the time all three came of an age to work themselves, they could read and then all would participate reading biblical excerpts to the rest of the family. When he returned from America, Nathaniel thought he had detected a slight glimmer of recognition in his father's eyes and a small suggestion of a smile on his face but he must have been mistaken because he had not seen it since. It was the husk of a man that faced him daily. His eyes distant, absent he knew not where. He hoped this person whom he loved deeply and dearly was still there, a soul trapped but still present perhaps in turmoil or self-recrimination, hopefully in some limbo of tranquillity. It was obvious he was not recovering from whatever it was that assailed him. Why had it happened? Had he been touched by the hand of God or smitten down by it, as many of the old-timers claimed. He couldn't believe there was anything in his father's life that would call for such punishment. On the other hand, there were more modern voices that suggested the mad had lost their reason because of some earthly affliction, nothing to do with God. They must try something. The Rev John Fletcher frequently in the early days tried to communicate with him, even to the extent of suggesting exorcism, but Sarah and Rachel would not hear of it, fearing it was too close to popery. Gideon had become an increasing burden for Sarah as he needed directing everywhere and whilst she felt able to leave him with her daughter for a short while, there was no one else that she felt able to call upon. From dawn till dusk he needed attention: dressing, feeding, washing and taken to the toilet. He was inert and didn't struggle but it was a constant demand on her time and energy, which after a few years had now begun to weigh heavily upon her. She accepted it all stoically, but Nathaniel was increasingly concerned for her health as well as his father's. They had been extremely fortunate from the support they received from the Reynolds, the Rev Fletcher and, after he'd returned, from the greater income he received as a director. When Rebecca entered the household as his wife, she was able to take some of the burden by running it and also by taking close care of Bright Eyes. But he knew even this couldn't continue as Rebecca was likely to be with child soon and need extra help herself. Then they would hire a maidservant for help with his daughter and in support of Rebecca. He decided to make wider enquiries about possible treatment and provision. The Rev Fletcher told him there were a few lunatic paupers whom the local Poor Law Guardians took responsibility for if they had no family to look after them. Increasingly, however, he learned that there were a few establishments specialising in provision for those who weren't physically afflicted but were quite incapable of fending for themselves. He discovered there was a place called Cleethorpes Manor about 25 miles distant, but when he raised it with his mother, she was at first quite reluctant to accept her husband going outside of the family. However, when he told her it was where some of the best families in the county sent family members, she agreed to inspect it with him. He sent a letter off to them asking for a suitable date to visit and at the same time spoke to Abia Darby on the issue. She offered to enquire amongst the Society of Friends scattered throughout the country.

When Sarah and Nathaniel approached Cleethorpes Manor they were favourably impressed with the formal gardens and imposing entrance. People of many ages appeared to be happily engaged tending the various plots. Stopping to take in the scene, they were startled to notice that these supposed gardeners were dressed in expensive silks with fine cotton stockings. They looked up at the four-storey building and Nathaniel thought he caught sight of a woman's face staring down at them with wild hair and a fearsome expression. When he tried to draw attention of this apparition to Sarah, it had disappeared. They were greeted affably by an elegantly dressed butler who immediately recognised the name and welcomed them inside. They were led into a large, bright salon which was expensively furnished and on the walls of which hung some well-known artists' work. They were soon joined by an agreeable young man in his early 30s who introduced himself as Dr Wilson. He instructed the butler to provide them with tea and sat down to talk about the establishment.

'As you can see, we have quite a number of guests, that's my word for the patients, who are of the better sort. They are free to come and go around the house as they wish, but I believe it is important for them to have some occupation and, as you will have seen, many of them choose to work in the gardens. Guests are welcome and arrangements can be made for them to attend and even stay overnight, when we have the room. You may also note that some of the guests have their own servants, for which they pay directly, of course.'

'There doesn't seem to be many attendants around the house,' queried Sarah, 'for such a good number of guests?'

'Oh, there really are ample, what with the private servants as well. At the moment, many of them are in the laundry, cleaning the rooms or working in the walled garden, where we grow our own food, or attending to the horses in the stables. If you would like a guided tour of the house, I would be very glad to arrange one for you. Yes?' They both nodded in approval at this suggestion. 'I'll just ask my assistant, Mr Strangelove, to show you around.'

The individual who appeared was definitely not quite what they'd expected, after speaking to the refined and well-dressed doctor. The man before them was heavily built, poorly shaven and with a slight odour of stale urine about him. He looked slightly flustered as though he had been disturbed in the middle of some strenuous physical activity so that his jacket was rumpled and misshapen.

He spoke with a broad rural accent, which was probably local, 'Aye Doctor?'

'Please show these good people around the house and grounds, Mr Strangelove, and answer any questions they may have. We have nothing to hide here.'

'Before we go Doctor,' asked Nathaniel, 'can you tell me who that lady was I thought I saw from a top story window just as we arrived? She looked quite young but somewhat dishevelled.'

'Oh, you must have been mistaken, sir, as there is no one residing on the top floor. Those rooms are in the process of being refurbished for further guests. I think it must have been a trick of the light.'

They followed their unsavoury companion who took them on a tour of the next two floors. He didn't bother knocking on a door before he opened it, explaining that all the guests were outside during the day. These rooms were tidy, well-furnished and clearly containing personal possessions of their owners. In one room on the next floor, however, they found an elderly lady cowering in her bed and fully clothed. She almost became hysterical when she was surprised by the door opening and the three of them coming in.

'Now then, don't go gettin' yourself worked up, Mrs Moffat. These folks are just 'avin' a look around.' There was a none too pleasant odour emanating from the room so they were glad to get out as soon as they could.

'Tother rooms art t' same.'

'And what about the top floor?' persisted Nathaniel, for he was sure he had seen someone at the window.

'There 'baint be anyone there, they rooms 'r all empty. Now I'll take thee to where the pauper lunatics are kept.' Sarah and Nathaniel looked at each other with alarm on their faces, as if to say hadn't they seen enough that was disturbing already? They followed Strangelove down the rear stairs which brought them out into a cobbled corridor where the wind whistled keenly through. Their malodorous guide explained they provided charity by keeping six paupers referred to them by the Poor Law Guardians. They went through the main stables where a number of expensive thoroughbred animals were kept, coming eventually to the end stable where they found six people, both men and women sitting around in the straw or in one case shackled to the wall wearing nothing at all. All were manacled, dressed in thin cotton nightshirts and when the visitors entered only one or two paid them any notice. When Sarah tried to talk to one of them, she stared back at her with mute stupidity. The guide explained that for the most part they were docile except for the one chained to the wall who could be violently abusive. The reason she was naked was that it was the best way to keep her clean without the staff being injured.

'This is appalling,' expressed Nathaniel in a quietly shocked voice. 'I cannot believe that human beings are treated like this.'

'They be treated very well 'ere,' re-joined Strangelove. 'They are fed regular and kept warm by the 'ossess. There is no other that'd 'ave 'em.' He seemed quite put out by the criticism and defended the establishment with some warmth.

'I really think we've seen enough here, Nathaniel. It's time we left,' said his mother in a tone of subdued horror. They couldn't bring themselves to return to the main house and see the doctor again, but left as quickly as they obtained their mounts. Neither of them spoke as they found the path homeward. They were too overwhelmed by what they had witnessed and both agreed when they returned home there was absolutely no question of Gideon being incarcerated there. When they described their visit in detail to the family, they were equally shocked.

'We must do something. There's something not right there,' emphasised Rebecca, 'but what?'

'And the woman's face at the window,' said Rachel, 'you clearly saw her Nathaniel and your eyes are very keen. Do you think she was being kept prisoner?'

'It's very possible. I think the very least we can do is to inform the Poor Law Guardians in that area of the inhuman conditions of their people and alert the Lord-Lieutenant of the County regarding the others.'

A little later, Nathaniel called around to see Abia where he related the account of their visit and asked whether she might have heard anything herself from the Quaker network. It transpired that she had indeed acquired some very useful information regarding a certain William Tuke, a member of the Society of Friends in York. He had a particular interest in the mentally afflicted and having made an extensive study of the phenomenon concluded that most current methods of treatment were barbaric and mediaeval. He was planning to establish his own facility in York for the treatment of such poor people based on his new ideas which emphasised warm baths, massage, a balanced diet, exercise and fresh air, as well being given purposeful work to do. In addition, be believed that talking with compassionate understanding to his patients was essential as was dismissing the notion that they were possessed of evil spirits requiring imprisonment and physical punishment. In fact, he insisted that his new premises would have no bars at the window nor locks on the door. Abia suggested that it might be useful to invite the good man to Coalbrookdale to see what he might be able to do for Gideon. She would be prepared to pay his expenses and make a good contribution to his new venture. The family were overjoyed at this level of support from the Mistress but it no longer came as a surprise to them that there were no limits to her charity. Rebecca undertook the task of writing to the Poor Law Guardians about the conditions and treatment of people at Cleethorpes Manor, whilst Abia wrote to the Lord-Lieutenant of the county regarding their suspicions of possible unlawful imprisonment there. Then all they could do was wait.

Two weeks later a letter was received by Abia from the Lord-Lieutenant thanking her for her intelligence which he was keen to investigate, since similar cases had been revealed in other parts of the country. A few weeks later, he wrote again to say that there had indeed been found a case of wrongful imprisonment at Cleethorpes Manor, along with other abuses. The proprietor was discovered to have had no professional medical training whatsoever and was charging enormous fees to the wealthy residents. Many of these it transpired wanted to stay on at the establishment because it was what they had become habituated to. Also, their relatives were not of a mind to take them back, but would rather pay to keep them where they were. As for the lunatic paupers, they were found places in other pauper mad houses in the county. He was also able to inform the Mistress that Parliament had recently investigated the whole issue and was going to introduce legislation to monitor and control such establishments. In the event, Dr Wilson was charged with false imprisonment and himself was incarcerated in the Fleet prison for up to 5 years. The new proprietor of Cleethorpes Manor deregistered it as a madhouse and ran it as a straightforward private hotel.

William Tuke accepted Abia's offer agreeing to visit for no longer than a month to see whether he could affect some improvement with Gideon. Abia put him up at her house and the plan was that he would visit Gideon every day for as long as he felt it was appropriate. He was a soberly dressed Quaker, short but stocky with a decidedly quiet and appealing manner. He had a rich North country accent and exuded a confident conviction that what he said could be trusted. His voice was almost hypnotic and was one of those that put listeners immediately at their ease, so that everyone liked him. Before he even met Gideon, he spoke to the family about the circumstances of the onset of his illness, which he insisted on calling it. He explained that his purpose was to try and get Gideon talking and eventually tell him in his own words what had happened and how he felt about it. That way he believed Gideon could recover. It all seemed very harmless. He began by asking Sarah to introduce him to her husband and explain who he was and what he was trying to do. Then he began to talk to Gideon himself,

'Mr Shawcross, my name is William and I would like to talk to you about the events of two years ago. I know that some of this may be extremely painful for you and I don't want you to tell me anything unless you want to. I'm not forcing you to say anything you don't want to. But perhaps you could tell me a little about your childhood and where you grew up.' He had asked Sarah and other members of the family to leave them alone for now. He waited to see if Gideon would respond, but there was no flicker from his continual blank expression. After a while, he said,

'Perhaps I should tell you something of myself,' and he continued in his quiet, captivating voice to talk to Gideon for the next half hour about his own childhood and family background. Then he left Gideon alone. William proceeded in this manner for the next three days and he was beginning to despair that his approach wasn't working, but on the fourth day Gideon's eyes began to move as though he had heard and understood what was being said. William then asked Sarah to be present, when he asked Gideon how he had met her.

'Tell me, Gideon, if I may now call you by your Christian name?' but didn't wait for an answer, 'What did you feel for her at the time?' There was a slight flicker of recognition.

'Do you love Sarah?' There was now a recognisable response and tears formed in Gideon's eyes. William had spoken to Sarah about possible responses and should this happen he'd suggested what she do next, which was to reach out and take him by both hands gently squeezing them and then to begin stroking one of them. As she did so, the tears began to flow more heavily until he began sobbing whereupon she took him to her bosom. William said this was a significant breakthrough and he wanted Sarah to be present each time he came. Gideon still hadn't said anything but William felt sure that now they had reached this stage it wouldn't be long before he did. This continued for a further two days, when on the third day Gideon addressed Sarah for the first time in over two years.

'Sarah, my love… I'm so sorry…' He couldn't say any more for being overwhelmed by emotion and hardly could she.

'No, no, my sweet love… You have nothing to be sorry for,' and she held him closely to her for a long time. In the next room, William said they were definitely making progress but the next stage was to get him to say what he was sorry about and this could be dangerous for him as he might recede even further into himself. The following day, William opened the session by reminding Gideon of what he'd said to Sarah.

'Gideon, you said you were sorry for something,' he continued gently, 'can you tell us, Sarah and I, for what it is you feel sorry?' William knew this was the determining moment, whether they succeeded or failed getting through to him. They could see Gideon was wrestling with something hidden and his mouth was trying to form words but no sound emerged. William thought they'd lost him, but then almost imperceptibly from a dry, hoarse mouth the words began to come, slowly in a whisper at first and then more rapidly, more strongly.

'Those men… Henry and Martin… Peter, Stewart… The others. It's my fault… It's my fault they are dead… I thought they were… Safe, but they weren't…' This was the most he'd spoken since the accidents.

'No darling, no… It wasn't your fault. It was the mine. You are a good, safe manager and you would not put any of them in danger knowingly.' Gideon wept heavily and she embraced him again as she had done before. It was working. He was talking about the past, the people who had indeed perished in those terrible accidents – but that's what they were.

'I know it is hard to reconcile that you live when others die,' said William, 'but it is God that chooses in these circumstances, not us.'

'But I should have read the signs. I was the manager, the experienced minor and they relied on me. I let them down.'

'No, you didn't,' insisted William, 'I've read the reports and spoken to the mine owner, Richard Reynolds, who thinks very highly of you and says you ran one of the safest galleries in his mines. It was an accident that no one could foresee happening. Those dangers are ever present underground. You cannot blame yourself, Gideon, that is an offence against God, who knows all and is a mystery to us.' These words appeared to penetrate Gideon's consciousness and he looked less agitated than he had. Now Sarah re-joined the conversation.

'Their families have all been well provided for. They often ask after you with affection and sadness to hear of your condition, but they will now be glad to learn of your recovery. Now, I have a surprise for you – someone you haven't seen for many years.' They had agreed that if Gideon responded positively and seemed strong enough, they would ask Nathaniel to enter the room, which he now did. As Nathaniel entered, Gideon struggled to his feet, apparently at a loss to remember who this was, but then he shouted for joy and rushed to his eldest son who embraced him passionately.

'Oh Father, my father…' Nathaniel himself was overcome with such feeling that he broke down in tears and struggled to speak. Gideon's face beaned with pleasure and it was he who now controlled the situation.

'Nathaniel, my wonderful boy – don't cry. I'm here, my son. I seem to have been away, but now I'm back,' and father and son remained closely hugging each other for a long while, whilst Sarah and William looked on with immense relief and pleasure. Thereafter, Nathaniel and Gideon had much catching up to do and they gained a great deal of satisfaction by spending much time together. Gideon became aware of the house they lived in and was amazed, but sincerely pleased by his son's success. he recognised also the pivotal role that Mistress Abia had played in their lives and as soon as he felt confident enough, he visited the Mistress to express his thanks. When he did, he was further surprised when she said,

'My dear Gideon, I'm so pleased to have been able to play a little part in your recovery. As you know, I think very highly of Nathaniel and his undoubted abilities. I don't know whether you have given any thought to what occupation you may take up now, but I would suggest it would be better not to return to the mines. How would you like to work for me? I could offer you a carpenter's assistant role working alongside Elijah Smith, whom you know well and is a great friend to your family.'

Thus, Gideon was returned from the dead and the Shawcross family order was restored.

Chapter 23
The Cannoneer

The noise was deafening. It was that more than the danger of the enemy fire that remained with Elijah all these years. He had spent five years at sea rising to become a master cannoneer aboard *HMS Tiger*, a Royal Naval ship of the line. They had destroyed the French fleet in Quiberon Bay and now 49 of His Majesty's finest were arranged along the St Lawrence waterway levelling anything which moved on the northern coast. Their enemy's batteries were superbly designed to withstand the cannonade and their own guns lost no time in firing on their aggressors. When the first wave of returning fire came, it was directed at the upper row of 42 pounder cannons which threatened them with the greater danger. Three balls smashed through the bulk work sweeping all before them. All that was left was a ragged gaping hole and the stack of orphaned cannon balls heavy and carefully locked into position to prevent them rolling away. Of his mates from those stations, he could recognise nothing from the flotsam of human limbs and chunks of bloody flesh that smeared the rear bulkhead. Two of the guns had been knocked completely off their stands disappearing over the side through the gaping hole that was a smaller image of the one through which they had entered. He counted himself lucky he hadn't been closer as those that were adjacent had been fatally skewered by thick shards of timber that stuck out from their bodies making them look like human porcupines. Those more distant were showered by needles that pierced their hands, their heads and arms which they had raised to defend themselves. The captain ordered the helmsman to steer them out of the direct line of fire to a distance just beyond the range of the French guns. He had mistakenly come to close when it was unnecessary, as their British made cannon had a greater range. There was now no serious threat from the French fleet taking them by surprise from behind and no individual ship would dare to challenge them.

As they rode at anchor, repairing their damage, now safely out of range of enemy guns, the captain allowed his men to take some rest. Elijah took advantage of the respite, after helping with the clean-up below, by getting rid of the stench of gunpowder, human waste and blood from his nostrils by clambering up to the main deck. Others were doing the same but there was little talk between them as they digested the terrible sights of their comrades torn apart below. It wasn't his first action, but he never got used to this part of the battle. Although the liberally issued quantities of rum anaesthetised some of the feeling, it couldn't remove everything. It was at those moments that he began to question what he was doing there. Why had he spent so long in that arena of death? Of course, he had been glad to get away from the rainswept heaths of Cumberland and the relentless tedium of farm life. Liverpool, Bristol and finally Portsmouth, where he was seduced to take the King's shilling by tales of faraway lands and the status of being a member of the best Navy in the world, were now his home. He had sailed the world from India to Jamaica, the Gold Coast to Nova Scotia, chasing and being chased by pirates, Spaniards, Chinamen and Frenchies. As a young man, it was a great adventure and whilst he had a good captain, a fair wind and silver in his pockets he wanted for nothing more – his sea mates were his family. But as war spread beyond policing actions to almost every part of the globe and its bloody tendrils spread everywhere, so the gloss of sailing the high seas and scanning new horizons tarnished. He began to search more deeply for something in life. He didn't know what it was but he came to realise what it wasn't – kneeling behind a 42 pounder to obliterate whatever he was told to.

He was ashore in Philadelphia for more substantial repairs to his ship. It was two weeks after the sanguinary engagement that had culminated in the taking of Québec, when his feet and unfulfilled soul-searching led him to one of many Quaker Meeting Houses in the city. His parents were strict Presbyterians and being of an independent mind, as soon as he was 16 years old, he broke away from their beliefs and narrow-minded constraints running away to Liverpool to find a ship. During the following ten years, he hadn't given religion a second thought. But now he was on the cusp of a significant change in his life's course. He found the tranquillity and unforced piety of the Meeting House deeply moving. He went again the following day where one or two recognised him from the previous day and chatted to him amiably. They knew who he was from the clothes he wore, but no one mentioned it until he did. It was then by gentle questioning that his unformed emotions were gradually given shape and he began to realise the terrible enormity his life was having on others. Until then, it had simply been his duty to obey the commands of his superiors, but it began to dawn on him that he was responsible for what he did and what he did to others. He knew he wasn't going to return to the ship so it was important he collect his things and money discreetly so as not to give any indication that he was about to abandon his ship, which was a capital offence at any time never mind in war. He found a cheap lodging place where he dressed in civilian clothes, destroying his uniform. He knew he would be sought by the Marines so his plan was to get away from the city as quickly as possible joining a small merchant seaman bound for New York. His aim then was to follow the coast northward to Nova Scotia to get a job aboard a whaling ship, which meant he would be at sea for long periods of time and away from the prying eyes of the Royal Navy. He also had time to read and think of the long boring days at sea. Fortunately, his parents had ensured he could read being sent to a nonconformist school for a few years before he became too useful on the farm. He had also picked up a number of pamphlets, a Holy Bible and a copy of Milton's Pilgrim's Progress. He had always been good with his hands and attached himself usefully to the ship's carpenter where he was able to extend his knowledge and skills. After a few years, he grew tired of the dangerous, stormy seas in which they often hunted for prey and decided to head landward. Landing in Bristol, he heard about the new developments and expanding prospects for skilled men in the Midlands so he decided to investigate, whereupon he was delighted to discover Coalbrookdale and the Darby family who led the small community of the Society of Friends there. When he showed them the products he had made in wood, he found no difficulty in obtaining work in the pattern shop. And there he remained, deepening his knowledge by reading pamphlets and newspapers, trying to forget his former life. It provided him with much joy when Nathaniel came to live with him and they could discuss the new political ideas that were emerging. He hadn't told Nathaniel about his early life and didn't know whether he ever would. When he returned after three years travelling through the colonies, he could see he was a changed man. He was more considered, confident in his own knowledge and ideas, but he also saw that he'd suffered. Furthermore, they no longer lived together and though he continued to be a frequent visitor to the Shawcross household it wasn't quite the same when they could excitedly pore over the most recent pamphlet he'd received. He was also a much more important person now as a director of the company, his obvious talents having been spotted and utilised by the Mistress. Not that Nathaniel became self-important, but he was just less approachable being busy elsewhere.

John Wilkinson was a bull of a man. He didn't suffer fools lightly and dismissed the company of fops and idiots who permeated the top ranks of British society. He'd been drawn into the area of Coalbrookdale because of the presence of the

Darbys and their expanding ironworks. He was a self-made man having made a success of the business of iron working unlike his father. He was excited by the prospect of smelting from coking coal and could see its amazing potential. He was sometimes referred to as "Iron-mad Jack", believing that the future would be dominated by the material. It was his faith and his life. He was soon invited to be a member of the exclusive Lunar Society, which was restricted to men like himself – men of invention, science and technology. It had emerged in the very centre of the Midlands industrial nexus, Birmingham. There was no restriction on their thinking and discussion, which extended to many areas of science, or natural philosophy, as well as social and political philosophy. Their ambition was to drive the new technology and scientific ideas into the betterment of all people. Wilkinson himself, like others of his ilk, treated his employees well on the whole, supplying them with housing and schooling for their children. But there was a disturbing flaw in the man, which probably derived from his ruthless push to make the world iron. He always needed money and perhaps he didn't scruple to engage in methods which came to make people distrustful of him. He married eligible ladies to obtain their wealth, he stole his father's ideas pushing him out of the business and paid his workers with his own tokens that they could only exchange in his shops. But he was a dynamic energy of entrepreneurial endeavour and had a genius for applying engineering ideas practically. He had contracts with the government to supply armaments and consequently flourished during the Seven Years' War. His undoing came when two fellow members of the Lunar Society, Matthew Boulton and James Watt, offered him a contract to supply them with cylinders for their new steam engines. He copied their designs making engines of his own which he then sold undercutting their prices. When he and his brother fell out, the latter revealed the theft and Wilkinson was successfully sued by the famous engineers and had to repay a great deal of money in settlement.

This was the background when Abraham Darby tabled a motion for discussion at a meeting of the Board of Directors in mid-1775.

'Gentlemen and Mother, you all know of our illustrious neighbour on the other side of the river, John Wilkinson. However, you may not be aware of his latest invention of a cylinder boring lathe which will revolutionise iron manufacturing. He has secured a virtual monopoly with the government to supply all cannon, other armaments and munitions because of this revolutionary device, which enables a cylinder to be bored to within tolerances hitherto not possible. I want the Board to consider purchasing a licence from him so that we can build a boring machine here.' As soon as he'd finished speaking, concerned looks appeared on all faces around the table. It was the name John Wilkinson that had evoked this response.

'But... You can't be suggesting,' Nathaniel expressed the thoughts of most of the others present, 'that we go into armament production, can you?' Abraham didn't reply at once, waiting to see how other members would react.

'I'm sure that Abraham doesn't have that in mind,' the diplomatic William Reynolds commented, although in the back of his mind he wasn't too certain. Abraham still remained silent.

'When your father entered into this line 30 years ago,' said Abia, 'I opposed it wholeheartedly but it took me 15 years to finally put a stop to it. We are Quakers and justly proud of our pacifism. We cannot sacrifice our values, our faith to Mammon.'

Now Abraham spoke, 'I didn't for a moment think that you would say anything other than that. No, I'm not at all suggesting we manufacture armaments, but that doesn't mean to say we cannot use the device for other purposes. In particular, it means we could produce the superior Bolton and Watt engines ourselves as well as any other items that might benefit from it. I knew his name would arouse consternation so

I thought we should get it out of the way from the beginning. Hopefully, you're all now reassured we are not going into competition with John Wilkinson to produce cannons.' There was visible relief and nodding of heads all around.

Elijah couldn't contain himself. He heard a rumour passing through the works that they were about to embark on producing cannons. His work stopped and the years of his youth flooded over him leaving him weak and despondent. Could it be true? Surely, the Mistress would not allow this. He had to find out. He waited for Nathaniel to return from the boardroom and as he walked out, pounced on him breathlessly.

'Nathaniel, friend,' he knew he couldn't get an answer to this question there and then, 'I must speak with you urgently, please.' Nathaniel was completely surprised by this approach and Elijah's dreadful state of agitation, but he wouldn't deny his old friend and promised to come around to his house in the evening about 7 PM. Until then, Nathaniel tried to think what it was that could have put Elijah into such a state, but whichever way he came at it, he could not come up with any idea.

In the time he had between meeting Nathaniel and leaving work, Elijah took himself off to the Meeting House, that place of solitude and nearness to God which never failed to calm his turbulent emotions. It was early evening, mid-week and there was no one else around. Just as he preferred it when he was in such a state. He sat for half an hour until the dimming light brought some calm to him and he began to think of the past 15 years of his life in this tranquil Vale. He brought to mind the people he'd come to love and revere such as the Mistress, the Young Master Abraham and Nathaniel. Eventually, he gained control of his feelings and in that mood, he departed for home. As he arrived, so Nathaniel did too. Once inside, Nathaniel began the conversation,

'Now, my old friend, what has you so worked up?' Elijah's past threatened to destroy the peace he had so carefully striven to achieve in the past hour, but he forced himself to remain coherent and controlled.

'There is a rumour abroad in the Works that we are about to begin making cannons and other armaments,' he said tremulously.

'Certainly, it was discussed at the last Board Meeting but not with any serious intention to produce weapons of war. There was universal condemnation of any such policy.' The relief on Elijah's face was unmistakable. 'The reason it was discussed at all was in connection with obtaining a licence to produce a boring lathe from John Wilkinson, whom you know from his many businesses in the area. It is a technology he has developed for cannon production, but it has many other applications for which it can be used and that's why we are interested. We want to build a boring mill on site which will develop our ability to produce much more precise items, in particular the new steam engine invented by Matthew Bolton and James Watt. But what I don't understand, Elijah, is why you have been so concerned about this? If I may say, it has put you in a state of agitation in which I have never seen you before.' He placed his hand on Elijah's shoulder to confirm the close bond between them.

'There are aspects of my past life as a young man, Nathaniel, of which you are not aware and of which I am not proud. Indeed, it shames me to think about it.' Nathaniel sat down waiting for him to continue. Elijah then told him about his years in the Royal Navy and his rise to becoming a Master Cannoneer in His Majesty's service. He referred to some of the bloody battles he had participated in and the destruction he had meted out. He was almost sobbing by this time until Nathaniel stood and embraced him saying,

'Enough, Elijah. It is a rare man or woman who regrets nothing of their past lives. There are things I haven't told anyone here save one about my time in North America when I killed men with my own hands. I too feel ashamed about these acts for which I will be personally responsible to the Lord. It is no different from what you have done. But rest assured, my friend, we will never whilst the Darbys are in charge embrace the production of armaments.'

Chapter 24
The Age of Iron

John Wilkinson surveyed all 16 trustees invited by him and Andrew Prichard to this first meeting of the Bridge Project. They were all significant men in the county, landowners, iron masters, businessmen or others of substance.

'Gentlemen, welcome. We are on the threshold of a pioneering step. Yes, we are building a bridge. But this is no ordinary bridge. It is no bridge of wood, which will catch fire at the slightest application of incendiary material. Nor is it a bridge of brick or stone, which will require many supports to hold it up and reduce the passage beneath it to one so small that no longer will our great waterway, the Severn, be a conduit of major traffic that is cut off at this headwater too early to be of any continued serious commercial use. No, sirs, our bridge is to be of iron – the material of modern times and of those to come. We know its uses, its true potential here on both sides of the river. We build our machines with it, our rails are iron, our houses are virtually iron. We use iron for our water cisterns, our window frames, our door and fire surrounds, even our floors. Our ingenious development of this wonderful material has given us beautiful steam engines. We clad our boats with it and soon iron boats will replace timber hulls – I already have a prototype fully iron made barge floating in the canal. Soon this will be commonplace. And for a long time now we have come to rely on hundreds of domestic iron items. Gentlemen, we are in the midst of a revolution – the iron revolution.

Of course, we all agree that we need a bridge to span this river of ours. This river, a force of nature that reminds us from time to time that we don't control it. Just two years ago it swept all before it, not a single bridge was standing, neither wood nor stone. We have struggled too long ferrying goods from one side of the river to the other, which is frequently impossible in the winter storms. And we know how unstable the banks are through the gorge, at times producing destruction of biblical proportions – remember that five years ago, a whole copse of new oak saplings slid into the river blocking it entirely, resulting in columns of water spouting many feet into the air. The destruction to commerce was lengthy and costly. We need, sirs, a bridge which is on strong foundations and high and wide enough to allow our largest ships passage. Therefore, gentlemen, I submit to you and endorse the design which has been produced by our eminent architect, Thomas Farnolls Prichard.'

Then, with a great dramatic flourish Wilkinson pulled back the canvas cover, which had up till now been hiding a wooden scale model of the proposed bridge. There was a gasp from the assembled trustees at the sheer detail and beauty of the model, which included green and wooded banks on both sides of the river. It was high, higher than any would have imagined with a great single arch spanning the total width of the Severn.

'Gentlemen, I give you our bridge of iron.'

Again, there were gasps but this time accompanied by expostulations of 'Impossible!', 'Too high!'. But also some of admiration 'Magnificent', 'Beautiful', 'Remarkable!'.

'There has never been built a bridge such as this,' undeterred, Wilkinson continued. 'It will be the marvel of the modern age, the envy of the world. It will demonstrate undisputedly that iron is king.'

Young Abraham Darby the third was the next to speak,

'I think it is a beautifully designed structure but I do have one question. What kind of iron will be used?' Wilkinson was ready for this question.

'It will be cast-iron.'

'In that case,' responded Derby, 'I have to ask whether you think it will be of sufficient tensile strength to take the pressure that will be exerted upon it from the sides of the gorge? You know, as we all do here, that the sides of the gorge are collapsing at a minimal but steady pace into the river. We see evidence of this regularly on both sides. The danger of the cast-iron bridge is well-known, that it will fracture under such pressure, whereas we know wrought iron has sufficient pliability to absorb these strains. How do you know the bridge won't collapse within a year or two?'

'That is a good question, Master Darby, and it's one I would have expected from you. Firstly, Mr Prichard's design makes it abundantly clear that the positioning of the bridge is crucial and should take place in the strongest and highest parts of the bank existing already. These are where the main ferry crossing is, but these foundations will be strengthened by brick and stone with the ends of the iron structure embedded in concrete. Secondly, the design allows for the replacement of any one of the 1700 parts in situ so that where any fracture, however small, is detected it can be replaced. The largest single part will be no longer than 5 feet and thus will not compromise the overall strength through repair.'

'Excellent,' replied Darby, 'May I congratulate you and Mr Prichard on an outstanding production of design.'

Although there were other questions, none of them were as pertinent as Abraham Darby's and there was agreement to proceed by inviting tenders for the work after which the project would be submitted to Parliament for its approval.

There were three members of the trustees who were able to speak directly to the bill proposing the building of the Ironbridge, Earl Gower, Lord Craven and the MP for Shrewsbury, William Pulteney. However, its reception in Parliament in both houses was far from encouraging. Members were obsessed with the idea that bridges could only be constructed in timber, brick or stone. Although there was no outright opposition to the idea of spanning the River Severn, the composition of it evoked widespread controversy if not ridicule. Wilkinson himself journeyed to London to lobby members of the house but he was regarded as quite an eccentric figure being referred to as "Iron-mad" Wilkinson. He was a very wealthy man, however, and he had various manufacturing premises in different parts of the kingdom via which he could exert some influence on members of both houses. But it was not enough. Furthermore, the importance of a bridge at that specific location could not be said to be enhancing travel and communication throughout the rest of the country. It was without doubt of absolute importance to the local landlords and industrialists in that area finally bringing together the two important centres of industrial development at Madeley and Broseley. To others elsewhere in the country it seemed less crucial. Some even suggested that it was nothing more than an advertising gimmick by John Wilkinson for his businesses and obsession with iron. In this way, his endeavours in London may well have backfired. Parliament did give approval for a bridge eventually, but it was one of brick and stone. He ranted to Abraham Darby,

'Our current parliamentarians seem to have the vision of pygmies and even less wit. My poor friend Prichard is on his deathbed and we seem unable to raise sufficient sums to build the most modest of bridges. At this rate, we will only be able to construct a bridge at Coalport or a reconstruction at Buildwas, neither of which will achieve our purposes. I really am become quite sick of the whole thing.'

'Don't despair my good friend,' replied the young but still very enthusiastic Abraham Darby. 'It can be done and if you wish I will purchase your shares in the venture to give me a majority in the Trust where I will continue to promote our cast-iron bridge.'

Parliament could find no takers to build a bridge in timber, brick or stone so when Darby's tender to build a cast-iron bridge at the very modest cost of £3150 was received, it was accepted. A few weeks later, poor Thomas Prichard died but Abraham threw himself into the project, along with his best designers including Nathaniel. Two years later they were ready to start thinking about construction which immediately faced them with a problem.

They had a design. But where should they build it? They knew they would require a lot of iron – 390 tons of the stuff which would take three months to produce. They then had to think about casting. Did they have the space? There were three possible sites where they could produce the amount of cast-iron required, but they all had pros and cons. At Horsehay they had their most recent furnace which was the largest and therefore the quickest. However, how on earth would they get what they produced the 3 miles to the river, over difficult and often unstable inclines? Cast-iron is heavy and although they had iron railways to carry coal and ore that distance, it was another thing to consider the problems associated with transporting a large unwieldy very heavy structure across this dangerous ground. No, Horsehay was out of the question. The best choice would have been the Bedlam Furnaces which lay only 600 yards away from the construction site. But these furnaces were the oldest and smallest so it would take twice as long to produce the iron that they needed. In addition, there wasn't much space between them and the riverbank, which was non-too stable itself. The structure was so large it would require a larger space for the moulding. So, regrettably this option had to be rejected.

'The Coalbrookdale Works,' suggested Nathaniel, 'is the only practicable option. We still have quite a lot of pig iron imported from New York state which we can use since it is of the highest quality and closely available. We will also have sufficient space to layout moulds in sand. Of course, we still have the problem of transporting it, but that is along a predominantly level surface with the slope in our favour.' The other members of the team digested this proposal and Abraham seemed to accept it.

'Yes, wherever we move it from it's going to be a challenge. Any suggestions?'

'Well if we were in ancient Egypt, we could use timber rollers,' someone said half-jokingly.

'It might well come to that,' replied Abraham testily, 'but we have to be extremely careful as the arch will be over 100 feet long and any sudden and uncontrolled movement could well fracture it.'

'What about two teams of horses with suitably cushioned wagons?'

'That just might work,' said Abraham. At that moment, his mother, Abia, entered the office, which was something she rarely did making them all look up in surprise.

'Abraham,' she said seriously, 'I need to speak with you urgently and in private.'

'Of course, we can go into my office.' When she was sure that none of the others could hear them, she began, 'Abraham, I saw John Wilkinson this morning who gave me some very disturbing news. He told me that you purchased all his shares in the Bridge trust giving you the controlling vote, but more to the point he said that you had promised to meet the costs of any overspend in the project. Don't you think that is rather reckless? We are already suffering as a result of the American war and the loss of our markets there. Others tell me that the estimates you submitted for the tender were on the low side so I'm beginning to wonder whether we might not be in for a difficult time financially. Or, am I wrong to fuss and worry?'

'No Mother, you're probably not wrong to have some doubts, but I am confident the bridge will be a great success and bring in much revenue from tolls. It may take a few years to recover our expenditure but our reputation can only be aggrandised by this venture.'

'I sincerely hope you are right, my son.'

When Abraham returned to the design team, he seemed to possess a quite different mindset.

'Gentlemen, I have been thinking about the difficulties of transport and I think we should use the shortest route. That means using the Bedlam furnaces. Yes… Yes… I know,' as Nathaniel and the others reminded him of why they'd rejected it. 'You would be right, if we were to try to cast it into a single large arch but we don't have to. Instead, we can cast it in much smaller and more manageable parts that we can then assemble on site when each is ready – rather like a jigsaw puzzle. What's more, we can ensure greater accuracy of fit by first of all measuring the actual gap between items and casting accordingly. Let's do a quick calculation from the main design as to how many parts we might need, their size and weight.' A few hours later they had the figures.

'Well,' reflected Abraham, 'it looks like we shall need between four and five hundred lengths for the ribs forming the main arch that will be about 5 feet long and weigh approximately five tons.'

'That's brilliant!' marvelled Nathaniel. 'It solves both weight and transport problems. The next question is, how do we fit them all together?'

'I've had an idea about that too,' replied Abraham. 'Why don't we use mortise and tenon joints as we do with wood? That way also allows for slight imperfections and movements, which we know the bridge will experience over time.'

'For the actual construction,' added Nathaniel swept up in the excitement of inventive genius, 'we should then build the brick and stone abutments on either side of the river and build them up equally on both sides. We should be able to work from anchored barges with our wooden derricks and cranes as the structure gets higher. But we will need men to climb up the ascending ribs to place the individual parts as they are lowered in and then to hammer them in firmly. That will require nerve and strength. Do we have men sufficiently skilled and experienced at working at heights for this task?'

'Not really,' commented Abraham thoughtfully, 'but there must be a few amongst our hundreds of workmen who have done similar work such as building the high chimneys. We will call for volunteers offering to pay a premium rate for dangerous work.'

'I've had some experience,' said Nathaniel to the surprised assembly. 'In America, I spent 18 months with a clan of the Mohawk Indian who proved their courage by scaling the great trees of the northern forests, which grow to lengths of three and four hundred feet or more. I learned from them the way of focusing closely on what is immediately in front of you and cutting out all else. In this way, you will not overbalance nor panic. I can teach this to a number of chosen men. We should also secure each man with a rope in case he does fall.' Thus the detailed plans were made, materials collected and men trained. But it was another 18 months before they could begin construction because the approach roads, even from the nearby Bedlam furnaces, needed strengthening before they could cope with the loads that had to be drawn to the river. Once there, man's ingenuity with mechanical physics made it much easier and the dream became reality.

Nathaniel's courage was an inspiration to the other men and he didn't ask them to do anything he hadn't already done first. The bridge builders also took comfort that there was a degree of stability right from the start as they braced the twin ribs growing up to the top of the arch. Working deftly in tune with the crane men, it was easier than they thought to fit the heavy sections together and hammer them, with muffled heads, into place. It was fortunate that they cast the pieces as they progressed because they noticed that the measurements were in some cases different by centimetres from the original design. During construction, hundreds of visitors arrived to watch in amazement at this feat of engineering. People from far-away lands, Royal dignitaries and the idle rich with money and time to spare to watch the work of others flocked to Coalbrookdale. Even before the bridge was completed, it had become a must-see item on any European tour of worth and the coffers of the good burgers of Madeley and Broseley began to fill up. The

Coalbrookdale Company was also congratulated on not having obstructed the course of river traffic at any time during the three months of construction. For Nathaniel, Abraham and the other managers the greatest achievement was not having lost a single man to accident. It was a remarkable feat and testament to careful planning and consideration for the company's employees. When the Bridge was finished, it was sometimes dubbed jokingly "the road to nowhere" because until they'd completed the approach roads on either side, it wasn't serviceable. However, even before the grand opening in 1781, thousands of pedestrians were more than happy to pay the toll for crossing, which vindicated Abraham Darby's faith in its ability to generate revenue. It was the marvel of the age – the first cast-iron bridge anywhere in the world.

Nathaniel didn't know whether he was awake or dreaming. Standing in the middle of the Bridge, he looked up and northwards at the great, billowing plumes of black smoke, darker than the night sky snatches of which could be seen filled with the twinkling stars of heaven. Here and there were coronas of bright fiery red from the dozen furnaces, which he knew were the powerhouses of this Satanic landscape. As his eyes grew accustomed to the oily black silhouettes, he thought he could distinguish hundreds of little white spots like termites in a termite hill forever disappearing and reappearing, turning over, sifting and sorting an eternal heap of growth and decay in a perpetual cycle of regeneration. He was shocked to realise these weren't insects but human beings. Later, during the day as he looked out from the great bay window of their Dale house, he could clearly see the sprawl of buildings that made up the Coalbrookdale Works. The overwhelming impression was that of an industrial cacophony: the screeching iron wheels from the wagons full of coal and ore as they descended Jiggers Bank and Cherry Tree Hill at a controlled brake; the blows of the great water driven hammers in the wrought iron shop; the screeching tear from the sheet metal sheds; the regular bass roar of the huge steam driven bellows that fed the hungry furnaces; and everywhere the men scurrying to keep up with the demands of the voracious beasts. Buildings in construction, steam engines working everything, here and there patches of deciduous trees and grass squares that so far had escaped the destruction. Flame and smoke spread everywhere, testament to one of the great industrial centres of the country. What would the Great Spirit think of it all, wondered Nathaniel? Acts of sublime creation to the betterment of all, or works of wanton destruction with the alienation of the many and aggrandisement for the few? His heart remained still with the Susquehanna.

The End

Bibliography

A Collection of Religious Tracts (1778) *Observations on Slavery by John Wesley*, PDF, University of North Carolina.

A P Baggs, D C Cox, Jessie McFall, P A Stamper and A J L Winchester, 'Madeley: Growth of Settlement', in *A History of the County of Shropshire: Volume 11, Telford*, ed. G C Baugh and C R Elrington (London, 1985), pp. 27–31. *British History Online* http://www.british-history.ac.uk/vch/salop/vol11/pp27-31 [accessed 29 January 2019].

Berthoud, Michael (1977) *John Wilkinson and Iron Bridge*, PDF, Broseley and Community History Society.

Encyclopaedia Britannica (2018) *Abraham Darby*, PDF

Gorman, P (1977) Sterling Iron and Railway Company Records 1740–1984, New York State Library, PDF

Historical Boston (2019) *Boston Tea Party Facts,* PDF

Historical Society of Philadelphia (2019) *Peaceable Kingdom Lost: The Paxton Riots* (Digital Paxton, www.digitalpaxton.org)

History (2019) *Ottawa Chief Pontiac's Rebellion against the British* 1763 (https://www.history.com/this-day-in-history/pontiacs-rebellion-begins)

Homberger, Margaret (2003) Madness: Wrongful Confinement, PDF, In *Deviance, Disorder and the Self*, Keele University

Intriguing History (2012) *The Lunar Society bringing brilliant minds together,* PDF //www.intriguing history/Industrial Revolution

National Humanities Centre (2009) *Becoming American: British North Atlantic Colonies 1690–1763*, PDF, www.//nationalhumanitiescentre.org

Paine, Thomas (2019) *Common Sense*, Independence Hall Association, *American History.org*

Pauls, Elizabeth Prine(?) *American Indian*, PDF, Encyclopaediabritannica.com

Pee, Ralph and Hawes, Maurice (1988) John Wilkinson and the Two Willey Ironworks, PDF, *John Wilkinson Society Journal, monograph one 1974.*

Quaker Info (1998) *The Retreat Mental Hospital*, PDF // www.Quaker info.com

Quakers in the World (no date) *The Darby Family*, (www.quakersintheworld.org/quakers-in-action/271)

Shropshire History Industrial Heritage (2005) *Solved – The Mystery of Ironbridge*, PDF, in Association with Timewatch BBC, 2002

Spence, Thomas (1775) *A Lecture Delivered at the University of Newcastle Upon Tyne On Land Reform* (University of North Carolina Archives digitised 2007)

Taylor, Alan (2016) *American Revolutions*, Norton Paperbacks 2017 (E-Book)
The Abolition of Slavery Project (2011) *Granville Sharp 1765–1815: The Civil Servant*, PDF

The Ironbridge Gorge Museum Trust (2019) *The Ironbridge*, PDF

The Nine Men of Madeley Project (2014–2019) *Religion*, PDF, www.//ninemen.org

Trinder, Barrie (1988) *The Darbys of Coalbrookdale*

Trinder, Barrie (2017) *Ironbridge and Coalbrookdale*, Phillimore & Co-Ltd

Wikipedia (Accessed 2019) *Susquehannock*, PDF

Wilson, David Robert (2010) *Church and Chapel: Parish Ministry and Methodism in Madeley 1760–1785, Special Reference to the Ministry of John Fletcher*, PhD Thesis Presented to Manchester University.

Timeline

1709: Abraham Darby I begins production of iron in the Coalbrookdale blast furnace forming the Coalbrookdale Company.

1716–1794: Abia Darby, wife of Abraham Darby II and mother of Abraham Darby III. Quaker leader and preacher in Coalbrookdale and Broseley.

1735–1816: Richard Reynolds, ironmaster at Coalbrookdale and interests with the Darbys in coal mines in Madeley. Quaker and businessman.

1750–1789: Abraham Darby III. Ironmaster and builder of the Ironbridge.

1755–1764: French and Indian Wars.

1757: John Wilkinson purchases New Willey Ironworks in Broseley, Shropshire.

1757–1789: Rev John William Fletcher Minister at St Michael's in Madeley. Anglican evangelical divine who laid the foundations for Methodism along with John Wesley.

1768: Treaty of Fort Stanwix between British Government and Iroquois Federation that all lands beyond the river Ohio were Indian territory.

1768: Conestoga/Indian Town Massacre.

1774: First Continental Congress – to discuss opposition to British Government by the 12 American colonies, in Philadelphia.

1774: Boston Tea Party.

1775–1783: American War of Independence, beginning in April.

1777–1779: Construction of the Iron Bridge.

1781: The Iron Bridge opens.